I0672154

FLOATING WORD PRESS

Praise for Doc Macomber:

"Insanely entertaining!"
– Editor, *The Skin Game*

"Doc understands the seamier side of life. His characters are complex, loaded with contradictions and wholly believable."
– Dan Schilling, Former Special Ops Commander, Co-author, *The Battle of Mogadishu*

"As addictive and satisfying as my first tattoo...
Wolf's Remedy left me craving more."
– Lyle Tuttle, Tattoo Legend and Historian

"Hard men, Wild women, and even a Love-sick Alligator
... it's a killer!"
– Retired Marine Capt. W.A. Montgomery

"It's always enjoyable spending time with Jack Vu."
– Bill Johnson, Teacher, Screenwriter, Author, *A Story is a Promise*

"An intriguing read that will hold your attention as investigators come up against dead ends and lies...where people aren't always what they seem. A fun read and something different by a talented author."
– Murder and Mayhem

"Adventure abounds in Costa Rica ... In his latest Jack Vu mystery, best laid plans for a quiet vacation get shattered when the drug trade becomes a genuine threat to the peace and tranquility of this otherwise idyllic country. Jack and Betty soon find themselves back on duty... Once again, Mr. Macomber has scored a winner!"
– Harley L. Sachs, Author of *The Mystery Club* series.

Riff Raff

Also by DOC MACOMBER

The Killer Coin

Wolf's Remedy

Snip

Riff Raff

(A Jack Vu Mystery)

by

Doc Macomber

Floating Word Press, LLC
Portland, Oregon

Floating Word Press, LLC

1017 SW Morrison Street, Suite 215

Portland, Oregon 97205

This is a work of fiction.

Any similarities to people, places, living or dead, is purely coincidental.

Floating Word Press logo is a registered trademark. For information about special discounts for bulk purchases, please contact Floating Word Press, LLC, Special Sales at 1-877-356-9673 or fwp@floatingwordpress.com.

COVER DESIGNED BY DIVERSITY DESIGN STUDIOS

Editor: Martha Cowen

Author photograph Copyright © 2008 by Serge A. McCabe

Manufactured in the United States of America

Printing Number

10 9 8 7 6 5 4 3 2 1

First Edition

Library of Congress Control Number: 2011933814

Soft Cover: ISBN –13: 978-0-9785717-9-5

For Birdie, my sweet girl of paradise...

Chapter 1

Lyman crouched low and squinted through the spotting scope. His target vaulted through the Costa Rican rainforest canopy fifty meters ahead, but was losing strength. The forest's chaotic symphony was silenced by a toucan's shrill warning as Lyman lowered the scope and pushed on through the heavy foliage. White bats glared and fanged spiders scurried in his wake.

Massive hanging strangler vines scraped his arms raw. Ducking beneath a low-hanging termite hive, Lyman snagged his large backpack on a barbed manchineel limb and stumbled. Cautious of the poisonous thistles, he slowly untangled himself and moved to more solid ground. He stared down at his muddy combat boots, the ground underfoot suddenly felt oddly hollow. He rocked forward, detected a brittle snap. Locking his weight evenly over both feet, he eased down, pulled a K-bar strapped to his ankle and carefully nosed the razor-sharp point of the blade under the saturated vegetation.

Lyman's mind ratcheted back to the invasion of Panama. The memory still haunted him. The jungle surrounding one of Noriega's hideouts had been choked with trip snares and explosives. One wrong step had taken a former soldier's life and nearly his own.

A spooked Kinkajou flattened his furry raccoon-like body behind a rotting log. The blade revealed nothing but a crumbling palm pod.

Lyman torqued down his caution and continued on. With his free hand latched onto a fig vine, he muscled his body onto a volcanic rock and maneuvered up a narrow ridge. Up ahead, a whiskered, white-face capuchin peered out from behind a mahogany trunk, his ancient eyes searching the forest floor.

Unseasonably heavy rains and mud slides had washed out much of the area near Manuel Antonio. Even the Ticos, Costa Rican natives, avoided the slippery mangrove swamps until the dry season arrived. It was simply too dangerous to traverse. This suited Lyman fine.

He jacked through the sodden wetlands until he reached a clearing. His clothes clung to his body like sap, weighing him down. He shrugged off his backpack, sluiced a handkerchief across his dripping face and contemplated his next move. He vibed their close proximity. He was sure of it. Tepid water from his canteen recharged his strength. Bracing his shoulder against an ironwood, his scope caught a glimpse of a capuchin chattering in a cluster of mangrove trees just ahead.

Not much further now. *Move your ass.*

* * *

Officer Maria Sanchez sensed escalating sound waves. She raised her modified AR-15 and peered through the laser scope. No clear sighting yet, but her eyes remained locked and loaded.

For the past decade, she'd been a drone for the *Policía de Fronteras*, the immigration bureau of Costa Rica. She'd heard a rumor that the "Mule Team," a notorious band of smugglers with ties to the Columbian cartels, had entered the area scouting new drug routes across the Central Southern wetlands to transport their product to Panama. Recent political upheaval along the Nicaraguan and Columbian borders had disrupted former routes through

Costa Rica. The idyllic beaches and rainforests of Manuel Antonio National Park now attracted tourists and drug runners in equal numbers.

Though thirty-five and a head shorter than most of her male colleagues, Sanchez could handle any man twice her size. Her perfectly tailored tactical uniform and flawless makeup belied her strength. But she was all business. Her father had taught her well. A veteran in the Bureau Of Immigration for nineteen years, he had been her mentor, until a modified hollow-point to the back of his head, courtesy of the drug cartel, prematurely terminated his career. His case remained unsolved.

After her father's death, she had transferred to the Drug Task Force. In less than a year, she'd gone through two partners.

"She burned me out," her colleagues had *officially* notified her superior officer.

But off the record, "Psycho Sanchez" was a "revenge crazy bitch hell-bent on nailing the bastards who killed her father." Nothing was too desperate or dangerous in that pursuit.

Despite passing three psychological evaluations with flying colors, no one would work with her. And she liked it that way.

Her index finger slid toward the trigger and froze as the target came into focus. *Aim, breathe, squeeze. Wait! Who the hell was this Caucasian? Where was the mule team?*

She ran the man's face through her mental databank of criminals and drew a blank. The cartel could have sent down new blood from Canada. Or perhaps he was American, a lone wolf hatchet man or a mercenary scouting the coastline for opportunity. Either way, she didn't like it. And neither did her trigger finger.

* * *

Lyman found his spot. One at a time, he watched a troop of monkeys swing down from the canopy of trees. A total of six: two males, two females, a newborn clinging to the back of its mother, and his favorite – a mischievous prankster he'd named Riff Raff.

Lyman was certain he would be the next alpha male. He'd chosen the name Riff Raff after hearing a park guide use the term in a derogatory manner when speaking about the pesky capuchins and their ability to steal from humans yet live in the forest. He had said they were inbred and not worthy to be a species. Lyman felt the same way about humans.

The leader of the clan, Gringo, the old capuchin he'd tracked through the forest, hunched regally on the sturdy treetop, scratching his bulbous belly, keeping a close eye on Lyman and the other primates.

From inside his backpack, Lyman removed his canteen and several ripened apples. As soon as he placed his canteen on the ground, Riff Raff raced up from behind and grabbed it. Lugging it to a nearby stump, he stood bowlegged and proud.

Amused, Lyman figured the young capuchin's interest would wane soon enough, and then he could retrieve his canteen and indulge in a much needed drink.

Lyman understood that this troop of primates did not fear him. They never had. Survivors all, an understanding existed between them. When war memories festered, he replayed mental loops of this primate family to quiet the echoes. He owed his tenuous sanity to them.

Lyman moved to a flat stump across from Riff Raff, munching his apple and watching the nimble monkey twist the canteen this way and that.

Riff Raff was unique to his breed. His right eye was brown, his left blue. Lyman had spent several afternoons researching this rare condition. But that wasn't why he was his favorite. He also lacked any protective instinct, racing from one adventure to the next, unaware of his surroundings and the dangers they held. Lyman admired Riff Raff's bravado, even as he recognized the danger. He felt strangely protective of the fearless youngster.

Lyman cut up the remaining apples and tossed pieces along the ground. Riff Raff tossed the canteen aside and snatched a slice. He carried it up a branch and ate it alone and then hopped down to attempt to steal a second piece from his mother, who didn't appreciate his poor manners, and boxed his ears. Riff Raff squealed and tore off through the woods.

Vigilant in the treetops, Gringo suddenly grew agitated at something near the ground over where Riff Raff had stopped. The sun was dropping in the sky as Lyman picked up his canteen and walked over to see what had the alpha male so upset.

Chapter 2

glistening pool had formed at the bottom of the tree, fed
by a trickling stream down the trunk. As Riff Raff sniffed
and Lyman approached, a blob of moisture plopped into
the puddle from above. The sound reminded Lyman of the water
features so popular in restaurants and spas, where trickling and
splashing sounds were designed to evoke inner calmness. All
similarities ended as both Lyman and the startled monkey gazed
upward to the source of the fountain. Lyman's smile flattened as a
macabre visage overtook him.

The body sagged in the fork of the tree. Wedged between two
limbs, the decaying body blended with the dense foliage. Insects
crawled over the bloated slick skin. The decomposing corpse stared
vacantly down. All that remained of the head were hollow sockets
in a face devoid of any recognizable features. A red baseball cap
slanted gangster-style over the forehead.

Riff Raff scampered up the tree and bounced back and forth
on a frail branch above the corpse, emitting a high-pitched excited
shriek.

"Get down!" Lyman shouted. Something in his tone stopped
the excited dancer, but didn't bring the monkey back. Riff Raff

leaned closer to his newfound treasure, bending the fragile branch under the weight. As he inched further out the limb for a better view, the branch snapped, jarring the corpse, and dumping money from its sodden lap to the ground below.

Riff Raff screamed a frightened call, unaware of another movement along the limb. Lyman reached for his K-Bar, calculating distance and speed.

The poisonous eyelash viper slithered out from behind the body, a foot from the monkey's hairless ear. Its point-blank tongue zipped out like a polished stiletto while heat sensing pits beneath the viper's moss green nostrils locked onto Riff Raff's warm scent.

Lyman cocked his arm back to throw, but before he could release, Gringo dropped from the canopy above and lunged straight into the viper's venomous jaws. The old monkey plummeted from the tree with the viper in his firm grip.

The two warriors hit the ground tumbling in a death match. Gringo's sharp teeth tore through the snake's tough skin but the viper's sense of survival was as fierce as anything Lyman had ever seen on the battlefield. Fangs slashed even as its head was torn from its spine.

Within seconds, it was over. In his jaws, Gringo victoriously held the bloody snake head. But, the venom released into his system had already begun to take hold. Confused and partially paralyzed, the primate struggled to walk before collapsing, his breathing spasmodic.

The other primates formed a protective circle around their ailing leader while Riff Raff hopped about at Gringo's feet wanting the old monkey to get up and play. Gringo remained still. The discord struck Riff Raff and he stopped toying, cuddled up next to the old monkey and howled lament.

Lyman put his knife down. If he was going to help, there wasn't much time. Quickly, he shooed the primates into the trees hearing escalating sounds and movement nearby as the denizens of the forest spread the word. Ignoring his desire to check the sounds, he bent down next to Gringo and lifted his limp head. The primate moaned faintly, but didn't open his eyes.

Lyman lifted Gringo's limp arm and examined the wound. He held tightly and used his sharp knife to slice below the row of puncture marks a small cut through the hairy skin. Blood oozed out. Gringo's eyes shot open for a brief moment and then closed and remained that way. Lyman pressed his lips to the wound and sucked spitting out blood and venom. He repeated it twice and then tore off a chunk of t-shirt and used the makeshift bandage to wrap the monkey's wound. The other primates stayed their distance, watching intently from the trees.

Carefully, Lyman eased Gringo inside his empty backpack and zipped it, leaving just the head exposed. Then, he picked up his scope and looked off toward the dense canopy where his instincts told him to look.

*   *   *

The humidity fogged the lens of Sanchez's scope. She used a corner of her t-shirt to wipe it clear. She could barely make out what was happening down at the forest floor. It didn't make any sense to her. Who was the corpse in the Mangrove tree? Could it have washed up there in a heavy rain? Possible. Or he could have climbed up there as a lookout for the mule team and been killed? It seemed as big a surprise to the Caucasian as to her. And now what was he cutting up on the ground? She dialed in the focus. What the hell? He was scoping her.

*   *   *

Lyman spotted her in the tree and suspected she'd been watching him the entire time. By the look on her face, she was as surprised to see him as he was to see her. So she probably wasn't tracking him personally. As far as he knew, nobody knew he was down in Costa Rica, least of all the cops. So what was she looking for? Guns? Drugs? But there was no time for that now. He had to fly.

After hiking up and down slopes for nearly half-an-hour, Lyman came upon a small stream, waded across it, and then started the final trek down out of the tombola formation of Cathedral Point. Bleeding from cuts on his legs and exhausted from his forced march, Lyman pushed on. Against his back he could feel Gringo's beating heart, a faint life-force softly drumming through the worn nylon material. Like mythical eagles searching for the sun, a pair of scarlet macaws circled overhead.

Lyman's throat was parched, but he didn't stop to replenish fluids. His enemy was not thirst ... it was time. From his training he'd remembered some key facts: when a human gets bitten by a poisonous snake, swelling occurs within forty-five minutes; and within three hours, if the bite is serious, the person will usually die. How rapidly the venom moved through a primate was unclear to him. This lack of knowledge unnerved him. If poison moved through an animal's system according to body weight, it meant he had less than an hour to save Gringo.

He reached the summit and looked out toward Playa Espadrille Sur where the endless blue-green waters of the Pacific beckoned. The end was in sight.

Chapter 3

The young assistant for veterinarian Dr. Phillip Ramos walked out of the back room and turned on a light in the narrow hall where, for the past hour, Lyman had been pacing.

"Do you like a Coke?" she asked.

The girl stood four feet tall, tipping the scale around eighty pounds. Beneath the oversized lab coat, which nearly dragged the ground, she wore a blue school uniform. Her dark hair and brown eyes were surely those of a Tico.

"No thanks," he said.

The girl frowned.

"Very well no coke. *Agua* then?"

"Nothing," Lyman said firmly.

And with that the girl sat down on a wooden chair beside the door and stared at him. Lyman ignored her and began pacing again. Worry creased his brow as he focused on the animal's fate. In the two years he'd been in Costa Rica, he'd never seen a poisonous viper in that area. Of course, he'd never seen a corpse in a tree wearing a baseball cap before either.

"You are like the caged jaguar at the zoo."

The girl was right. He did have that captive feeling, trapped in this narrow hallway. Lyman looked down. Now with the light on, he noticed the ingrained trail of muddy boot prints running the length of the hall.

"Sorry."

He presumed the girl was the veterinarian's daughter, that she helped out after school. The clinic wasn't much, just one room off the main house. Earlier, two school-age children burst through the doors and disappeared through an adjoining room where on several occasions their laughter carried through the thin walls. The house sat back from the highway surrounded by trees, and had been the closest veterinarian to Manuel Antonia that he knew of. The sign on the highway indicated it was the Quepos Animal Hospital.

"My name is Sabrina. What's yours?"

"Lyman."

"That's a funny name."

"I'll take that Coke now." Anything, he thought, for a few moments of peace and quiet.

Sabrina hopped down from the chair and disappeared through a side door leading into the main house. In a few minutes, she returned with a bottle of Coke, which she handed him before returning to her chair.

Lyman sipped the cold soda. "Don't you have homework to do?"

"Papa said I should stay here until he is finished."

Lyman walked over and sat down with his back toward her, hoping to finish drinking his soda in silence.

"Is the monkey your pet?"

"It's against the law to keep them as pets."

"Yes, but everyone does."

"I don't."

"Then you are different. But you're from the United States, aren't you?"

"Yes."

"Which state? I have memorized all of them" she said proudly. "Would you like to quiz me?"

"No."

The girl made no reply.

Lyman immediately regretted his short response. "Okay. What state connects to Mississippi?"

The girl hesitated. "You are from Louisiana?"

"No."

She scratched her head. "But I'm correct? Louisiana is next to Mississippi?"

"Yes, it is. And so is Alabama."

"You're from Alabama?"

"No. I'm just testing your knowledge of our geography.

"I would very much like to see New York City and Disneyland. Oh, and maybe Hawaii and Hollywood. Do you live in any of these places? I could visit you." The girl swatted at a fly buzzing her head.

"I grew up in Kansas."

"That is in the land of tornados, right?"

"Occasionally."

"Why did you come to Costa Rica?"

"It's beautiful here."

She frowned. "You chose this place" she looked around her shabby environment "over Disneyland?"

"Yes." Lyman smiled at the thought. It was not like he could tell her that he'd stayed for personal reasons, long after his woman had returned to the States. How simple choices seem when you are young.

His smile vanished as the office door opened and Dr. Ramos entered the tiny hallway, drying his hands on a small towel. Sabrina solemnly took Lyman's hand in hers. "I'm afraid I have some bad news."

Chapter 4

The 727 out of Miami made a descending turn, slicing through the clouds as it began its final approach into San José.

Jack Vu stared out the port side window surprised by all the buildings below. For some reason he'd imagined they'd be landing on a remote runway in the middle of a rainforest. The Costa Rica he'd pictured had beachside huts, coffee plantations, banana trees, howler monkeys, tropical birds and pungent flowers, all in a luscious green paradise. His friend, Detective Hill, thought it would be filled with dark-skinned natives dancing around topless in brightly colored skirts, chanting to bare-chested tattooed tribesmen, roasting pigs on a spit over a blazing fire. Jack didn't have the heart to tell him Tahiti wasn't located in Central America.

Instead, what he saw was a crowded city with skyscrapers, smog and filth. The rainforest was there all right, hidden within the green hills and spewing volcanoes, but he couldn't see it from the window.

"Jack, move your head. I wanna see."

Vu sat back, allowing his girlfriend Betty to press her face against the glass. She twisted a strand of her long red hair in her hand like an excited teenager as she stared out. Vu stared at her hunched shoulder leaning across him. He loved her pale skin, which erupted into a riot of freckles at the slightest exposure to the sun. By his feet he heard a loud thud and noticed the guide book, previously balanced on Betty's lap, had fallen to the floor.

He reached over Betty to pick up the book. Once he retrieved it, he sighed. The book had several hundred marked pages with dog-eared corners, torn newsprint, and a stained cocktail napkin wedged between the pages. It looked like a puppy had chewed it, he thought. Attempting to untangle the crumpled maps, Vu smoothed torn and wrinkled pages. In just two hours, Betty had mangled the guidebook.

As Vu removed a sticky cherry stem from the cover, a stewardess strolled by, instructing him to return his seat and put his tray to its upright position.

"Look, there's Cathedral Metropolitano!" Betty excitedly pointed out. "Wasn't the original structure toppled by an earthquake in 1821? Let me see the book."

Vu clutched the savaged tome to his chest. But Betty's enthusiasm won out.

While Betty thumbed through her marked pages with her glittery nails, Vu reminded himself that this was a vacation. A long overdue one. It had been well over a year since either of them had a break from their hectic careers. Since Katrina and then the oil spill, it had been nonstop for both of them. Betty had spent seven days a week identifying bodies from the disasters, in addition to her usual homicides, suicides and undetermined deaths in a seemingly unending corpse parade. In the past year Jack, a military investigator, had caught moments with her in between probing all modes of crime inherent with a disaster, including death, forgeries, insurance scams and identity theft. You always learn the best and worst of humanity in times of crisis.

It's time to loosen up and relax. He was going to enjoy this, sticky book covers and all.

He had to admit he took pleasure in the disconnect between the precise serious woman who headed the New Orleans Forensic Department and the laughing scatterbrain who shared his bed at night. He admired her ability to study death in all its ugly faces, and still embrace life so fully.

After surviving the war and making his escape from the internment camp following the fall of Saigon, he had relied on karma to explain the twists the fates had handed him, but dancing with joy still eluded him. Maybe this vacation would bring out the "inner child" psychologists are always talking about. Certainly his work as a military investigator didn't.

"Jack, I'm so excited," Betty said. "Did you remember to bring the itinerary?"

"Yes. Did you remember the suntan lotion?"

"You betcha." Betty leaned close and nibbled his earlobe, leaving a smear of lipstick on his cheek, which she playfully rubbed off. "What's the name of our yacht again?"

"*Sea Gypsy.*"

"*Sea Gypsy* ... just like you, Jack."

Before Betty unfolded her legs, she was distracted by a tiny fray on her skirt hem. Then like a giddy child, she pointed to her big toe, upon which she had painted a glittery "J" and blew him a kiss. Childlike, unconventional, joyful – that was Betty.

"Did we bring Dramamine?" Vu asked.

"We can ask the ship's steward for some. I did remember the Bushmills."

Betty leaned over and kissed Vu's cheek. "Why Jack, is that stubble on your face? What would the Air Force say?"

"I'm taking a shaving vacation for the next two weeks, honey."

"Really?"

"Yep."

"Then I'll take a break from personal grooming too!" Betty enthused and clapped her hands.

The plane touched down as Vu tried to determine which of Betty's grooming routines was being tossed to the wind.

After the airplane turned onto the crowded tarmac and headed toward the terminal, the pilot came on the loud speaker.

"Ladies and Gentleman it appears another aircraft is at our gate. It'll be just a few minutes while we talk to the tower. Until we receive further instructions, please for your safety, stay seated with your seatbelts fastened."

Ten minutes later, the engines turned off. As the time ticked by in the rapidly heating plane, Vu cursed all the tea he'd drunk. After 30 more minutes, he made a decision. He unbuckled his seatbelt, and climbed over Betty.

"What are you doing?" Betty asked.

"I'm making a run for it."

Vu hit the aisle. While the stewardess protested, he sprinted into the lavatory and locked the door. By the time he exited the bathroom, there was a line forming as other passengers followed suit.

Vu sat back down and buckled his seatbelt.

Betty shook her head. "You're such a bad boy. See what you started?"

Passengers now choked the aisle.

The pilot came on the loudspeaker. "Please stay seated. We can't move the aircraft until you are all back in your seats. We expect instructions any minute now."

Vu detected a worried undertone to the pilot's voice as he focused his attention out the window. Vu counted a total of thirteen airplanes randomly parked on the tarmac, awaiting gate clearance. Other aircraft in various states of repair were lodged in overcrowded hangers or under scaffolding. The only gate that appeared to be operational was blocked by the same plane that was there when they had landed nearly an hour before.

Bored baggage handlers and airport personnel stood about with hands in pockets. Even the security personnel looked like they were taking extended smoke breaks.

Vu read the lips of a frustrated pilot swearing into his microphone. He watched another aggravated 727 pilot throw his hands up in disgust. They were going nowhere. The airport was locked down and the employees were on strike.

Long after the water was gone and the toilets had flooded, the pilot came on.

"Ladies and Gentleman," the pilot announced, not bothering to hide his irritation, "I've never seen anything like this. Now the tower says we'll be unloading from the tarmac and taking a school bus to the terminal. It is still unclear how your luggage will be transported. Just hang on a bit more. We do appreciate your patience."

Twenty-five minutes later the engines revved up, the plane crept forward fifty meters and then stopped for good. The pilot killed the engines, then announced, "Folks I guess this is it. We'll be off-loading here. Again, my apologies for this utter chaos."

When the aircraft doors opened, humid air rolled in like a tsunami. The stewardess gave the go ahead to the first passengers to de-plane. Betty held Vu's hand as they stepped out of the aircraft and descended the stairs together.

"I hope this isn't a sign of things to come," Betty said, pushing a strand of matted hair from her face. The scorching wind kicked up dust clouds that swirled across the tarmac.

Vu squeezed Betty's hand reassuringly. "Remember, when we go off plan that is where the adventure begins."

They boarded the stifling bus, packed forty deep, sweaty bodies pressed together. Betty clutched a handrail still wearing her intractable smile, albeit without its sparkle. Finally, the driver closed the doors. They were moving. Hurray!

After a short jaunt to the terminal, the bus off-loaded at ground level. Everyone was directed inside by officials standing at the terminal doors. Vu followed Betty inside into an ocean of fuming tourists. There were bodies as far as you could see.

Following the herd toward Immigration for an hour and a half, made the 30-minute wait to pass through Customs, seem like a skip in the park. By the time they were free of bureaucracy, and heading toward freedom, the sun was nudging toward the low lying mountains.

Outside the terminal doors, hustlers zeroed in. Hungry and tired, Betty tried to pick a fight with loud American blocking the sidewalk.

"Hey, move your fat ass." she shouted.

Vu put his arm around her, traded positions, putting a body between her and the testosterone tank. A sign mounted on the wall behind the man's head read: *"In Costa Rica it is illegal to have sex with a minor."*

Obviously the hustlers working the sidewalk couldn't read English. Okay, he was grumpy too.

Vu spotted a teenager in a tan uniform holding a sign from their travel company. "Over there, Betty!" he pointed.

Vu signaled their eager attendant who guided them through the raucous crowd and introduced them to a friendly female in the same colored uniform holding a clipboard. Betty reached into her purse, fumbled with her camera, and squeezed off a picture.

"Buenas tardes. Welcome," the attendant said, "I see here on my list you are with Windward Expeditions. Allow me to help you find a seat inside our air conditioned bus, and enjoy a snack."

It would be another hour before the entire tour group boarded the bus. A different tour guide, also Costa Rican, introduced himself.

"Felicidades! Congratulations," he announced cheerfully. "You have all made it. My name is Billy Delfaro. I will be your host for the journey to your boat in Herradura. Rather than wait for your luggage to find us, we will leave men here to gather it and bring it to the boat as soon as possible. Now, did everyone receive a sack lunch?"

Betty turned to Vu, now happy as a clam. She'd torn into her lunch, cramming the turkey sandwich into her mouth. Vu took out an apple and rubbed it on his pant leg, smiling. She was a girl with voracious appetites.

Betty slurped mustard from the corners of her mouth. *"Dáme un beso!* Give me a kiss." she enthused between bites.

The two-hour drive from San Jose to the pier at Playa Herradura in many ways reminded Vu of traveling through Vietnam. The Capital of San Jose, perched among a crescent of mountains and volcanoes, bore a resemblance to the Saigon of his youth, a city shackled by frantic pedestrians, heavy traffic and blaring horns. The splendid architecture also bore a striking similarity to his homeland, revealing the disparity between rich and poor.

"Look!" Betty pointed out the window at a busy freeway. Vu looked but didn't share her enthusiasm.

"What is so special about an interstate?" he asked.

Betty eagerly pointed out that they were following the *Carretera Interamericana Highway*, a stretch of famous interstate which connected Costa Rica to her northern neighbor, Nicaragua and to her southern neighbor, Panama. Betty pawed through her guidebook again, adding a bright smear of mustard to the pages.

While the entire trip excited her, it was all just foreplay to the main event crossing the Panama Canal, a childhood fantasy stemming from a Cary Grant movie she saw as a kid. The main plot involved two spinster aunts killing men and having their crazy brother bury them in the basement, telling him that he was working on the Panama Canal and they were yellow fever victims. Only in America would this plot be considered a screwball comedy.

Vu wondered what part that movie played in the development of this beautiful forensic pathologist with her high IQ and low cut dresses.

"Just think, Jack, in just one week we will transit the Panama Canal." Her face became serious. "For the next seven days, there'll be no work, no phone calls, no emails. Just us."

Vu looked her in the eye. "I give you my word."

Betty stared at him for a long time before she sat back and relaxed. And before Vu knew it, they were out of the city and traveling on Highway 3.

This narrow, treacherous and twisting road humped out of the Meseta Central plateau at an elevation of 4000 feet and descended to nearly sea level before ascending again like a wild carnival ride.

The highway forged across what remained of the Central Plains, but what made the ride thrilling, were the enormous potholes and steep drop-offs on the sides of the road, both of which the driver tried to avoid. Zigzagging through dairy farms, plantations of macadamia, fields of Mangroves and *viveros*, flower farms, they descended before darkness encompassed them.

Amazingly they arrived at the pier unscathed, slightly dizzy, but eager for the next adventure. It would start sooner than they anticipated.

"Jack," Betty said, after she climbed down out of the bus and stood on the deserted dock. "Where's our boat?"

Chapter 5

Vu stood on the dark pier and stared toward the water. Behind him Betty paced back and forth. She was not alone. Five other couples from the bus stood about fidgeting with their carry-on bags or swatting at insects. In the marina, adjacent to the pier, luxurious yachts settled into their slips for the evening, their colorful flags blowing gently in the breeze.

"Do you see anything?" Betty asked for the third time in five minutes, pressing a tired squeak out of the dried wood on the dock as she stood on tiptoe and searched the horizon.

"I see the moon and stars, but no boat."

"What do you think happened to it?" she asked.

"I don't know."

"Maybe pirates took it. I read there is a problem with pirates."

Before Vu could reply, their tour guide appeared and told everyone to gather round; he had an announcement to make.

"Ladies and Gentlemen, I have some very good news," he shouted. "Our ship is coming. It was delayed because another vessel needed to unload passengers just before we arrived. If you look out toward the water now, you will see its bow light. We apologize for the inconvenience. We will be boarding just as soon as it ties up."

Sure enough, Vu turned and spotted the shining light in the distance. The frustration of traveling seemed to evaporate with this happy news. He pulled Betty in close and hugged her.

All passengers gathered on the pier to watch the cruise ship glide toward the dock. Out of the darkness, the vessel appeared with the mysterious charm of an old steam locomotive easing into a sleepy depot. Vu estimated that the ship was about eighty-feet longer than the *Arctic Wing*, his boat, which would make her about one-hundred and seventy feet from tip to tail. Its three decks were lit up like a stage set. They'd reserved a top deck cabin and Vu quickly counted back from the bow to see if he could see which cabin would be theirs.

"More passengers are arriving!" someone from the back announced excitedly.

A taxi skidded onto the pier. A couple from England, it turned out, had taken a later flight and had also been delayed at the airport and missed the bus. The couple bailed out, eager to join the others on the dock.

"Ladies and Gentleman," the guide announced from the pier. "Please step back. The crew will be throwing lines ashore. We do not want anyone to get injured."

Betty slipped behind Vu and wrapped her arms around him. Together they watched the crew heave the heavy ropes ashore. The lines were secured to cleats and drawn snug. A hatch opened. A slender man in a white uniform stepped out and waved.

"Hello, everyone!" he shouted. "On behalf of the captain and the crew of the *Sea Gypsy*, I'd like to welcome you aboard."

* * *

Vu and Betty's cabin lights were soft as moonlight capturing the rich warm teak interior. Betty fell onto the queen-size bed and fanned her arms out along the soft comforter like a child falling into a snow bank. "Oh, Jack, this feels so good."

After two days of travel through two cramped and annoying airports, they'd made it. Looking around the spacious room, Vu sensed that booking the first class cabin had been the right move. Vu was perversely proud of his frugal nature, but when it came to Betty, he had no such restraint. He wanted to give her the world, or in this case the best room on the boat.

Betty patted the bed. "Come here, big boy, let's cuddle. We got time. The others are still boarding."

The offer was tempting, but Vu was afraid if he relaxed back into the big bed for even a minute, he'd never get up again.

Before he could decide, the cabin's speaker system requested all passengers join the crew in the dining area on the bottom deck for dinner. Tonight's meal would be a choice of sea bass, ginger chicken or pesto pasta with chocolate bread pudding for dessert. Red or white wine could be purchased with the meal.

"Yummy, sea bass," Betty said and popped up, licking her lips. "I didn't know I was so hungry." She glanced down at her turquoise blouse and slacks. It was evident from the wrinkles and spots of dirt that she'd been traveling all day. "Look at me," she said, attempting to brush wrinkles from her blouse before slumping in defeat. "I don't feel like changing. I'm going like this. We're on vacation, right?"

Vu smiled. "We're on vacation." And that would come to be their theme line. Vu checked his appearance. Cotton slacks, a soiled white shirt and dusty deck shoes. His armpits felt like pools of salt. *To hell with it, they'd go as the stinky couple.*

"We embarked with no luggage and big appetites."

Stepping out of their cabin and onto the narrow deck area, Betty lost her balance, swaying with the boat, her arms pinwheeling. Vu caught her before she did a somersault over the railing.

"Oops! I gotta be more careful," she said playfully. "And I'm sober! Think what could've happened after a few glasses of wine?"

"You'll have plenty of chances to get it right."

Vu closed the cabin door and realized it couldn't be locked with a key from the outside, only from a knob on the inside. A maritime rule, apparently. Yet, it still concerned him to leave their possessions unsecured.

Betty stretched her kinked neck up toward the sparkling sky. "Look at all the night stars, Jack. Aren't they beautiful?"

He turned and glanced skyward. It sounded corny, but he wished upon a star for their safe journey in this foreign land. Buddha spirit – be with them.

After reaching the stern they rounded the deck to the port side of the vessel and descended steep narrow steps to the lower level.

The dining area was at the stern on the bottom deck. It was divided in half with a rosewood self-service counter in the center and teak tables lit by brass table lamps. Setting off the rich décor were statues carved out of hardwood. Mounted on the walls were historic black & white photographs of sailing ships and famous explorers. The polished hardwood flooring emitted a pleasant lemon-blossom scent. Vu figured the room filled to the brim would hold a hundred people give or take. Most of the guests were getting acquainted at tables. Betty and Vu took a seat at a round six-top, joining another couple, already sipping on wine and chatting amongst themselves. Vu recognized the couple from the bus. After the host left the table, they introduced themselves. Their names were Fred and Carol Doff from Texas.

Fred was a retired engineer. His wife of thirty plus years was a retired teacher. This was their second trip with Windward Expeditions. Their first was to the Galapagos Islands.

"I'm so excited to be aboard," Betty said. "I don't think I'm going to be able to sleep tonight."

"Did you bring earplugs? These boats can be quite noisy," Fred said, setting his wine glass down so the waiter could refill it.

"I brought my sound deafening headphones. Jack reminded me. He always thinks of that sort of thing. I usually wait until the last minute to pack. When I get to my destination it's always a mystery to see what I actually brought."

"What is it that you do, Jack?" Carol asked. Vu noticed that Carol sat rigid like a board propped her up from behind. Her brown eyes were almost too intense to look at. Vu suspected she had a medical condition.

He was not eager to talk about himself. As a rule he much preferred to listen and observe. But he felt like he had to say something. As he opened his mouth a waiter stopped at their table,
introduced himself as Ernesto. After he read off the menu choices,
he asked them which entrée they preferred.

"I want the Chilean sea bass," Betty said, smiling, "and what
comes with that?"

"Chayote and red rice," the waiter replied.

"Chayote?"

"Sautéed water squash. Your *Corvina a la Chorrillana* also
comes with a ginger passion fruit sauce. I'm afraid it does not come
on the side. Would you also like wine with your dinner? We are
serving two semi-dry wines this evening. Red or white. A Char-
donnay or Cabernet. They are both from Argentina. We also have
wines by the bottle, if you prefer."

Vu ordered the *Gallina Rostisada en sus Jugos*, garlic roasted
chicken in natural juices and told the waiter to hold the squash.
Rice was fine.

The waiter took the Doff's order next. They ordered the pesto
pasta. Afterward Fred asked: "Have you two traveled with Windward before?"

Vu was relieved he did not have to discuss work. "No, we are
virgins, so to speak."

"I noticed you have an anchor logo on your pocket. Are you a
sailor?"

Betty jumped in. "Jack lives aboard a ninety-foot wooden boat.
It was decommissioned back in the eighties, and purchased by a
Japanese businesswoman, who planned to convert it into a floating
hotel. But her plans dissolved following Katrina. It's in dry dock
now being repaired."

Carol sat up. "We're boaters too. Our home port is Houston.
My husband and I own a Monk Trawler. We travelled to Scandi-
navia to see it being built. We've put over twelve thousand miles
on *Dream Spirit* since we bought her in 2000. We took two years
off and sailed down the entire Atlantic coastline, circled the Keys,

then back up Florida's western coastline. We entered the inland waterways and continued until it spit us out into the Atlantic again. It was quite an adventure. Most of the marinas where we stayed are gone now – destroyed by Katrina and the oil spill. So many lives were ruined. I'm glad we made the trip when we did."

"When you get our age," Fred continued, "you realize that time is not on your side."

The rest of the evening's conversations progressed along the lines of boating, current politics and how wonderful dinner tasted. Vu was not a connoisseur of grape wines and would have preferred a rice wine, like sake, but the ship's hotel manager said they were fresh out.

Dessert was served.

Everyone at the table with the exception of Vu dug into the decadent bread pudding. Vu seemed lost in thought, staring at a passenger across the room. Betty turned to see who he was looking at.

"Jack – what is it?"

"Nothing," he said, resuming his composed posture. He picked his fork off the table and began eating his dessert.

Betty looked at the man he'd been studying. An American with rugged good looks, built like a brick wall, and their age.

Betty leaned over and whispered in his ear. "Tell me you aren't turning gay on me."

"No such luck. You're stuck with me." Vu was ashamed to admit it but his mind was on an old case. He chastised himself.

Curious, the Doffs stopped eating and put their forks down.

Vu looked Betty in the eye. "He reminds me of someone."

"Probably looks like one of those cop characters on TV you guys like to watch," Carol said. The Doffs chuckled.

The man reminded Vu of an old adversary. For several weeks prior to leaving on vacation Vu had had a recurring nightmare about an old murder case involving a former Special Ops soldier named Jim Lyman. Lyman had been tortured and presumed dead in Southeast Asia when his fingerprints mysteriously turned up at a grisly murder scene in New Orleans. Vu had tracked the soldier as he made his escape on a trawler off the Oregon Coast. When wreckage washed ashore days later everyone presumed the soldier had perished at sea. Yet, Vu had a feeling Lyman had once again survived. The fellow sitting at the table across the room reminded him of Jim Lyman.

Vu quickly changed the subject and faced the Doffs. "You think we'll see any Howler monkeys on tomorrow's hike?"

Fred smiled awkwardly. "I would like to see a jaguar. I hear they've been spotted at Manuel Antonio."

"What about you, Carol?" Betty asked.

Carol had a smudge of chocolate on her lip. She wiped it clean with a napkin before speaking. "I would very much like to see a Sloth. I can't imagine what it would be like to spend your life hanging upside down. Can you?"

Betty perked up. "I read somewhere that they only come down out of the trees once a week to poop. Is that true?"

"Yes," Carol replied appearing dismayed by Betty's uninhibited discussion of bowel movements at dinner.

And then, as if on cue, a number of guests stood and started trickling back to their cabins. The brass clock on the wall near their table read 2200 hours.

The foursome stood. Betty and Vu wished the Doffs a good night and left. When they reached the upper deck, Betty slipped her arm around her man and directed him toward the lounge.

"Care for a nightcap, sugar?" he asked playfully.

"I think champagne's in order, don't you?"

Chapter 6

The next morning inside the laboratory of the *Instituto Nacional de Biodiversidad*, Dr. Gaston Trujillo removed his rubber gloves and apron and dropped them into the biological waste container. He then stood over a stainless steel sink, turned on the faucet and let the water heat before washing his hands and cleaning the specks of fresh blood from his eye glasses. Gaston readjusted his tie in the mirror, noticing the dark circles around his eyes. His *café au lait* skin had taken on a pasty gray hue. He ran a tongue over his teeth. The bitter aftertaste of espresso still lingered. *How much longer could he use caffeine and other less innocent stimulants as a substitute for sleep? As long as it took...*

He returned to the small operating table and stared down at the rare mono titi, the baby red-backed squirrel monkey, no larger than a pair of his mistress's panties and no less endangered. Its tufted red, orange and yellow fur shined under the bright florescent lights. So did its fresh patch of shaved skin at the base of its neck where the transmitter had been inserted.

It'd been a relatively routine procedure. After he'd anesthetized the animal, he'd implanted the electronic device a few millimeters beneath the dermis in an area where the monkey couldn't pick at it. His fellow primates, although highly intelligent for their size, might be curious about the implant, yet he doubted they would try to tear it out of the skin. Grooming each other, he'd been assured by the manufacturer, would not dislodge or damage it. During testing, the transmitters functioned far better than his homemade models he'd used many years ago when the experiment first hatched in his subconscious.

It had begun when the government demanded that all civilians feeding or keeping wild animals as pets release them back into their natural environments. It was one of the first efforts of the environmentalists and PETA advocates to attempt to return Earth to its natural order.

As a child, his beloved Capuchin playmate, Jake, had been unceremoniously stolen from him while he was away at a school science fair. Unable to fend for itself and never having laid eyes on a fellow monkey, Jake returned to Gaston starving, lice infested and mangled just days later. He knew he couldn't keep the little fellow hidden from his mother, so he devised a plan to save his friend and restore the environment. His idea at transitioning Jake into a strong Alpha Male, with a band of loyal soldiers and mates took shape as only the mind of naïve youngster could conjure raised on cartoons and superheroes.

He outfitted Jake with a radio transmitter. He explained to his friend that he would track him at all times and place safe bedding and food along his path. It seemed so simple.

He carried the bedding and food a mile into the woods and returned home. Jake was there waiting for him. Determined, he ignored his monkey and slowly saw through his GPS that the monkey began to eat from the feeding station. But he never learned to forage on his own. Although he became more feral with each passing week, returning less and less to the boy's home, his eyes slowly changing from joy, to fear, to anger, Gaston learned one of his first adult lessons: There is a difference between a tightly held belief and the truth. He truly believed he could give Jake the life he deserved, but the truth was the creation of a crazed defenseless animal.

It all ended when he returned home to see his father carrying a dead monkey to the garbage. His father said, "I shot this little bugger before you could adopt him." Later that evening, he lifted the lid of the can and with a sob he could not contain, removed his transmitter from the neck of his once closest friend on earth. And when he buried Jake under his bedroom window that evening he also buried the soft childlike core of his heart. All his prayers hadn't helped save Jake. Only science could do that.

Thank God I'm an atheist.

Gaston stifled a yawn. The young primate began to twitch and flutter its eyes. The effects of the anesthesia began wearing off. Spittle drooled from his black-capped mouth. He had to hurry now. Gaston picked up the handheld tracking device, turned it on and waited impatiently for the screen to display. Once the image popped up, he punched in a series of numbers and was pleased to see the implant was transmitting a strong signal. He stowed the device in a lower locked cabinet, slipped on a clean lab coat and carefully carried the groggy animal over to a row of metal cages. He placed it inside the last one on the end and secured the door.

Next he checked in on the other captive monkeys, the three white-faced capuchins and two spider monkeys who'd had the devices installed the day before, as did the Howler monkey, segregated in a cage across the hall. All were eating well and looked to be recovering nicely.

Across the room the laboratory door opened. A middle-aged man in a sports jacket and slacks followed by a young woman wearing a lab coat walked in and greeted the doctor. Gaston recognized the man immediately. He was a veterinarian from the Animal Clinic in Quepos. The woman was one of Gaston's new assistants. No one got into the laboratory without an escort.

"*Buenos días. Cómo va, Doctor Ramos,*" Gaston said. "*Que opinás?* What do you think of them wanting to tear down our favorite restaurant? I just read of it today. Where will we have our *cervezas* now?"

Gaston walked over, shook hands and excused his assistant, who left quietly.

"It is bad everywhere, this construction," Dr. Ramos said. "This new marina – what will it do for men of education I ask you?"

"It will do nothing for our minds, I'm afraid, but it will have a disastrous effect on our alcoholic tendencies. Perhaps we can exploit tax revenue and fund research with the profit it makes from us."

The two doctors continued talking in the spirit of *el Dia de Independencia*. As they spoke, outside the windows, school bands were on the march getting ready for the traditional Independence Day parades all over the country. Nearly two centuries ago, messengers from Nicaragua brought the word of liberty to Costa Rica. Until that time the country was a backwater of the Spanish Crown.

The boisterous conversation excited the primates. Cages were rattling and the room was filled with dog-like barking sounds. Dr. Ramos looked concerned.

"Come with me," Gaston said. "I was just getting ready to feed them. You can assist."

Dr. Ramos raised his hand. "Yesterday an old capuchin was brought to my hospital. It had been bitten by a poisonous snake. I'm afraid I was unable to save it."

"Why on earth did you even try? Snake bites are fatal."

"Because an American brought it to me. He said he found it in Manuel Antonio."

"How did this man come in contact with the primate?"

"He was in the woods and saw a viper attack it."

"Vipers haven't been native to this area for decades."

"And he tried to save the monkey by sucking out the venom."

"He cut into a wild capuchin?"

"Yes – along the arm. Most unusual, don't you think? It was one of the reasons I tried to save it. After an hour of hiking to my clinic, it was still alive!"

Gaston found the news fascinating. Perhaps his experiments at strengthening the breeds were working.

"Are you certain it was a wild capuchin and not a pet that had escaped?"

"It had many scars and even though it was dying, it attempted to bite me, but I am uncertain of its origins. That is what brought me here."

Gaston's mind locked on an irregularity he had spotted in his tracking system last night. He knew with certainty why Ramos was here. "What is troubling you my friend?"

"He had a transmitter in his neck."

"A what?" Gaston held his expression carefully.

"As I was examining him, I found an old surgical scar. Upon closer examination, I found this and removed it." Ramos handed the metal chip to Gaston.

"I've never seen anything like this." Gaston's innocent expression belied the mental files he was combing through in an attempt to direct the conversation a certain way. He'd recognized Gringo's chip immediately.

"Do you think the man inserted it?"

"No, he is new to the area and the scar was old."

"Possibly some international animal rights group?"

Ramos shrugged.

"This man that brought the capuchin into your hospital, do you think he is a tourist?"

"No."

"What can you tell me about him?"

"His name is Lyman. I believe he is a former military man. My daughter says he is from Kansas and has fled the United States for crazy reasons. But she has a very vivid imagination."

"I would like to know more about him. You will inform me if he visits your clinic again?"

Dr. Ramos nodded and scratched his chin.

"Did you keep the remains? I'd be most interested in examining them."

Dr. Ramos shook his head. "No. The American insisted I return them to him immediately. I did manage to retrieve a vile of the monkey's blood and tissue samples where I removed the transmitter." Ramos removed them from his jacket pocket and handed them to Gaston. "Maybe you can find out more about the monkey's ability to withstand the viper's bite with your sophisticated equipment?"

"Did he say what he was going to do with the carcass?"

"No." Ramos paused in thought. "I didn't know if I should even bring the device here today. Since we don't know who is tracking these monkeys, I didn't want to involve you in something we know nothing about. But then I thought that they would know the monkey was dead or else they would think it had learned to drive a car and had come to pay you a visit.

Gaston attempted to chuckle. "Let's go discuss this over a *cervezas* next door before they tear down that building. I'll have my assistants handle the feeding."

As he draped his arm across Ramos' shoulder he was already worried about how many more people to whom Ramos had told his story.

Chapter 7

Across town, Sanchez woke up with a hangover and to the sound of pounding parade drums outside the small apartment overlooking Main Street. She rolled over and checked her watch on the nightstand.

Shit!

She bolted upright, facing a blazing sun glaring through the French doors. She swung her short, bare legs over the side of the bed and dangled her feet on the hardwood floor. She was too dizzy to get up yet, so she eased her head down between her legs to see if the room would stop spinning.

"*Porquito*? Where are you going?" It was a male voice, scratchy and tired, stirring on the other side of the bed. At first, she had no idea who the sleepy voice belonged to. Then the evening's events flooded back in a wave of nausea.

"Go back to sleep."

Her male companion rolled over and closed his eyes instantly.

The slight vertigo passed and she climbed from bed. She stood naked on shaky feet and had no idea where she'd taken off her clothing. The surroundings weren't familiar. It was a loft apartment. Large and well furnished. Oriental rugs. Enormous oil paintings.

A leather sofa. Imported tables. Scattered across the room were bits and pieces of her uniform. She found her bra hooked over the bedpost, her t-shirt in the center of the room draped over a wooden statue of an eagle. Her jeans were crumpled on the floor near the kitchen like she'd just stepped out of them. Her shirt flung across the sofa with one of the buttons torn off socks strewn by the bathroom door. But her shoes – they were nowhere to be found. Nor could she locate her underpants.

She gathered up the clothing and bungled it on. In a living room mirror she noticed her t-shirt was on inside out and flipped it around. Her eyes were bloodshot. Her tossed hair looked like some animal had made a nest in it during the night. Her gun belt and revolver lay neatly on the kitchen table. She strapped them on next and noticed the handcuffs were missing from the pouch. She checked the floor and then turned back toward the bed. The shiny cuffs were clamped onto the brass headboard above her companion's side of the bed. The activities, although still fuzzy in her mind, slowly returned after her eye lit upon the empty bottle of Scotch on the night stand. That would explain the throbbing headache. She rubbed her neck and stared down at the naked guy sprawled out atop the silk sheets, purring like a drugged tiger. He was handsome enough and his hair was dark like she liked them. Not overly muscled but firm. Tight abs. A fine ass. So this Tico stud had been her one night stand….

She took another look at his attractive face. Hell, he was just a damn kid. What had she been thinking?

Then she remembered the corpse. How it troubled her. How it triggered memories of her father's murder. That explained the blackout drinking and need for distraction.

Sanchez tip-toed to the bed and retrieved the cuffs. She found her underpants beneath the nightstand, next to the trash can, where she found a fresh condom wrapper and several crumpled Kleenex. At least one of them had the good sense to use protection.

She stuffed her panties into her purse, then entered the kitchen and made some instant coffee. After slugging it back, she immediately felt sick to her stomach. She needed to eat something, soak up the booze and she desperately needed a shower. But she'd already wasted enough time. She found a pair of men's sandals by the door and slipped them on.

Outside the stranger's apartment the bright sun was a thorn in her eye. The street was noisy and crowded. Excited school children in colorful uniforms waved paper lanterns, flags and banners, all of which were in celebration of *el Dia de Independencia*. Tourists darted through the streets snapping pictures of the donkey parade.

Sanchez crossed the street behind the crowd and headed into the next block where people were folding up their chairs in front of a few businesses and leaving the area. She remembered stopping at Nick's Sport Bar to calm her nerves. She'd been wound up after the hike into Manuel Antonia and what she'd found there. After a couple beers and some conversation, she followed the rookie back to his place. He seemed harmless and hot, the perfect distraction for her pain. He said he was a cop so she felt okay about it. She vaguely remembered that he had joked about living above an Italian restaurant and that his place always smelled of Lasagna. But she couldn't for the life of her remember if she drove? Somehow it had all seemed more attractive than driving back to her apartment in the next township since she'd scheduled a meeting in Jaco the following morning. To drive eighty miles round trip when she was already in the area made no sense. Or at least that's how she justified it at the time.

Through the harsh light she made out the old jeep up ahead, illegally parked at the curb, covered in confetti and dried mud, awaiting her like the carriage of a princess, albeit an immoral and hung-over one. The rust bucket government-issued vehicle would hopefully start and its bald tires would hopefully stay inflated long enough to get her to the office of the Judicial Investigation Organization in the Central Providence.

She fumbled around in her purse until she found the key. Knocking some confetti from the windshield, she unlocked the door and climbed in. She checked by rote the special locked compartment behind the seat and saw that her rifle and two-way radio were safely inside the metal box.

Wedged down between the passenger door and the seat she spotted her satchel and camera. She took her underpants out of her purse and stuffed them into her satchel. She didn't need to lug them around. She quickly donned a pair of dusty sunglasses from the dash before searching the glove box for smokes. She found a partial pack of unfiltered cigarettes, lit one and tossed the match out the open window. The quick rush of nicotine eased her nausea and provided a false sense that the day ahead was going to get better.

Chapter 8

The surf splashed over the Zodiac's bow, showering the eight passengers. The salty water striking Vu's bare leg brought back old memories. As a teenager he'd escaped from The Killing Fields in a homemade boat similar in size, but not nearly as seaworthy. The harrowing weeks at sea had killed nearly everyone. He was one of the few to survive the ordeal, ending up in Malaysia where he was granted political asylum. All the suffering had eventually subsided. None of it mattered any longer. The remarkable journey from his former homeland to freedom in the United States and to the woman who sat across from him now, had all been worth it. He'd never felt more in love.

Betty leaned out over the water, enjoying every minute of the thrilling ride. Vu smiled affectionately toward her while she tightened her grip on the side-rail. Her daypack was tucked between her legs and her pants were soaked. Her hair danced in the breeze. The warm glow washing over her face brought out the best in her complexion. She looked vibrant and happy. Other passengers paled in comparison.

"We are getting near now," the guide said, pointing out the small island ahead. "You see the small beach off your starboard bow? That is where we shall make our first wet landing. Does anyone have any questions?"

An unhealthy looking women sitting beside him moaned and clutched her stomach. She lowered her head and closed her eyes. Beads of perspiration rolled off her forehead and her pasty skin suggested she was struggling to keep breakfast down.

"Look out to the horizon," Vu said. "It will help."

The woman opened her eyes and peered into the distance. Vu retrieved a peppermint lozenge from his vest pocket and offered it to her. "This will relieve the nausea."

The woman hesitated, reached out with a shaky hand and took it, prying her lips apart in order to swallow the lozenge. "Thank you. What is your name again?" Vu told her. "You're the military investigator, aren't you?" A hint of life returned to her face now. "I overheard your wife mention it to one of the passengers at breakfast."

Vu had done well keeping that part of his life quiet. But he couldn't keep Betty from talking about him. He cringed at some of the classified military stories she prattled on about after a glass of wine or two. Of course to be fair, she also happily discussed the most grisly aspects of her cases over morning breakfast.

"Yes. I have two years until I retire," he told her and then changed the subject. "If I may ask, are you traveling alone?"

"Yes." She kept her eyes riveted to the horizon. "For years my husband and I had planned this trip together. But, three months ago, he was killed in the line of duty. Our children insisted I come anyway."

"Was your husband in the military?"

"No. He was a policeman in New Jersey. It's a long story. And quite frankly, I'm tired of telling it." Vu understood that statement more than she could ever know. She paused a moment then turned toward him. "Thank you for the mint. I believe it helped."

Vu nodded.

As their boat neared land, the pilot made a one-hundred-eighty degree turn pointing the stern toward shore and within seconds the inflatable was scuffing the bottom and shuttered to a halt.

One-by-one the passengers began to scramble from the boat, stepping into the warm knee-deep splashing surf. Vu assisted the sick woman ashore.

"My name is Elisabeth," she said to Betty, who hurried over to help, "but please call me Ellie," the woman offered in reply. "You have a nice husband."

Betty didn't correct her and smiled wickedly at Vu.

"Would you like some water?" Betty asked.

"No thanks. I just need to sit down for a minute."

Vu looked around and spotted a log that had washed ashore. He pointed it out to Betty who led the way. Once they had the woman sitting on something solid, her color slowly came back and a hint of life returned to her eyes. The native biologist from the boat strolled over to them.

"I know you are all scheduled for the Birds of Costa Rica hike." He then turned toward Ellie. "Perhaps you should take the Sloth Walk today," he said. "It is a flatter two-mile walk and might be easier on you physically."

Ellie looked at both Vu and Betty and smiled, "I kinda feel like a sloth right now. Thank you. I will." Ellie turned toward Vu and Betty, "You two go ahead. I'm fine."

"Are you sure?" Betty asked. Vu knew that Betty had been looking forward to this hike which she'd read about in the travel books. Yet she put her own needs aside.

"Yes. The longer I am on dry land, the better I feel."

"Then we'll see you at lunch."

Vu took hold of Betty's hand and led her toward the small group that had collected at the trail leading into the rainforest. The guide explained that it would be a difficult three-mile hike around the area known as Punta Cathedral.

"She's seems fragile, that one," Betty said, after they were out of earshot.

"Her husband recently died."

"How awful. I don't know what I'd do if something happened to you, Jack."

"I'd hope you would do just like Ellie and take your trip to the Panama Canal."

"And what about you? Where would you go if I died right this minute?"

Vu rolled his eyes skyward. "I'd go find my Blue Footed Boobies. And when I did, I'd name the biggest Boobie of all after you."

Smiling like a delighted child, Betty leaned forward and kissed Vu's cheek.

* * *

Beyond Punta Cathedral, Lyman slipped off his backpack and sat down on a familiar flat stump. He took out a handkerchief from his pocket, wiped perspiration from his face and took a long cool drink from his canteen. He read the screen of his handheld GPS. He was heading in the right direction but the signal was weak. Even with electronic devices, conditions in the rainforest often changed overnight. The terrain could appear quite different from the day before – shifting contours, darker soil; even trees and foliage could change colors. Strangler vines grew, twisting endlessly through the forest floor hidden under deep vegetation like giant nooses waiting to trap their prey. Overhead, the thick canopy altered with each rising sun, each leaf wanting to extract as much sunlight as possible. If they could obtain enough sunlight, plants thrived in these moist conditions. Wildlife was also unpredictable, moving from location to location, leaving behind only the subtlest traces, too minute for him to usually detect.

Eventually, Lyman recognized the balloon-sized termite hive that had nearly taken off his head the day before. This time he tripped over a decaying ficus branch as he spotted Kinkajou tracks along the way, followed by other broken branches. Someone else had been in the area since yesterday. And he knew who it was.

Lyman rested. A blue-winged butterfly drifted down out of the trees followed by a clickity-clackity chatter of a red-eyed tree frog. The mating call of a toucan could be heard far away beyond the ray of sunlight that ignited a small area of the lush forest. For his own edification, Lyman began to recite the Latin names of the flora straining toward the light and the various trees around him. The living breathing rainforest was a network of opposing elements. Somehow those elements found a way through the millennium to co-exist – to be an essential part of a bigger whole. One could not exist without the other. It was also true of the insect world. The life of a colony of leaf cutter ants co-existed with nature supplying soil with necessary nutrients while removing decaying vegetation from the forest floor. Each had their unique role. Worker ants converted the waste matter into life-giving fuel, without which the entire rainforest could not survive. It was a miracle so pure. A feat of nature so basic, yet so essential to everything that grew here. If only he could have seen the same interconnectedness in human life. Human life seemed absurd to him. One endless struggle after the next. No reason behind the absurdity except absurdity itself.

The longer Lyman studied the rain forest, the better he felt. It was reassuring to know that something had meaning. But where did the decaying tree corpse fit into the "Grand Plan?"

He continued on until he found the tree where the body still sagged on a branch undisturbed. Traces of Gringo's blood spattered the dirt. A predator had evidently carried off the snake's body, which was fine with him. And the money was gone. That suggested a different kind of predator. He had one more thing to do before he put Gringo to rest.

He walked fifty meters to the southwest – toward a square strand of hardwood trees where he noticed broken twigs and scuff marks in the soil. He studied the tree trunks and found a few rubber scuff marks on one trunk base suggesting someone had recently climbed the tree. Next he studied the towering limbs. Many of the new starts had been broken off, evidence of where the person would have propped themselves up. At the base of the stand of trees, he examined a small mossy area flattened by footprints and uncovered two cigarette butts and four matches that someone had gone to the trouble of covering up with a light dusting of topsoil.

He brushed them off and put them into his front pocket. He then returned to the area to say goodbye to his old friend.

He reached inside the backpack to remove Gringo's body, wrapped in camouflage material. That morning he'd taken an old BDU out of hiding, cut it up using a portion of it as burial cloth. The uniform somehow seemed fitting for an old warrior like Gringo. He couldn't think of a better way to honor the primate's bravery.

He used a small folding shovel to dig a hole in the earth in the shape of a coffin and deep enough to make it impractical for most wild animals to unearth. A mysterious breeze kicked up and part of the cloth fell down from Gringo's neck. He stooped over to re-wrap it when he noticed a small hole about the size of a nickel along the primate's neckline. It seemed strangely out of place. He would have to query the veterinarian later about this.

He had just sat back to say a few closing words when he heard them swinging through the forest from vine to vine like a chorus of acrobats. One by one, the family of six primates dropped down and hobbled over to him, with little bow-legged Riff Raff leading the way.

Chapter 9

Sanchez splashed some cold water on her face and stared at the restroom mirror inside the Judicial Investigation Organization building. She looked as terrible as she felt. Her eyes were bloodshot. The bags under them could double as nut sacks. No amount of makeup would hide this hangover.

The Records Department was in the basement. A crowd waited to reach the counter to speak with an overworked clerk. Sanchez marched up to the front of the line and flashed her credentials, but the man told her to step aside and wait her turn.

Usually Sanchez would have pushed harder, but today she felt like a wimp and took her place in back.

Twenty minutes later, it was her turn at the counter. She requested files on six individuals – names she'd committed to memory.

"You're kidding, right?" the clerk said.

"No."

The man pointed over his shoulder. "See that line out the door? Today, two files maximum."

"You're kidding right?" she said, gritting her teeth. She needed that information.

"Two files. That's it."

"C'mon, you can squeeze in a few more? This is a federal matter." She gave him her best seductive smile, but it didn't seem to have the desired effect.

The clerk was middle-aged and about thirty pounds over-weight that not even a pressing of his wrinkled uniform could hide. Her father would have been about the same age. But he would have never let himself go like that. Despite a disheveled appearance, the clerk was courteous, but firm. She handed him the list with all six names, which he grunted at and then disappeared for five minutes before returning with three folders that he plopped down on the counter to Sanchez's surprise.

"Looks like you had a rough night," the clerk commented.

Sanchez just nodded. "This it?"

"All we have. You can take a seat at the table behind you. If you need to use the toilet, return all the files before you leave the area."

"You're positive you don't have the other three?"

"As a departmental courtesy, I checked all six names off your list. The others are missing."

"Where are they?"

"Beats me."

The clerk waved the next person forward. Sanchez put up her hand. With a surprised look, the man behind her stopped in his tracks.

"Have records turned up missing before?"

"It happens," the clerk stated, then quickly changed the subject. "Hey, I understand they arrested 11 gunmen in your area. Part of the Sinaloa Drug Cartel. You figure they're coming through Costa Rica with their shipments?"

"What are you talking about?"

"Your office is on this, right?"

Sanchez couldn't afford to be rude if she wanted the clerk's cooperation in the future. Questions like this made her head hurt. "We're working on it." She glanced down at the clerk's name badge. "Frank – could you do me one more huge favor? Re-check the names on this list again. The files should be here. I've driven from San José."

Sanchez's smile appeared to impress the clerk. Perhaps it was the fact that she unbuttoned her shirt to cool off while offering up a little more flesh, which the clerk duly noted. He took the paper back.

When he returned empty handed, he said, "That's all we have. Check upstairs with Vice. They have a regular habit of removing records without filling out the proper paperwork."

"Could you call them? You know how they hate to have an unannounced drop-in."

Sanchez didn't know if this was true or not – but they would certainly be more responsive to an inquiry from one of their own rather than an outsider from another agency who just popped in.

"Let me take care of this line. Then I'll make the call."

"Thanks, Frank."

Sanchez carried the files over to a crowded table in the corner, nudging in between two legal assistants, both appearing to be working divorce cases, and sat down. The cramped quarters added to her hypersensitivity to loud noises, certain colognes, and the flickering overhead lighting. One of the men at the end of the table removed his jacket and accidentally fanned cheap cologne in her direction. As she scanned the incomplete files, the sickeningly sweet scent nearly proved to be fatal. Adding to her disgust was the lack of professionalism the detectives handling the cases had shown. Just when she thought she had uncovered something of interest, the overhead florescent light directly above her chair burned out and now she couldn't read the fine print. She said something to the guy across from her. He told her the light had malfunctioned before. He'd also requested that it be fixed. They had told him it'd be a few weeks before maintenance could replace it. *WTF?* Sanchez wondered. Hadn't she recently read in the local paper that the Judicial Investigation Department had received government funding for five-hundred new hires. Yet, it couldn't afford to spend a few colons to replace a bulb?

Sanchez got up and moved to the window for some much needed fresh air. She raised the blinds and looked out. The parade goers were still at it down on the streets. A few school kids lit off fireworks in front of the station and ran off. Kids...

She sat down again and opened the last file. She jotted notes, studied the mug shots, background information, crime sheets, detective reports and any notation added by the courts. None of these guys were her man. The guy she was looking for was probably untouchable. Sending her on this paper chase, she figured, was just a ploy by her supervisor to keep her out of the field. She'd show 'em. Wait until she called in with her latest discovery. The shit would really hit the fan.

She looked up, rubbed her dried eyes. She gathered up the files and dropped them off with the clerk.

"You really ought to get some air conditioning in this pit."

"Yeah."

"Hey, you heard any rumors about a guy trying to save a monkey in Manuel Antonio yesterday?"

"Save it from what?"

"A snake."

"You're joking." The clerk laughed, shaking his head. "Those missing records aren't in Vice. I checked a few other possibilities. They aren't here."

Sanchez figured there was no point dropping in on the local Narcotic's Division. If there'd been any new reports about drug dealers hiding along the remote beaches of Manual Antonio Park, or of using the new corridor as a transport route across the inland, she'd have heard about it by now. Her information would be the most accurate.

The corpse – that was a whole different matter altogether which she needed to first discuss with her supervisor. She would go back out and take another look, then call. Although her Intel was a week old it was unlikely the Judicial Investigative Organization would share information with the *Policía de Fronteras* once word got out that a body had been discovered. Agencies were as tight-lipped as a virgin on Prom Night. She figured it was the same in the United States and Europe. Fact was, all government agencies were hoarders of power. The CIA, the FBI, the DEA, the NSA, the SAS, Customs, even her own department. They all hoarded information because if they didn't crime would drop, and jobs would be cut. The governmental machines had grown too big, both in the United States and abroad. Even in Central America her father had warned her to tread lightly. Once you create a bureaucracy it's self-sustaining. It devours any attempts from outsiders to weaken or destroy it. Sharing information was the same as committing treason.

The stairs to the lobby dumped out along a marbled corridor that some poor schmuck had actually mopped recently. Several orange cones blocked entry. So she headed for a different exit, passing several small offices with frosted glass doors. Near the last office, she stopped at a drinking fountain and bent down to suck up some water. The door across the hall marked Narcotics Division opened and she half-assed listened to the raised voices spilling out into the hallway. She choked as she recognized one of them.

Chapter 10

I n addition to steep, the trail was wet and slippery. Betty's boot caught the edge of a volcanic rock and slid off, causing her to sway sidewise toward a jagged cliff. In the nick of time, Vu grabbed her arm and pulled her to safety.

"Geez," Betty uttered, shaking out the stiffness in her ankle. "That was a close one."

Vu let out a deep sigh. "You want to take my hand?"

"Don't be silly, Jack. I just got a little off balance that's all. My body's still trying to adapt to being on land."

Ahead, the group stopped to look at several wild birds. After Betty appeared confident she would be OK on her own, Vu pulled out his binoculars and studied the colorful birds perched in the trees.

"Look, everyone," the guide explained. "Over to your right. See the pair of blue-crowned mot-mot. Extremely rare for this area."

The blue-headed bird had light-green wings and a mustard-colored body. Its long blue tail hung several inches below the branch on which it rested. Vu passed the binoculars to Betty who took a quick look and then passed them back, looking bored.

Vu zeroed in on a different bird further away – a raucous keel-billed Toucan, which was common in Corcovado, but not here. Vu was hoping to see what some consider the "Holy Grail" of tropical birds, the quetzal, an exotic and elusive species that drew many birders to Costa Rica. As of yet, there had been no sighting of the emerald plumaged bird that Mayans worshipped as a god called Quetzalcoatl, or the "Plumed Serpent." Vu knew the iridescent endangered bird was usually spotted at elevations above 3500 feet.

Betty grew impatient, anxious for the bird watching to be over. With the exception of Vu, the entire group had moved on ahead, eager for the next spotting.

"Jack, what are you looking at?"

Vu had turned his attention to what appeared to be a shiny reflection deep into the heart of the rainforest. The reflection was moving. "Hang on a minute."

Vu adjusted the binoculars. The image came into clearer focus. It was not a stationary reflection but what appeared to be a man, shoveling dirt into a hole. How strange.

"Betty, take a look."

Betty sidled forward. "You know I'm not the bird nut that you are. I like bats."

"It's not a bird I'm looking at."

"Jack – we're falling behind. Let's go."

"Just take a look, please."

Betty looked through the binoculars. "I don't see anything. What am I supposed to be looking at?"

"There's a man in the forest. He appears to be burying something. Look over by that group of ficus."

"Where?"

Vu did his best to show her. And, Betty took another look, shrugged and then lowered the binoculars.

A ways down the trail, their guide shouted back: "Mr. and Mrs. Vu! Are you coming?"

Betty chuckled at the marital reference. "Troublemaker."

Betty grabbed hold of Vu's hand to lead the way. Vu desperately wanted another look. Betty was having no part of it. She marched along steady on her feet like the trail had miraculously turned into asphalt and she was not slowing down for anyone.

Near the end of the hike, the group stopped to take pictures of a sloth hanging upside down in the tree tops, nibbling on vegetation. The long-snouted hairy animal blended in so well with its environment that members of the group had to be shown just where to look.

Betty turned to Vu and returned the binoculars. "Go ahead I know you're dying to get a closer look."

Vu grinned gratefully and took the eyeglasses. He held them up but when Betty wasn't looking, pointed them toward the forest, not up at the trees where they belonged.

In the far distance, he made out a large man bedecked in professional hiking gear, trekking out of the forest with a small shovel strapped to his backpack. Vu focused in on the hiker recognizing him immediately, the rugged face so embedded in his memory that he could have recognized the ex-soldiers' chiseled features in total darkness. Even though he had always sensed it, knowing firsthand that Jim Lyman was alive, rocked his world. The dreams which had preceded this trip seemed a harbinger of this exact moment. Vu had always known they would meet again. They were old souls with unfinished business together in this world.

"Jack? You're doing it again."

Vu said nothing. He simply faced Betty, the color draining from his face. He held out the binoculars. "I'm through with them. They're all yours."

Worried about his abrupt change of behavior, Betty was reluctant to make a move.

"I think we've had enough nature for one morning," Betty said finally. "Shall we head back to the boat?"

At the beach, Vu stooped over and picked up a pair of lifejackets and handed Betty hers. Several passengers milled about waiting for the Zodiac to return to shore. Jack searched their faces.

"Is something wrong?" Betty asked finally. Vu cinched the waist strap on her life jacket and looked off down the beach. "Jack, did you hear me?"

"Yes. I'm sorry," he said, leaning forward and kissing her cheek. "Don't make me hit you."

Vu was silent for a few seconds. "Remember the case I had when we first met?"

"The one where I thawed the frozen hand in the microwave for you?"

"That's the one."

Betty touched a finger to Vu's lips and looked him in the eye. "I'm going to give you the benefit of the doubt here. We're not about to discuss work, are we?"

Vu nodded. Betty removed her finger, but kept it within reach of Vu's lips.

"I saw Lyman," he uttered.

"I much prefer it when you look at birds."

"Betty. What's Lyman doing here?"

"Who cares? We're on vacation. So what if he is here bird watching? If you mention Lyman's name again, I'm divorcing you."

"But..." The sputtering sound of an outboard motor brought their conversation to an end. Betty marched off.

...*we're not married.* Vu finished the joke to himself.

Chapter 11

The intercom sounded in the bridge. The captain of the *Sea Gypsy* put down the logbook and answered the onboard phone.

"*Qué es*? What is it? What? Say again? Slow down, Raymon. Repeat? Yes, yes. Very well, I shall come down at once."

Captain Leo Spartacus signed off and turned to his first mate standing at the helm. "Inform the crew we may be delayed."

"Yes sir."

The bridge door flung open. Captain Spartacus stepped out into the bright sunlight and breathed in the salt-scented, humid air. Off the portside bow, the first Zodiac of returning passengers from Manuel Antonio crashed through the rough surf. Off the starboard bow, the view was different; in all directions, nothing but miles of endless, boundless, blue-green sea.

Captain Spartacus remained calm. He'd been the onboard Commander in Chief for the last three years. Mechanical problems, weather and delays were just part of the job. He remembered his first year as a junior ship's mate, fresh out of maritime college, eager for sea time experience, cocky but wet behind the ears. All week the vessel he'd been assigned to had been in dry dock. Finally, they had been given clearance to leave port. He'd drawn the third watch. The small cargo vessel had motored all day without incident. Seas were calm. Wind was out of the north. No other vessels on the horizon. It had been difficult to stay awake but he'd drunk plenty of coffee earlier hoping the caffeine would keep him alert.

Just as the watch waned, he heard a startling sound. At first the eerie echo below deck sounded like engine trouble. He moved outside and looked off the starboard bow where he thought the noise had originated. Out of the great depths of the Pacific a humpback whale appeared. The great mammal broke surface within a few meters of the hull. Spouting several times it kept pace with vessel before it swam away as silently as it had appeared returning back to the mysterious depths of the early morning sea. Later, he had mentioned the sighting to a fellow crew member. It seemed no one aboard had seen the whale but him. He'd spent many years at sea attempting to replicate the experience.

"Our luggage was taken to the Caribbean rainforest by mistake?"

"Yes, Captain. We have just received the luggage for a group from Japan on the dock."

"This is very unfortunate. How soon can we get this baggage confusion straightened out?"

"Twenty-Four hours."

Captain Spartacus's brow furrowed as he thought over his choices. "All right, if we must be delayed, this is a very good place. Inform me the moment the luggage arrives."

"Yes sir."

"While I go inform the passengers of our delay, please deliver all our promotional clothing to the lounge. And open the bar for complimentary drinks."

Following the Captain's announcement over the intercom, a crowd began to gather in the upper-deck lounge. Betty and Vu entered late and the crowd's eyes were on them as they searched for empty seats. Betty quickly spotted a pair near the back and led the way. They sat down at a table with a couple from Virginia and exchanged introductions.

Over the last twenty-seven years, Scott and Betty Nelson had traveled all over the world. Scott said he overheard one of the crew mentioning something about baggage trouble to a co-worker. That's why the meeting had been called. Betty shot a worried look at Vu, who remained quiet but held onto her hand as Captain Spartacus entered the lounge.

Just standing before the crowd, Captain Spartacus had the natural presence of a leader who commanded respect. "Ladies and gentlemen, thank you for your patience," he said calmly. "If everyone would please take a seat, I'll explain why I've called you here."

A few stragglers were still filing in. Once they found seats, the Captain began.

"I have just learned that your luggage delivery has been delayed twenty-four hours. Unfortunately, this will keep us from departing Manual Antonio on schedule. On behalf of myself and the crew I'd like to extend our apologies for this delay. We have washers and dryers on board if you need to wash some items. I have made available to you, free-of-charge, the resort clothing line for Windward cruises to supplement your wardrobe."

"That stuff is hideous," Betty whispered to Vu. "Thank goodness I over packed and have plenty of clothes in my carry on."

Vu looked at his two-day-old wrinkled clothes. He did seem to recall the resort clothing was all Pepto Bismol pink and purple.

"If any of you are interested, we have contacted the local travel agencies and they have arranged free tours to the village of Quepos. There are plenty of opportunities for sight-seeing in this quaint sport fishing village. We will be offering a shuttle service to shore every half-hour. For those of you taking the tour, your guide will notify the crew when the group is ready to return and we will send a Zodiac to shuttle you back to the ship. We request that you fill out the sign-up sheet on the bar if you're interested. For those of you that are not interested in participating on the guided tour, feel free to explore more of Manual Antonio Park. The park officially closes at dusk but our shuttle services will be available to bring you back. All guests must be aboard by 2230 and a head count will be conducted by cabin numbers."

Someone from the front of the group asked, "What if we want to hike for a few hours and then go to Quepos for sight-seeing? Is that an option?"

The Captain glanced at his clipboard. "I will see if I can arrange it. Please check with the hotel steward at 1300. He will have an answer for you. Are there any other questions?"

The crowd stirred in their chairs, but no one spoke.

"In that case, thank you for your patience, and while you select vacation wear from our gift shop, we will be serving complimentary drinks at the bar. Please enjoy the rest of your day."

After Captain Spartacus left the lounge, guests filed up to the bar to wait their turn for the sign-up sheets. Others slid their chairs together to gossip. Guests were fretting about missing some of the scheduled stops along Costa Rica's southernmost coastline not to mention the stops planned for Panama. Would there be time remaining to explore *Parque Nacional Corcovado*? Or, what about the *Peninsula de Osa*, *Golfo Dulce*, or *Isla del Caño*? What about snorkeling and kayaking off *Coiba Island*? The bitching had begun.

Once they were alone at the table, Vu turned to Betty. "They don't appear to understand that this situation is beyond their control."

"If I didn't know you better, I'd accuse you of stealing the luggage." Betty attempted to smile. "I suppose you want to go look for your ghost, Lyman?"

He could not lie. "The thought crossed my mind, but I've let it go. I'm happy spending the day with you, doing whatever you want. We can go hiking, sight-seeing or even stay aboard, lounge in the sun, read or do whatever. I don't care."

Betty looked surprised. "Really? Whatever I want?"

"Yes."

"Good. Let's get some lunch. I'm starving. And then, I want to go sight-seeing in Quepos and I want to have a cocktail made with lots of rum and fresh fruit with one of those paper umbrellas sticking out of the top."

"That would be a Mai Tai."

"That would be splendid. Then we could go shopping."

Vu's enthusiasm waned.

"I also want to take a picture of you drinking one of those foo foo drinks in a Panama hat."

"I don't have a Panama hat."

"I'll buy you one. That's why we need to go shopping. See, I'm practicing my Buddhism. Everything is interrelated—"

Chapter 12

As the icy water splashed her face, Sanchez snapped out of it. She stepped back from the drinking fountain in time to swipe her wet lips before her man bolted from the office. He hadn't noticed her before exiting a back door.

She figured she had two choices. Flight or fight. She opted for the latter and caught up to him in the parking lot.

"Hey! Wait up!" she shouted.

The man stopped, and turned around. "Maria?"

"Tell me you aren't spying on me?" she asked.

"I told you last night I worked for the Judicial Department. Don't you remember?"

"Is this some political bullshit between divisions?"

He shook his head, confused. "Not that I know of."

Sanchez brushed a few loose strands of hair from her face. Perhaps it had all been her mistake. Her confrontational behavior was getting her nowhere. She changed tactics. "Look, I'm embarrassed to admit it, but I don't remember your name."

"I must have made quite an impression." The man turned to leave, but Sanchez latched onto his shoulder.

"Wait a minute…"

"My name is Carlos," he said, then cracked a sarcastic smile, as if the whole scene seemed ridiculous.

"Look Carlos, I thought … hell … let me explain … I'm not usually that fucked up."

"Forget it."

He looked her in the eye. "Actually, you kind of forced your way into my place last night. You'd had a rough day. You remember any of it?

She studied his expression carefully. "No."

Carlos pulled up his sleeves and showed her his wrists where the reddened handcuffs marks were still apparent. "Now?"

A jagged memory of wanton release surfaced, "Sort of," she said, and felt her face blush.

Now, Maria, if you don't mind …"

So he'd been coherent enough to remember her name. What other information did he acquire?

"Tell me you don't work Narcotics?"

"Would it matter?"

"Shit. Perfect."

Carlos frowned. "You didn't divulge any top secret information while we were thrashing around."

Some of the tension in the air faded. Sanchez felt like a stupid kid again and hated the feeling. How could she have been so blasted that she didn't remember any of the events from the previous night? In daylight, this guy wasn't someone she'd usually go for. She liked them more beat-up, scarred, dirty, even a little mean. This guy was way too smooth for her.

"There was one thing," he blurted out. "Did you really find a dead baseball player in a tree?"

Sanchez held his eyes. "I must have been telling you about a movie I saw."

"It didn't sound like a movie I've ever heard of." He studied her face.

"I guess our taste in film differs," she replied in a controlled voice, and inadvertently glanced down at his crotch. Why yes, there was a rather nice bulge down there. Too bad she couldn't remember enjoying it.

"Where are you heading now, Carlos?"

"Work."

"Really?"

"Look, after the ass-chewing I just received from my Sergeant, I'm lucky to have a job."

"Hey, Carlos, nothing personal, but I don't think I'll be seeing you again."

"It's just as well. You're a little too kinky for my taste."

Carlos grinned proudly and then walked off and climbed into a white unmarked sedan.

Sanchez gave Carlos one final glance, then headed off in the opposite direction until she heard a whistle from behind. Carlos was waving her back over to the car. Sanchez reluctantly turned around, and strolled over.

"Now what?" she asked. "You wanna kiss and make up?" The driver's side window was down and Carlos held out her missing shoes.

"I'll trade you."

* * *

The Quepos Animal Hospital sat quiet. The narrow entryway that doubled as a waiting room was empty. Lyman figured his children were still in school, which meant Dr. Phillip Ramos would likely be working alone.

The good doctor looked up with surprise when Lyman walked through the office door.

"Good day, Mr. Lyman."

"Is it?"

Dr. Ramos stood up from behind his desk. "Is something the matter, sir?"

Lyman cut to the point. "What did you do to the neck of the capuchin last night? I saw the wound. It was not there when I brought him in."

"Please, have a seat."

Lyman remained standing and glared across the room.

"I assure you, the capuchin would have died in the hands of the world's best veterinarian, with or without that incision. Primates cannot survive poisonous snake bites. Your efforts to remove the venom probably gave him a few extra hours of life. In that, you should find satisfaction."

"I'll be the judge of that," Lyman said. "I want to know what you did."

"Very well."

Dr. Ramos crossed the small office and opened an overhead cabinet, the contents inside were mostly surgical supplies: small prescription bottles, wipes, gauze, tape, even a few stainless steel tools. On a lower shelf he removed a manila folder and carried it back over to the table.

After Dr. Ramos opened the file and studied the notes, he removed a digital photograph, which he held out as a peace offering.

"This is what was beneath the skin," Dr. Ramos explained. "I believe it is some type of tracking device to monitor the movements of the animals."

Lyman took it from the doctor and studied it. "Did you insert it?"

"No."

"Who then?"

"I am trying to discover that myself. I took it to a colleague of mine to study."

"Why are people tracking primates."

"I don't know."

"How many of these have been inserted into the monkeys around here?"

"Your capuchin was the first one I have found."

"Do you think it is just monkeys they are tracking?"

"I don't know, but I have been doing some reading on our region. Goober I believe you American's call it."

"Google," Lyman corrected.

"Yes, well Google says a private company is proposing to build a 50 kilometer corridor connecting Manual Antonio with the Central Plateau region."

"Why?"

"The corridor will allow primates and other species of animals to move outside their natural habitats. It is an attempt to restore a more natural order to our rainforest by allowing old predators to re-enter the environment. Many species have been isolated and inbred for years. Scientists feel that in the end it will strengthen the surviving species."

"Survival of the fittest," Lyman mused. "Didn't you tell me that the snake that killed the monkey wasn't natural to this area?"

"Yes," the doctor nodded.

"So my monkey died as a result of some scientific experiment thought up in some University."

"Technically he isn't your monkey, Mr. Lyman, any more than he is mine." The doctor corrected.

"He's dead just the same." *You'd think monkeys could just live in peace, but no, someone has decided to draft them into a war against their will. Sounds familiar. Well this was one war that he was not going to let go unchecked.*

Chapter 13

The chaotic Independence Day celebration festivities had the street blocked off in both directions. The thunderous blasts of bottle rockets and firecrackers charged the area and the crowd wanted more. A stringy haze of gunpowder floated down out of the sky. Sanchez stepped over the yellow tape, posting the area was closed to all but foot traffic. She crossed Main, followed a side street to where it ended, and turned left on Second. Christ she hated the chaos holidays caused. She hadn't been able to park within a mile of the Judicial Investigation Organization building.

After a half-block of fighting her way through drunken tourists, and screaming kids, she spotted her vehicle ahead, and the pile of glass shards along the curb.

She cautiously stepped over the broken glass and peered through the missing passenger window. The shitheads had made off with her satchel, camera and cheap sunglasses. Fortunately, though, they'd not been able to break into her metal compartment behind the seat, though it looked like they gave it a try.

All in all, Sanchez thought, this was turning out to be a very shitty day.

After about ten minutes of scouting the area for any witnesses, and coming up empty handed, she pulled out her cell and dialed the police. She spoke with an operator, got put on hold, waited, and eventually got fed up and disconnected. Then, she dialed her supervisor's number in San Jose, to pass on the good news.

Lieutenant Browning wasn't in his office, but answered his cell on the fourth ring. Sanchez could hear background restaurant noise coming through the receiver and figured Lt. Browning was taking a lunch break. She made a calculated decision to tell him about the break-in after she told him about the corpse discovery.

"You did ... you did what?" Lt. Browning asked.

"I found a body."

"Have you reported it to the local Judicial Department?"

"Why? We have jurisdiction. It's a National Park, which makes it Federal."

There was a pregnant pause on the line. "We'll need their cooperation, Sanchez."

"Look, once we match dental records–"

"So you already have an idea who it is?"

"I have an idea who it might be."

"You're telling me he's with FARC, *The Fuerzas Armadas Revolucionarias de Colombia?*"

"I'd bet my life on it. Our latest Intel indicated they were operating in the area."

"Christ, you're just like your father," he said. "No. I take that back, you're worse than your father. At least he knew how to follow orders. I don't suppose you found time to obtain the information I requested?"

"I found some of it."

"What's that mean?"

"Several of the files are missing."

"Great," he said, and then sighed heavily into her ear. "Anything else you want to tell me?"

"Yes. As a matter of fact, there is..." She then hesitated,

wondering if she should put a spin on it, but opted against it. "My camera was stolen."

"How?"

"While I was inside the Judicial Investigations building, some shithead broke into my jeep."

"You left your equipment unsecured in your vehicle?"

"I locked up what I could."

"Then you should have taken the rest with you," he snapped. "Have you filed a police report?"

"I'll take care of the paperwork, later. I need to go back out to Manuel Antonio. There may be some identification still on the body. He's stuck up in a tree. So I've either got to train a monkey to look for his wallet or get hold of some rope, and climb the tree myself."

"I'm sending Jiménez down to assist," Lt. Browning said. "Don't make a move until he gets there. Understand?"

"What am I going to do for the next three hours?"

"After you file a police report, you mean?"

"Sir, no disrespect but I'm heading back to the park before someone else discovers the body and destroys the crime scene."

"Sanchez? Don't push me."

"I only have about five hours of daylight left." Sanchez checked her watch. "Tell Jiménez I'll meet him at the Park's entrance tomorrow at 0800 sharp. And tell him to bring some rope."

"In the meantime, you've got plenty to occupy your time while you wait on backup. Go check with the Coast Guard. If there's been any suspicious activity noted in the waters off the Central coastline, they might know about it. Also, try talking to a few of the Ticos down there. See if they've seen anything suspicious. Hell, even hit up the tourists. I don't care what you do, but stay out of the park until Jiménez arrives tomorrow."

* * *

Nothing had prepared Vu for what he was about to see.

The aft-deck, or what was once referred to in sailing vessels of Columbus's day as the *poop deck*, is where Vu stood, breathing in the warm marine air and intently staring over the portside railing at the calm water while he waited on Betty to arrive.

One of the more adventurous guests had opted to take an early afternoon swim. Ginger, who Vu had met earlier while waiting in line for lunch, was now down in the water swimming circles around a life ring the crew had thrown in for a marker. Traveling alone didn't seem to bother her in the least. Having journeyed from England to make this trip, and in her own words, determined to take advantage of the ship waylaid in nothing-less-than paradise, Ginger paddled around gleefully in the calm water. Vu guessed Ginger's age to be sixty. She was well endowed and filled out her one-piece bathing suit quite nicely. A crew member on the upper deck pretended to be keeping an eye on her while allowing his eye to wander toward the ship's doctor – a young female with a slender body sunbathing on the lower deck. He failed to notice the pair of dolphins arriving. The playful pair swam up, taking turns darting over and under Ginger. She reached out and touched their sleek bodies as they zipped by. It was all so perfect, the sunny skies, the dolphins, the clear jade green water.

Until that is one of the dolphins grew amorous.

Ginger appeared to find the mammals lewd gestures humorous at first. But she soon grew tired and swam over to the life ring. After slipping the ring over her head, she relaxed back, allowing her shapely legs to float to the surface.

All of a sudden, Vu watched as one of the dolphins re-appeared, circled her twice, before mounting and excitedly humping her leg.

Vu didn't know what do. It was sort of freakish and yet seemed perfectly natural all at the same time.

About then Betty appeared at his side shrieking with laughter over what he was wearing. "You look like you're ready to join the Gay Golfer's Tournament. Betty slapped his pink plaid buttocks.

"If you think I look hilarious, check out what's going on in the water."

Betty peered over the ship rail, broke into a toothy grin and looked back at Vu in disbelief.

"Should we intervene?" Vu asked playfully.

"Jack, go tell the crew to help her," Betty said, but was unable to keep a straight face, and broke out in laughter.

Down in the water, Ginger was helplessly adrift with a sex crazed dolphin, until as suddenly as the dolphin had magically arrived, it found its satisfaction and disappeared back into the deep water.

Ginger began swimming back to the boat.

"Are you alright?" Betty shouted down to her.

Between strokes, Ginger shouted a response. "I bloody hope someone caught that on video."

Chapter 14

The two white panel vans from the *Instituto Nacional de Biodiversidad* pulled into the remote rainforest location a few kilometers south of Manual Antonio Park and stopped. Gaston climbed from the driver's seat and headed toward the other van and instructed his assistants to begin unloading the primates. Ten minutes after the animals were released back into the towering foliage, a black suburban drove down the same road and parked in a clearing nearby. Gaston removed his briefcase from the cab of his van and began the short walk.

When Gaston approached the Suburban, the tinted rear passenger window lowered and a set of big white teeth gleamed out at him. The two body guards, sitting in front, kept a close eye on him.

"Hello, Doctor," Senor Héctor greeted. "It is a lovely day, is it not?"

Gaston placed his briefcase at his feet, without smiling back at the well-groomed Columbian businessman. "That all depends."

"On what, Doctor?"

"On if you were able to deliver the cargo as promised."

Senor Héctor ignored the challenge. "Doctor, have you ever wondered about power. It has no fulcrum point. It is like an elusive and deadly mistress."

"Are we discussing the innate power of the jaguar? Or men?" Gaston stared beyond Héctor at the attractive female companion sitting beside him, fussing with ribbons on her low-cut summer dress. "Or, women?" he added.

"Does it matter?" Héctor remained calm, despite the obvious innuendo and glanced down at the briefcase.

"You will not take this to be discourteous if I ask to see the cargo before I provide you with the deeds?"

"Of course, as long as you can prove they are in your possession first."

Gaston stooped and retrieved his briefcase. As he raised it toward the window, the front door opened, and Héctor's body guard climbed out. Gaston popped the latches and the lid sprung open. Inside were legal documents, land leases mostly, and the most coveted documents, those granting maritime rights to coastal land. It had taken Gaston many months to secure the appropriate signatures and to acquire the leases. But his position with the Institute had always given him access to the right officials.

The bodyguard shuffled the papers around, and after taking a precursory look through it all, nodded to his superior that it was safe, handing the briefcase through the open rear window to his employer.

The drug kingpin casually placed the briefcase down on the floorboard, and then retrieved a large stack of cash, wrapped in brown paper, and passed it through the open window.

"Here is money we agreed upon as compensation."

Gaston tossed the stack of U.S. currency back into the car and it landed on the lap of Héctor's companion. "Please allow Cecelia to count it."

Dismayed that Gaston knew his companion's name, Héctor nodded. "As you wish."

Cecelia hesitated for a moment before digging her long, red nails into the thick, brown paper. Peeling back the edge of the wrapper, Cecelia revealed stacks of hundred dollar bills, some brand new and others stained and wrinkled. Counting the bills, her lips moistened, glistened even, as did her cheeks. Money, whether dirty or clean, was Cecelia's *sexo*.

"Remove two bills from the center of two different stacks," Gaston instructed, "and not from the top or the bottom."

Cecelia frowned.

Héctor smiled. "*Coca*, do as he says."

Cecelia fought with the tightly wrapped bills until she had removed two from the center. She passed them to Héctor to pass through the window.

Gaston glanced at them. "Okay, return them to your *Coca*. And then I will take the remainder."

Héctor was not amused by the doctor's antics. He was unaccustomed to taking orders from anyone, particularly in front of his crew.

Gaston took the stack of cash, placed it by his feet. "This is the last phase of the project. By this time next month, the corridor will be complete and my experiment will begin. You can begin transporting shipments through the new areas. The institute will provide you the necessary clearance. You should have no future distribution problems as long as you meet your obligations."

Héctor motioned to his bodyguard to open the rear doors. Gaston stared into the two large metal cages inside the luggage compartment. Agitated, the sleek animals paced inside their cages. These were two of the finest jaguars he'd ever seen.

Gaston snapped his fingers and his two assistants nervously hurried over and helped unload the cages and placed them on the ground. Then, the bodyguard closed the doors and returned to the front cab.

Gaston walked back over to the rear passenger window.

"The specimens are spectacular. I assume this concludes our business."

Héctor nodded. Turning to Cecelia, he said, "Return the money to the Doctor."

Gaston put his hand up. "I insist she keep it."

Gaston picked up his stack of cash and moved closer to the window and leaning toward Senor Héctor whispered, "I don't think I tipped your whore enough the last time she shared my bed."

It might not have been a prudent move, but Gaston had not been able to control himself. Seeing the animals had arrived safely was a relief. The last two had been stolen from a private compound, and they had been worthless to him. These looked wild. However, he'd sold his soul to the devil, and the price extracted much.

Gaston watched the suburban drive away. He wondered if he'd been too harsh on his former mistress. But, soon enough, it wouldn't really matter. Men like Héctor already knew the facts. Women like Cecelia were a dime a dozen. Until today, Gaston had been just another *putana* in Héctor's stable. Shaking it off, he returned to the van where his assistants were cautiously staring down at the jaguars.

Yes, there was a balance to power, Gaston thought, as the flickering radio needle picked up the released primates' signals.

Chapter 15

The hypnotizing hum of the 4-stroke outboard had Vu seeing visions far greater than those of the Costa Rican shoreline. This vibrating mantra expanded his world with each breath. His altered state halted abruptly with the Zodiac's jarring wet landing.

"Jack?" Betty jostled him back to reality. "You coming?"

The mystic had to come down off his mountain. "Right behind you, sugar," he said, taking her hand as he climbed from the boat.

The other passengers, several of whom carried miniature Costa Rican flags for the Independence Day celebration, disembarked and followed single file to shore. There were plenty of folding chairs to sit on along the beach as well as fins, masks and snorkels laid out for those that wanted to play around in the water before dark. While the others began removing their life jackets, Vu and Betty split off from the group, and followed the tree line until they came to an empty log near the park entrance. There, they sat down in private to wipe sand from their feet before putting on shoes.

All of sudden, somewhere far away, they heard an odd series of explosions, or perhaps one very loud echoing one.

"Were those fireworks?" Betty asked.

"If they were, the Ticos sure don't scrimp on gunpowder."

In the distant sky, Vu spotted a long dark trail of smoke drifting toward the ocean.

"Maybe it was a giant bottle rocket," Betty replied, grinning happily. "They probably don't have the restrictions we do in the U.S."

It didn't sound like fireworks to him, but he sure wasn't going to worry Betty with it, nor let it get in his way of having a good time in Quepos.

Their boat operator walked up, having overheard Betty's concern about the fireworks. "It is the farmers. They protest every year about one thing or the other. Mostly about the prices the market will bring. There is no need to be alarmed."

"What do you think they blew up?"

"Nothing of value, I can assure you."

"Oh, shit, Jack – did you bring any cash?"

Vu nodded, and waited for the operator to walk off. "More than enough for several rounds of cocktails."

"And you're sure you don't mind going into town?"

"We're on vacation."

"Good." Betty leaned over and kissed Vu, then retied her shoe. "You ready for action, Jackson?"

Although the bus ride to Quepos had been a jerky, sweaty affair as the bus negotiated steep terrain and volcano sized potholes, Vu enjoyed the view out the window. The town was coddled by forested hills and according to their guide there was a small bay two miles away, southwest of Highway 34.

"In the 1930s," their guide explained, "banana plantations were erected and Quepos became a key shipping port that lasted for about twenty years before a severe blight devastated the crops. After that, Standard Fruit Company switched its interests to African palms. But in 2004, an earthquake changed everything. Today, our fortunes rest on tourism. If you look out your windows, toward the right, a new marina and possibly a casino are going to be erected within the year. That is both good and bad, yes? Good for bringing dollars and jobs to this area, but very stressful on the environment. Some say, it is the ultimate gamble."

Now as they entered city central, small hotels, hip restaurants, and nightclubs dotted Main Street. Vu had just gotten used to the bucking bronco-style bus ride when it smoothed out and came to an end. Their guide instructed everyone to disembark, for they had arrived at their destination, the Rattleman Hotel, home of the world famous *Blue Moon* cocktail.

"Please watch your step…" their guide announced. "You are free to sightsee or join us at the bar for a very special treat indeed. The bus will be leaving…" he checked his wristwatch, "… shall we say 9 pm? According to my watch, it is now 5 pm. Meet back here by then please. For those of you that would like to go on a limited walking tour of Quepos, the tour company will meet you in the bar in fifteen minutes to discuss tour details."

Someone from the back of the bus shouted. "Is the town safe?"

"Oh, yes, very – but as I always say," the guide added "do not leave valuables unattended. Oh, one other thing. It has been known, and this applies mostly to the men aboard, that prostitutes frequent the nightclubs. Men have been known to invite these ladies back to their hotel room. But a big surprise awaits them. It is not the one the gentleman anticipates. Under pretense, the prostitutes slip a date rape drug in his cocktail. Once the tourist passes out, their room is ransacked. One man lost ten thousand dollars of jewelry and a very valuable laptop. So, I do not recommend accepting solicitations of any kind."

Vu noticed several of the wives in the group whispering to their husbands but he could not overhear what they were saying.

The guide added: "Unless there are more questions, I will see you in the bar. Again, watch your step de-boarding."

About half opted to go sightseeing on their own. Vu didn't have to ask Betty if she was interested in having a drink. Once they entered the noisy bar, she pushed her way to the front of the line and ordered.

The bartender was a native of the area. Dark and handsome and he knew how to work a crowd. He paid a little too much attention to Vu's gal while explaining what liquors went in a *Blue Moon*. His hypnotic recital of concocting spirits transfixed Betty but Vu lost interest quickly. He shifted his attention toward bikini tops of mixed sizes and colors pinned to the wall. Some of the garments even had writing on them.

"What's the story with those?" Vu asked, as the bartender whipped up their cocktails.

"After several *Blue Moons* the girls get a little crazy, no?"

"They remove their tops?"

"*Si*. And, then they receive a complimentary cocktail for their trouble."

The bartender topped off their blue drinks with fresh slices of pineapple, red straws and little paper umbrellas.

Vu dropped a twenty down on the counter, grabbed the two drinks from the bar and started to walk off. The bartender quickly told him that it would be another five dollars.

We're on vacation, Vu reminded himself. He handed Betty the drinks while he removed his wallet.

"Woo, they must be good for that price," Betty teased. "Jack, I see a table opening up. I'll be right over there."

Vu paid the tab and left a measly tip. This sort of made him feel better. The guy had been blatantly flirting with his girl. When he caught up to Betty she was weaving her way through the crowd. Another tourist lost in the funhouse.

Betty flopped down at a table and spilled a bit of her drink, causing a tiny pool to form around the base of her frosted chimney glass. "Jack, would you mind getting me a napkin?"

He spotted a pile of paper napkins on a table beside them and took them all, anticipating further spillage.

"Ah, better..." Betty sighed, mopping under her glass. "So that's pretty wild about the bikinis. I can't wait to try this concoction."

Betty removed her little paper umbrella from her drink, then used her straw to stir the colorful contents. After she sipped, she looked up, smiling. "Yum, yum – go ahead Jack. It's really good."

"Promise me you won't pin your bra to the wall."

"No worries there. I'm not wearing one. The girls are on vacation too."

"That should make me feel better, but for some reason it doesn't." He stared protectively at Betty's breasts.

Vu glanced out over the crowd. Most of the male customers sported tans, wore shorts and brightly colored Hawaiian shirts or tight t-shirts. A number of the younger female patrons wore bikini tops, but their bottoms were adorned in either cut-offs or short wrap skirts. Every man's fashion scheme seemed to include underwear suspended above the waist of their pants.

Vu continued his observations.

"Look over there, Jack!" Betty said excitedly. "Isn't that Jack Nicolson?"

Vu turned his chair. There was a striking resemblance to the actor, since the man had the same build, the same self-confidence, the same dark glasses – but it was not him lounging in the corner booth with two attractive women on each arm, sharing a bottle of champagne.

"Think we ought to warn him?" Betty asked, smiling.

"He's old enough to know better. Besides, attempting to alter his karmic path would be sacrilegious. It's pretty dark and smoky in here. Do you want to move to a table outside?"

Betty slurped her drink like a kid with Kool-Aid. "Naw, I like it here in the dark with my guy."

She slid her chair over closer. "You see the waitress anywhere?"

Vu spotted her across the room waiting on a table of four.

"Hey, look, there's Ginger!" he pointed.

"Let's invite her over. I'm dying to know what it felt like to be humped by a porpoise."

Betty stood up and waved Ginger over to the table. Vu noticed she wore a bright red summer dress that showed off her tan legs. Her hair glistened in the light but Vu realized it was still wet, yet it looked stylish pulled back off her face, tied in back with a green scarf. As she strolled up to their table, gold bracelets dangled from her wrists.

"Why, hello there," Ginger said. "May I join you?"

"Of course," Betty blurted out.

"That bloody bus ride was something else, was it not?"

"The roads are a mess."

"Forgive me, but I don't remember your names?"

After a proper introduction was made, Vu scooted his chair back and stood. "Can I get you a drink from the bar?" he asked Ginger.

"As a matter of fact, after that little fiasco I had earlier, I think that sounds splendid. What is it the two of you are drinking?"

Betty told her. "That sounds lovely, if you'd be so kind."

Vu made a move to leave when the waitress walked up to take their order. Vu ordered another drink for Betty and one for their guest. He had only taken a few sips of his, and it was really not his thing, this fruity rum punch. He told the waitress to bring him a local beer instead. She jotted it all down on a notepad and left. Vu removed his wallet and took out a pair of twenties and handed them to Betty.

"You seem to always be in the water."

"I'm from England where warm outdoor swimming doesn't really exist. So I'm going be a mermaid as often as possible on this trip, despite the risks of mammal sexual abuse."

"Maybe it was your siren song that they heard." Betty laughed.

"Lord knows, I've been trying to get properly laid for years now…"

The conversation had now drifted into chick chat. Vu stood up. "Excuse me ladies, I'm going to step outside for a minute and check out the neighborhood." His exit was not noted by the new BFF's.

The air outside Rattleman's bar was just as smoky, but it wasn't coming from cigarette smoke, rather from fireworks sounding off in the streets. Children ran about, shouting gleefully, tossing confetti on passing pedestrians or releasing balloons into the sky. Somewhere a loud speaker droned. Then a youthful voice rattled off a political speech in Spanish.

Vu kept to himself under the awning and watched the activity. Across the street, a group of youths were milling about an alley, smoking cigarettes and drinking beer. One of the youths threw his empty at a brick wall, shattering glass everywhere. The noise alarmed a pedestrian who stopped, glanced around briefly and then continued walking.

Since he didn't want to attract trouble, Vu took a little stroll along the sidewalk. It was never good to hang around and witness juvenile delinquency. The kids wanted a fight. He'd been around enough of them to know. Punks in Saigon, Iraq or Chicago were no different. Boredom bred brutality. Where was the cotton candy stand?

Down the block something else caught his eye.

He saw a tourist stumble drunkenly out of a convenience store and make it to the curb before puking. Vu assumed the Independence Day celebration had begun its toll on party-goers. Not unlike the third day of Mardi Gras in his hometown. People had sex on the street, urinated on the street, passed out on the street. But he'd never seen a donkey being led down the sidewalk by a young girl carrying a rainbow snow cone. Vu stepped to the curb to allow the pair to pass.

A few moments later an unmarked sedan skidded over to the curb across the street. Two well-dressed men jumped out, but ignored the drunk and instead headed toward the convenience store. Vu noticed gold badges pinned to their belts. Plainclothes detectives, he figured. The men entered the store and after a few minutes Vu heard a commotion inside. Sounded like a scuffle. His interest peaked and yet he waited on the sidewalk, kept watching the exit. He predicted at any minute somebody or something was going to fly out the door.

It happened almost as he had envisioned. The doors burst open and the detectives strong-armed two handcuffed, tattooed punks against the hood of the sedan, patted them down, removed a small bag of white powder from one of the men's shirt pocket, and tossed it on the hood of the car before stuffing the two in the back of the sedan. One of the officers spoke with the clerk of the convenience store who walked out to hand him a black satchel that the punks had left behind. The detective placed the handbag on the hood next to the dope, took a moment to casually tuck in his white shirt and repaired a cuff that had unfurled during the arrest. He then pulled out a notebook from his hip pocket and began to take the clerk's statement.

His partner who had been keeping an eye on the sick drunk at the curb walked over and dumped the satchel's contents onto the hood and went through the items one by one. What stood out to Vu were an expensive camera and a pair of women's underpants. Oddly enough the detective seemed very amused when he found a business card in the handbag. His face broke out into a big smile after reading it. He looked down at the women's underpants and examined them more closely.

Back inside Rattleman's, Vu returned to the table where Betty had moved to Vu's chair to get closer to Ginger. They were in the middle of a heated but friendly exchange about male genitals. They were also on another round of drinks. Ginger suddenly posed a question. Who has the biggest – Brits or Americans? The girls determined that the biggest were not always the best...

Vu sat down and took a sip of his warm beer. His other drink was still sitting there, watered down, but untouched.

Betty turned, "Oh, hi Jack. We were just discussing–"

Vu put his hand up. "I heard."

Betty tossed back her drink, "I gotta pee."

"Bloody fine idea," Ginger agreed, and stood. The girls looked around for the restrooms. Vu pointed to the area behind them. A sign hung over the entrance to the restrooms. The two girls giggled off in that general direction. The waitress came by and asked Vu if he needed anything. Vu closed out the tab and asked for a round of waters.

The water arrived before the girls.

Vu was sipping when the girls returned. During the potty break, the topic had switched from penises to shoes. They were going shopping.

Chapter 16

The following morning, Sanchez's jeep rumbled along the narrow dirt road leading out of Boca Vieja, an assemblage of stilt-legged wooden shacks perched along the polluted bay. With the window down, the humid morning air was ripe with the odor of sewage. She cursed that the car's air conditioning was on the blink and she had to breathe in this stench. She'd driven out there at the crack of dawn to talk with some of the locals who fished the water's off the central southern coast. But she had learned nothing. It had all been a big waste of time.

So when her cell rang, she didn't sound or act her best. "Yeah! What'd you want?"

"It's Carlos."

"Who?" she snapped, as she raised her voice over the loud road noise. "I can't hear you! Hang on a minute. Let me pull over."

After she stopped along the shoulder, she picked up the cell again. "OK – who is this again?"

"Your boyfriend Carlos."

She detected the humor in his voice. "So did you call to tell me you missed me last night?"

"Something like that," he said. "I am driving east, a few kilometers from Jaco. How would you like to meet me for breakfast in say one-half-hour in Quepos? I have something of yours I'd like to return."

Sanchez laughed. "What'd I leave behind this time?"

"A satchel."

Sanchez gasped. "How did you—"

"It was recovered during an arrest last night. I recognized your underwear immediately."

"Very funny," she said. "What about my camera? Is it still there?"

"Yes, it is there also. As a matter of fact, you have taken some very interesting photographs I'd like to discuss with you."

"Who else saw them?"

"It is our little secret."

Sanchez felt her palms get sweaty. "Look, I'm meeting a colleague at the park entrance at eight sharp. Let's skip breakfast. Meet me there. And, Carlos, it might be better if he didn't know about any of this."

"You mean the handcuffs or the photos?"

Before Sanchez could reply, the line went dead.

When the familiar sedan drove up the dirt road to the park entrance, Sanchez dropped her cigarette butt on the ground and checked her watch. Jiménez was right on time, the only Tico she knew who was ever on time. She wondered how long it would take Carlos to get there and resisted the urge to call him. A little free time with Jiménez was probably better. She could fill him in on a few things that Carlos didn't need to know about.

Jiménez parked beside Sanchez's jeep and climbed out, balancing a Styrofoam cup of coffee. He was careful not to spill on his pressed beige uniform.

Jiménez walked over and shook hands.

"How was the hotel?" Jiménez asked, as an icebreaker.

"Small and dirty. How was your drive?"

"Long and bumpy."

Jiménez calmly drank his coffee, staring at her.

"How much did the Lieutenant tell you?"

"He said you found a body."

Sanchez didn't know Jiménez well. He was a typical bureau-crat. She'd heard he was married to a nurse and had a son in high school but Jiménez had never discussed details of his personal life with her.

"Did you bring a rope?"

"Yes, it's in the trunk."

"What else do we have to work with?"

"Enough. I brought a body bag, some evidence tags and bags, an ice chest which holds an evidence kit and some tools."

Sanchez followed Jiménez to his car and popped the trunk. As she inventoried the gear, Sanchez watched him remove a backpack and set it on the ground.

"Let's get going," Jiménez said as a white sedan appeared over the hill and headed in their direction.

Sanchez glanced at Jiménez. "I'm expecting company."

"Who is it?"

"One of the local police. My car was broken into yesterday and he's returning what was taken."

"I'm impressed."

"Don't be. I told him in exchange for returning my gear, he could go along with us."

Jiménez closed the trunk and watched the white sedan in the distance. "He knows about the body?"

"More or less."

"What does that mean?"

"It means he's seen photographs of the body."

"How?"

"They were in the camera that was stolen that he is returning. He peeked."

Jiménez raised his eyebrows.

"Let's drop it for now."

Once the sedan was parked, Sanchez walked over and greeted Carlos outside the car.

"You were nearly on time," Sanchez joked.

Carlos pulled back his wrist to reveal that he wasn't wearing a watch. "There's a small shadow over the sundial, today."

Sanchez half-assed grinned and then visually searched the car's interior. She didn't see the satchel and figured it must be locked in the trunk.

"You want your property I assume?"

"What do you think?"

"I'll get it."

Carlos walked to the trunk and inserted his key. He popped the lid, removed the satchel, and held it out. Sanchez went through the contents. Everything was there. She removed the camera and a notebook and tossed the rest back in the trunk.

After Sanchez introduced the men, she briefed them on what she wanted to accomplish.

"What about firearms?"

"I'm taking my rifle," Sanchez said. "I suggest you do the same if you brought one. If we run into a mule team, I doubt they'll have slingshots."

Carlos smiled. "I've never heard of the cartels using mule teams to transport their drugs through this area of the coast. Their corridor is in the Central Highlands. We have intercepted vessels out of Nicaragua near Tortuguero. But never here."

Sanchez disagreed. "Last month the Coast Guard intercepted a vessel with four hundred kilos off the Pacific, near Dominical. We believe the vessels are transporting to key coastal islands where the teams pick them up. The shipments are going overland, through federal protected lands."

Jiménez remained silent, listening.

"You're suggesting they're using these corridors?"

"I know they are."

"How?"

"The same way animals use them to move from one habitat

to the next. The corridors provide undisturbed access across the highlands."

"Okay, perhaps," Carlos said. "But these corridors are undeveloped, not easily found and are treacherous."

"All the more reason to use them."

"You sound certain of this."

"My father was shot because he stumbled onto their plan."

Jiménez stared at his shoes. Carlos didn't take the bait.

"I guess the corridors could be suited to this sort of activity."

Jiménez finally spoke up. "I don't mean to break up the chitchat but tourists could be arriving soon. We should do this."

Chapter 17

The rainforest dripped with humidity. Excited, Sanchez fought her way through the thick brush and vines, leaving the two men lagging behind. When she reached a clearing, she bent over to catch her breath.

"C'mon you two," she shouted. "This isn't supposed to take all day."

For the second time, Jiménez had managed to entangle his trouser leg in a thorny bush. Every attempt to move elicited a scream as the needles tore into his shin. "Did someone bring a pocketknife?"

Carlos removed a small knife from his jeans.

"Don't hurt yourself." Carlos teased, as he tossed his knife to Jiménez who missed the catch, losing sight of it in the underbrush.

Sanchez was losing patience. She let out a loud sigh and stomped back through the forest until she reached Jiménez. Within moments she had located the knife and cut him loose.

After slicing through the bristly branch, she said, "Now you think you can stay with us?"

The comment didn't sit well with Jiménez, but he didn't reply. Sanchez walked over to Carlos and returned his knife. "If he causes any more trouble, shoot him," she said with a straight face.

Sanchez trekked on for another twenty minutes. When she came to the clearing she stopped, pulled out her notebook and flipped through the pages until she found her scribbled map of the area. Through the foliage she glimpsed the ocean and the rock of ages as she called it, an unusual cross-shaped stone jutting from the sea. She lined this up with an old Guanacaste tree, rising out of the rainforest. She then made out the cluster of purple orchids she used as her third marker. She returned the notebook to her pocket and started moving again.

From the back, Jiménez shouted. "How much farther?"

"Another couple hundred meters or so…"

* * *

Earlier that morning, Lyman had been in a different part of the rainforest, searching for his primate family. Using the internet, he'd discovered that the *Instituto Nacional de Biodiversidad* had recently purchased a number of transmitters like the one used on Gringo for an upcoming research project. What was not clear was the nature of the research they were planning to conduct. From what he could gather, it had something to do with a genetic experiment. He was not allowing his monkeys to become scientific guinea pigs.

Lyman spotted several different primates in the southernmost portion of the forest near Manuel Antonio Park. Many of whom had never been in that area before. Through his rifle scope he was able to see fresh neckline incisions on several. He even witnessed one incident where, without provocation, a spider monkey attacked a capuchin, and nearly killed it. Indeed, something rare. How would he protect Riff Raff and his brood? And who exactly was the enemy? He needed to identify that target before he could fight it.

But right now he just wanted to find Riff Raff and family. And the one location where he'd usually had success was just down the ridge a few hundred meters. He wondered if the body still clung to its perch there and if monkeys mourned their dead, or would now avoid that spot altogether.

*   *   *

Hot and tired, Sanchez reached the tree first and removed the backpack she'd taken from Jiménez, who'd lagged behind, slowing the group considerably. Carlos, his face drenched in sweat, was out of breath when he arrived.

After a moment, he walked over to Sanchez and handed her the water bottle. "So, where is he?"

Sanchez took the bottle, drew a long pull of water and nodded toward a mahogany tree looming above her.

Carlos looked up. "Oh, yeah… It's gonna be a bitch getting that down."

"That's why we brought along Jiménez," she joked. "You think he's any good at climbing trees?"

"There must be something he's good at."

As if on cue Jiménez lumbered into the clearing. He was winded and had trouble breathing. "This fucking humidity," he grunted, swiping the back of his hand across his sweaty forehead.

Sanchez grinned at Carlos. "How long before you're ready to climb up there, Jiménez?"

Jiménez gazed up into the treetops, scratching at the bare skin on his neck. "Why don't we call the Coast Guard? They'll send a helicopter. Drop a guy right down on it."

"They'd never be able to get close enough," Carlos pointed out.

Sanchez capped the open water bottle and tossed it to Jiménez. "Here! Drink something before you pass out."

Then he really ticked her off by guzzling at the contents of the bottle.

"Hey," Sanchez shouted. "That's got to last us."

Jiménez lowered the bottle and stared at her. "I'm not doing it."

Couple of pussies, Sanchez smirked.

"OK. I'll climb up there. First, we'll need to try and hook the rope around that big limb. Can either of you throw?"

Carlos stepped forward. "I played baseball in high school."

"What position?" Sanchez inquired.

"Third base."

"A pussy position."

Jiménez snuck in another drink of water.

"Hey – didn't I warn you?" Sanchez snapped. "Give me that!"

Jiménez slunk over to return it, but Carlos interceded, grabbing the bottle out of Jiménez's hand. "What do you mean a pussy position?" he asked Sanchez.

Carlos raised the bottle to his lips, egging Sanchez to do something about the fact that he was going to take the last of the water. Sanchez's just stood there, arms folded, staring at him, face reddening in anger.

"No one hits it to third base. All a third baseman does is stand there playing with his nuts."

"What would you know about the game?"

Jiménez stepped in between them. "Can we get on with this?" he said, scratching more of his neckline where a rash had blossomed.

Sanchez cooled her jets, slung her rifle and walked over to remove the rope from the backpack. Once she had it out, she offered it to Carlos. "Go ahead… I bet you throw like a girl."

With his head held high, Carlos snatched the rope away, then positioned himself underneath the limb and made his first attempt, which came up short. He looked at Sanchez, but she remained tight-lipped. He coiled the rope up quickly and tried it again, this time taking more time to calculate the distance before throwing. He missed again, the rope striking the underside of the limb before falling back to his feet. After he picked up the rope for the third time, he hesitated, as if he were determining what he needed to correct in order to succeed.

"Well?" Sanchez prodded. "Are you going to throw it or fuck it?"

Carlos grunted as he flung the rope overhead for the last time. The rope hooked the branch, but fell short of reaching the ground.

Jiménez, the tallest of the three, jumped and swiped at the elusive rope, finally managing to snag the end and pull it on down.

"Good job, boys," Sanchez said.

"Now it is your turn to impress us," Carlos said.

Sanchez walked over to Jiménez and took the rope. "Not a problem." She stared at Carlos. "Don't let go of the rope."

It took no time at all for Sanchez to scale the tree. Carlos and Jiménez watched with dumbfounded envy.

After she flung her leg over the limb where the corpse sat, she smiled down at the men on the ground. "What was my time?"

"Time?" Carlos shouted. "What are we, in high school?"

Jiménez laughed. "Well getting up was the easy part."

"That's what all you men say."

Now it was time for Sanchez to figure out how she would recover her body. She stared at her silent rotting ball player. From her training at the academy, she remembered one of the instructors telling the class about a dead body he stumbled onto in the jungle, very similar to this one. "The thing exploded," she heard him say again. "Like poking a water balloon with a penknife."

Before deciding to make a loop to slip under the corpse's shoulders, she inspected the body for snakes, spiders, or any other pests who had taken up residence that could harm her. The memory of the viper attack was still fresh in her mind, as was the man who had tried to save the monkey. The greenish body was teeming with larvae and fungi, but nothing that could inflict a bite as far as she could see.

In a serious tone, Jiménez asked, "Do you see any evidence of foul play?"

What an idiot. Sanchez mused. The body was badly putrefied and bloated. It would take a specialist to make that sort of determination.

"Carlos. Is there a pathologist attached to the Quepos Judicial office?"

"No, except for maybe our Veterinarian."

"Shit." Sanchez said. "We're not going to be able to determine squat unless we have an expert on hand."

Carlos seemed to remember something. "I have a relative aboard the *Sea Gypsy*. It is anchored off Manuel Antonio. There is a new doctor aboard. I can call the captain. She is young, but she might be able to help."

"She's probably just a general practitioner. That's not what we need here."

"It is worth a call, no?"

"Just get it down here, so we can have a look." Jiménez said impatiently.

"Okay." Sanchez leaned closer and winced at the odoriferous cloud that formed above it.

Having already looped one end of the rope around the end of the branch, Sanchez wasn't really listening, and dropped the other end down for Carlos to hold on to. Carlos had his cell phone out and was punching numbers when the rope hit the ground by his feet, startling him. He spoke quickly to the captain of the *Sea Gypsy*, and then hung up.

Sanchez repositioned her foot on the limb so that she could lean out over the corpse to attach the rope over its head. As she moved closer, her foot slipped on the slick bark and she momentarily lost balance and fell back, but managed to grasp hold of a branch, and steady herself. On the ground, Carlos flinched, as a piece of moss fell from above and struck his forehead. "Careful, up there," he said.

"Yeah, yeah … I've almost got it … just a little bit more. What'd your relative say?"

"You were correct. The doctor is not qualified. But, there is someone on board who is."

* * *

Lyman squatted low and watched the scene unfold through his rifle scope. So the government had been called in. It was just as well. He certainly wouldn't have gone to the police with it, not with his background. They would have locked him in handcuffs before he left their office. Still, he was curious about what had killed the young man.

Lyman sat back and watched. Then, out of the corner of his eye, he saw a family of capuchins coming his way, swinging from vine to vine through the towering trees. He immediately recognized the leader.

Oh, shit – Riff Raff! Not now!

*   *   *

Securing the rope around the corpse's head and managing to loop it beneath the arms, hadn't been easy, yet Sanchez had done the job. If she was careful, the flesh wouldn't separate from the body. Now she just needed to shift the corpse to the side by a half-meter and the body would dislodge itself from the tree. As Sanchez shuffled her position, something appeared out of the treetops startling her. Instinctively, she spun around and ducked, fearing it was a poisonous snake swinging down from above.

Instead, a small screeching capuchin swung by, bumping her and abruptly knocking the body off its shelf. The corpse swung out in an arcing pattern, the rope burning through Carlos's hands. He finally grabbed hold, removing all slack from the rope. As the body ceased its downward descent and jerked back upward like a disjointed bungee jumper, a spewing stream of fluid blew from the body showering the ground like candy from a piñata.

The cocked baseball cap flew off the head into a nearby tree. Sanchez held her breath as the body narrowly missed the tree by inches, swaying from side to side. Even though it missed striking the ground or surrounding vegetation, the jettison from the bough caused the body's skin to begin a slow shimmy as skin and muscles strewn down like confetti on a parade.

Sanchez struggled to regain her footing even as she tried to slow the arc of the body's swing.

"Did you see where the cap landed?" Sanchez shouted to the men below.

Since Carlos had his hands full easing the body to the ground, Jiménez searched around. Although looking up risked getting more jizz in his face. He spied the cap in the neighboring tree, just as an agitated capuchin snatched it up and did a triumphant dance.

"Over there." Jiménez pointed.

Jiménez threw a stick in its direction as Sanchez fired off a round, missing the animal by a long shot. As the shot's report echoed, the forest silenced. The monkey froze. The men wiped slop from their eyes.

And in that moment as the fleshy cargo swung like a metronome, a strange, eerie, manmade bird-like sound echoed through the jungle. Riff Raff cocked his head and took flight.

"What the hell was that?" Sanchez looked through her rifle scope.

"Tarzan?" Carlos said.

"God knows what we've been exposed to," Jiménez replied, wiping putrefied tissue off his lips.

Chapter 18

When Vu opened the cabin door, Betty bolted upright in bed. She squinted at the bright sunlight and attempted a smile which resembled more of a grimace. Vu closed the door.

"You must be experiencing what the locals refer to as *funk*."

"Is that why I think you are still wearing plaid pastels."

Vu bowed. "I'm starting to think this shade of pink brings out my eyes."

"Let's hope the luggage appears soon or I may be forced to join the plaid parade myself. And I know what that makes my ass resemble."

Vu wisely changed the subject. "Want some coffee? I'd be happy to fetch some from the lounge."

"That would be great."

"Earlier, I saw a platter of pastries. Would you like me to bring you a croissant?"

"Betty grimaced and wagged a finger. "Something chocolate." She rubbed her hands through her hair.

"What time is it?"

"Eight-thirty."

"When did you get up?"

"Six. I wanted to practice my tai chi at sunrise."

"My idea of a perfect vacation is never seeing the sun rise." Betty yawned and stretched. "What's on the schedule for today?"

"How does kayaking sound?"

Betty's eyes opened. "Lovely. But I'll need to eat something first."

"I'll be right back."

Down in the lounge, Vu approached the bar and drew a cup of coffee from a large silver urn and then walked over to view the pastry platter. The pastries had been picked over pretty good, but there was something that resembled a tart and a chocolate cupcake. He picked up a napkin and placed the cupcake on it and then headed back to their cabin. On the way he ran into Ginger who had just stepped from the shower. Her hair was wet wrapped in a towel and she was wearing a white bathrobe and flip-flops. She smiled and stopped.

"My lioness has awakened," Vu said. "I'm taking her some nourishment."

He rebalanced the coffee cup slightly.

"On your way then." Smelling of sweet lemon and citrus, Ginger brushed Vu's shoulder squeezing by, her touch unnerving Vu, a memory hovering just below the horizon. He nearly dropped the cupcake, making a saving catch in mid-air and recovering a most pleasant sexual snippet involving lemon colored silk sheets at the same time. After he found his center again, he moved on.

Up ahead, Captain Spartacus who'd just left the bridge stopped at his cabin door. He wanted a private word with him.

An hour later, Betty had finished her breakfast. She had changed into some beige shorts and a clean short-sleeve shirt. As she stepped inside the Zodiac, which moved unpredictably beneath her, she clutched Vu's hand for balance.

Still tied to the stern, the inflatable rocked to and fro in the current. Ricardo, a crew member from the ship, stepped aboard last, instructing the pilot to start the engine.

Betty shouted to Jack over the engine "So what are your feelings on this request the captain has made?"

Vu put his finger up to his lips, indicating they shouldn't discuss it in front of the crew.

"It's kind of ironic, don't you think?" Betty whispered in his ear. "Here, I've been nagging you about work and Lyman and now I'm the one that broke the promise."

"It was an official request. That's different."

"It's still work."

Vu raised his finger to his lips again and whispered back. "Don't worry. I won't let you have all the fun."

As the crew aboard shoved the Zodiac's bow into the water, Ricardo pointed out the splendid mountains in the foreground and then a brown pelican floating by in the sky. The Zodiac sliced through the waves. In a matter of minutes they had reached shore.

Since Carlos had given Captain Spartacus exact coordinates from a handheld GPS, the guide told them it would not be the same difficult hike they had made before. In part, because they had put in at a different location. Now it was just a matter of tromping over wet sand to higher ground, crossing a sandy ridge, and then traversing a few hundred meters of rainforest.

Easy, Vu thought. For a bird.

A difficult hour later, they thrashed through the last of the vines and entered a clearing. Up ahead, Vu spotted the three officers. One of them, carrying a rifle, paced about mumbling what sounded like curse words in Spanish. The other two were ignoring the lunatic.

"There they are," Vu announced.

"Yes, I see them," Ricardo replied. "Betty, how are you holding up back there?"

Betty had fallen a few paces behind the group but Vu had remained at her side. "I'm okay, go on ahead."

"It is not much further. I'll stay with you."

"Do I have sweat stains under my tits?"

Vu smiled at his vain woman with amusement. They were all dripping wet with sweat. Ricardo dropped back to check on them.

"Shall we stop a minute?"

"No, Ricardo," Betty said, swiping a handkerchief over her forehead. "Not with the end in sight."

After the introductions were made, and everyone had cooled down some, Betty had Jack mark off the crime scene area and instructed the others to stay outside the perimeter. Jiménez walked over and handed Betty a pair of latex gloves he'd removed from his evidence box. Betty stared at his contaminated hands and shook her head.

"Did you bring plastic sheeting and bags to collect evidence?" Betty asked Jiménez. "Anybody have a blanket in their car?"

"I have one in my trunk," Carlos offered.

"Ricardo, would you please collect the blanket and get a list from Mr. Jiménez so you can collect everything from his car?"

Ricardo pulled out his notebook and after a brief conversation, headed down the trail.

Looking over at the body, Jiménez remarked "I can smell that rancid stench all the way over here."

"Me too," Carlos agreed.

Sanchez turned to the two sodden men and informed them that they were the source of the ghastly smelling cologne.

Jiménez balked. "Well, he's all over the place."

Betty looked over at the two man crew. "Yes he is. I'm afraid you two are evidence. When Ricardo returns, I'm going need all your clothing."

"Officer Sanchez, were you gloved when you were recovering the body?"

"Yes."

"Jack, please bag her gloves and mark them, and then look over Officer Sanchez's clothing for trace evidence."

After removing Sanchez's gloves by peeling them backward off her hands and putting them in a plastic bag, Vu had Sanchez stand with her arms spread and legs apart and carefully searched her.

"This just gets better and better." Carlos leered at Sanchez.

"She's clean," Vu reported.

"Great."

Ricardo returned carrying an ice cooler and piles of plastic.

"Now Officer Sanchez, please have your officers stand on that blanket over there on the ground and bag your fellow officers' hands and cover their heads so we can comb through their hair when we get to a lab. Next, remove each piece of clothing and anything else on their persons, including guns, phones, everything that might be contaminated."

"My wife loved this uniform," mourned Jiménez.

"Jack – please donate that lovely pink plaid ensemble you're wearing to the cause."

"With pleasure, sugar."

Thirty minutes later both officers were standing with bags on their heads, hands and feet. Carlos was wearing Vu's pants, which reached mid-calf, and Jiménez had fashioned a diaper out of Vu's shirt, with his legs jutting from the armholes and buttoned up the front. He held the tail of the shirt around his waist with a belt made from plastic sheeting. Vu stood proudly in his yellow silk boxers.

Sanchez had been photographing the scene with her camera while she collected evidence and surreptitiously clicked off a few pix of The Three Musketeers.

While she worked, Sanchez explained to Betty that she had not disturbed the corpse, with the exception of retrieving it from the tree. They'd even chased off a family of monkeys to preserve the crime scene.

"What kind were they?" Betty asked, "I'd like to see a squirrel monkey. I hear they are very rare."

"Capuchin, but they're gone now," Carlos informed her. "It's a good thing because I believe if they would have stuck around any longer, Sanchez would have shot one."

Betty turned to Sanchez, "Where was the body when you found it?"

Sanchez handed over some digital shots from her camera. "He was sitting on a limb above you. I found no weapons. My guess he's a scout or was one." Sanchez then explained her drug smuggling theory to Betty.

Betty turned her attention to the corpse. Vu had seen plenty of bodies in his time. Burned ones. Flattened ones. Chopped ones. Even ones with skin peeled back from the bones. But, this one was unique because much of the skin and hair was missing. What remained on the body was green and bloated.

While Sanchez was talking with Betty, Vu stepped in closer to examine the area around the base of the tree.

If there had been evidence, it had been destroyed by their efforts to retrieve the body. Vu continued to search for clues as to what had taken place.

Something tugged at the back of his mind. Hadn't he seen Lyman in this general vicinity yesterday? Given the distance, Lyman would have been in the approximate area where he stood now. Perhaps a few meters one way or the other. Further from the tree?

"What happened to his shoes?" Betty asked.

Sanchez shrugged. "Beats me. Guess he wasn't wearing any."

"Maybe the monkeys took them," Jiménez said.

"The cap in the photo ... was it removed?"

"Ah, yeah..." Jiménez began.

Sanchez cut him off. "It flew off his head and the monkey made off with it."

This was the worst preserved crime scene Vu had ever seen and that included one body found in a room full of cats after a week. And these were cops!

"I find this unusual," Vu interrupted, staring at the ground. A few feet away, a fresh earth patch the size of a small grave, immediately captured his attention.

"What have you discovered, Mr. Vu?" Carlos asked.

"I believe something has recently been buried here." Vu glanced behind him. "May I use that?" he said, pointing to the shovel next to Jiménez's backpack.

"Be my guest."

Betty paused and watched Vu, who now appeared lost in his own world, carefully removing the fresh dirt. "Carlos, does Costa Rica have problems with immigrants?"

"Yes," he said. "Until recently, they had not been a problem. But now even Costa Ricans want to live in the city. It stresses our resources. There was a day when everyone didn't desire a cell phone or television. Costa Rica was content. People still worked the fields. But now even farmers are moving to the city and countries like Nicaragua and Columbia. They are flooding our borders. Even our water supply is threatened. Even with over hundred inches of rain last year."

Betty returned to the body, "The reason I asked is look at the thick calluses on what remains of his hands and feet. They're hard as volcanic rocks. It suggests this person spent a considerable amount of time barefoot. The calluses on his hands could indicate metalworking or farming."

"I want to know what happened to his eyes?" Jiménez said.

"The monkey got 'em." Carlos laughed.

"Is there any way to tell how long he's been out here?" Sanchez interrupted.

"It's difficult to determine without tests. Usually body temperature, especially if you can probe the liver, will reveal a close approximation. In this case, however, it doesn't apply. Based on the degree of decomposition, if I had to guess, I'd say he's been dead approximately a week, maybe more. I'd put his age at 13 to 16. His coarse hair and dark skin," Betty waved her hands to the hair and slime spread over the entire area, "indicates Indian bloodlines. What tribes are in this area?"

Carlos and Jiménez shrugged. Sanchez thought about it for a moment. "There are the Cabécar. However, they do not live near this area. You'll find them in the remote jungle-covered Chirripó Indian reserve a few hours from the village of Quetzal. Most of the indigenous people remaining live in remote locations largely separated from the Tico majority."

"You're certain, no other indigenous people live near here?"

"There might be," Sanchez guessed.

Carlos added, "Indians only became official citizens of Costa Rica in '91, when they were given permission to have a *cédula*, what you in the States call, a Social Security number."

Vu had removed several piles of dirt and took a breather. He turned toward the others. "Betty, do you see any identifying marks on the corpse?"

"You mean like tattoos?"

"That or perhaps scars or traditional jewelry."

Carefully inspecting beneath the corpse's clothing, Betty said, "No ink and only a few scars. His belt buckle is the only jewelry he's sporting. It does look handmade. I'd guess silver."

From a distance, Ricardo pointed out. "I've seen buckles like that for sale before, at the markets and mostly in the highlands." Carlos called Ricardo over for a moment.

"Look, what killed him?" Sanchez asked impatiently. "You got any guesses, doc? We're kind of spittin' in the wind here – talking arts and crafts."

Betty gave the corpse another examination. "We'll know when we get him to a lab and cleaned up. I don't see any bullet holes or knife wounds. His legs appear fine. Let me take a look around the neck area. Ah, I see something up here..."

Sanchez strained to see what Betty was looking at. "What is it?"

"Jack, come look at this."

Vu put his shovel down and walked over. He stooped over the corpse and examined the area just above the hairline at the back of the neck.

"They look like bite marks," Betty said.

"Yes, they do," Vu said.

"Human or animal?" Carlos asked.

"You're shitting me," Sanchez said, shuffling Vu aside so she could get closer to the body. "Let me see."

"I can't be certain until I get him to a lab," Betty clarified. "But, I'd lay odds they're not human punctures. We'd see teeth indentations, even with tissue decay. These are just puncture wounds. I'm thinking reptile or maybe sloth? Yet sloths aren't aggressive by nature."

"Besides," Betty continued, "he would have heard a sloth coming. A snake, that's another matter. Since I see no other indications, I'd say your guy died from whatever caused those wounds on his neck. If it was a poisonous snake, then the cause of death would likely be respiratory failure."

Within a matter of moments, Sanchez's murder theory had been flushed down the crapper.

"He could still be a lookout." Sanchez kicked the dirt and walked off disgusted with the results.

Jiménez looked at Carlos and shrugged.

Carlos swatted at a fly buzzing his head. "I should see if anyone has filed a missing persons report, say in the last six weeks, just to be safe."

Vu walked over and picked up the shovel and continued digging. After removing several scoops of dirt, he struck something.

Chapter 19

"**W**hat is it, Jack?"

"Mr. Vu," Jiménez said "May I be of some help?"

Vu squatted to his knees and used his hands to clear dirt from the object. The others moved in to see what he had found. Everyone had their backs turned, totally unaware of the rugged man who stepped out from behind the thick brush, packing a rifle, and zeroing in on them.

Vu brushed aside more loose dirt, exposing a piece of cotton material. "It looks like a sleeve—"

Before he could finish, Lyman raised his rifle. "Sergeant Vu, I'd stop doing that if I were you."

Vu didn't have to turn around to know who it was. He recognized the voice immediately. Slowly, he turned and faced the former soldier, pointing a 30-06 at him. "I see you haven't lost your element for surprise."

Curious who the intruder was, the others turned. Lyman kept an eye on the agent's weapons. "Let's not get excited here," he warned.

Sanchez appeared to be sizing Lyman up. Then, it dawned on her. This was the guy she saw rescuing the monkey. "Sergeant Vu? You know this guy?"

"Officer Sanchez, allow me to introduce you to Jim Lyman. He is a former Navy Seal who later transferred to the 42nd Air Force Special Operations Unit, earned a distinguished cross and was twice recommended for a silver star before he decided to leave his unit and the United States."

"I believe I'm officially dead, Sergeant." Lyman quickly removed Sanchez's rifle from her shoulder. He looked at the other two officers. "I don't know what kind of tea party you boys are having around here but it apparently doesn't involve weapons."

Sanchez, fuming that someone had actually snuck up on her, said: "I remember you. What'd you do with that monkey you kidnapped?"

Lyman's face hardened. "I didn't kidnap him. I tried to save him. He was bitten by a poisonous snake which was hiding near the body. I brought him back for a proper burial." Lyman stared down at the exposed cotton material. "Sergeant, pick up the shovel and fill in the hole."

"Officer Sanchez perhaps you'd like to ask him some questions regarding the corpse in the tree," Vu offered.

"Sergeant," Lyman said, tension swelling his neck muscles. "I'm not going to ask again. "Rebury my monkey. Then we can talk."

Vu picked up the shovel, and filled in the hole. He carefully flattened and smoothed the area, removing all traces that the site had been disturbed. Then, he tossed the shovel aside and stood staring at Lyman.

"Okay, Sergeant." Lyman said, and took a few steps back. "You've got two minutes."

"What do you know about the corpse?"

"He was dead when I found him."

"Did you see anyone in the area who might have had a reason to send him up the tree?"

"Nope."

"Hey," Sanchez interrupted. "This is my case, I'll do the asking."

"I believe this is also my case," Carlos said, glaring at Sanchez.

Lyman turned the rifle on Sanchez. "You two work it out later." He glanced at his watch. "Your two minutes are about up."

"Wait!" Sanchez blurted out. "You're familiar with this park. What do you know about mule teams in the area?"

"They have made three trips in the last six weeks. You should know this. You left something behind on your last scouting expedition." Lyman tossed the butts at her feet.

Sanchez shook her head. "I gotta quit smoking."

Lyman turned his attention toward Vu again. "What are you doing in Costa Rica?"

"One might ask the same of you, except I believe I know what you are going to tell me. Allow me to introduce you to my friend, Ms. Betty Caan. She is not only my traveling companion, she is also a forensic pathologist who works for the New Orleans police bureau."

"Sergeant, if you have intentions of trying to take me back…"

"That is old business, and besides as you've already said, you were officially presumed to be lost at sea," Vu said. "We're here on vacation. Yes, it's true I did see you yesterday and was curious about you. But I have no assignment or desire to return you to the States. Our ship, the *Sea Gypsy*, was delayed and the ship's captain asked if we could offer assistance to the officers. Since Betty is a forensic specialist and I know a few things about crime investigation, we volunteered."

Lyman cleared his throat. "Just as long as you understand I have no intentions of returning to the U.S. with you or anyone else. We clear on this?"

"Yes."

"If any of you attempt to reach for that shovel or a weapon before I am out of range, I'll show you how good of a marksman I am. Got it?"

Lyman scanned the group. Everyone nodded.

"Wait!" Sanchez cut in. "Why don't you help us? With your skills, we could locate the routes the mule teams are taking?"

"Team players turn against you." Lyman stared at Vu. "Sorry, officer, but I have my own plan. It doesn't include helping your department or my own government. Officially, I'm dead. I want to stay that way."

Lyman started backing away. "Besides, I don't work with thieves."

"What is that supposed to mean?" Jiménez blurted.

"Ask Sanchez where the money is?"

All heads turned toward Sanchez.

"I don't know what the fuck he's talking about."

An uneasy stare down triangulated between the officers.

"Now turn your backs to me and don't move until you receive a signal."

And with that he was gone. Moments later an excited capuchin dropped a red baseball hat at their feet from the tree above and swung away.

"He's a fucking monkey whisperer too?" Sanchez shook her head in disbelief, collected her weapon and tried to resume business, keenly aware of Carlos and Jiménez exchanging looks. "We're going to need to pack this corpse to a lab," she added. "Carlos, you think the institute has a place for it?"

"I'm way ahead of you. I sent Ricardo an hour ago to prepare for our arrival and bring a panel van to transport us and the body to the Instituto."

"Let's hope it doesn't have any windows. I wouldn't want anyone to see me in this outfit," Jiménez said.

"Good idea," Sanchez said. "So, what are your plans after we get out of here?" Sanchez stared at Vu and Betty. "We could still use your help, doc. We really don't know much about this guy. If he is Indian, we'll need to get an idea of which tribe."

"As long as our ship is in port," Betty said, "and if the institute has the right equipment, I'm willing to run a few tests."

"Do you intend to pursue Lyman?" Vu asked, with a tone of seriousness.

Carlos said. "I've got no reason for an arrest. He was simply preserving animal remains."

"Was he serious about the legally dead shit?" Sanchez asked.

"Yes."

"He's just another nutcase in my books," Jiménez said. "If he's got no outstanding warrants in our country, then he isn't worth the trouble."

Vu cautioned. "He may be legal down here, but he's still lethal. He's serious when he says he wants to disengage."

Chapter 20

Pulling onto the shoulder of the road, Gaston killed the panel van's engine and retrieved his medical bag from under the front seat. He closed his eyes and rolled his neck and shoulders. Opening the clasp, he removed a syringe, held it up to the light, examined the contents and then placed it on the dash. He opened a bottle of rubbing alcohol, rolled back his sleeve and poured the disinfectant over his arm just below the elbow, then put the cap back on the bottle and returned it to his bag. Afterward, he held the syringe filled with B12 up to his arm and inserted the needle under the skin. A tiny drop of blood rolled down the inside of his wrist and fell onto the floorboard. The injection would combat his fatigue, so he could press on through the day. He closed his eyes, sat back in the seat, and waited for the drug to take effect.

An hour earlier, he'd received a call from his secretary at the Instituto, informing him that the *Policía de Fronteras* were requesting use of the facilities to run tests on a corpse found in Manual Antonio Park. Gaston agreed to make his lab available, but also made it clear that he would not be available to conduct the autopsy or run tests himself. If all went well, he hoped to be back at the institute within 48 hours.

Feeling more vigorous now, he made a quick check on the jaguars. He noted in his charts that the tranquilizer he'd given them earlier hadn't worn off completely but the animals didn't appear to have suffered any adverse side effects from the powerful drug.

He pressed on.

The light slanted toward the horizon now. Rain fell hard. Gaston followed a rutted road that narrowed and became treacherous. The vehicle muscled deeper into the forest. He turned the wipers on high and clicked on the high beams. As the headlights lit up the muddy road, he glimpsed several rodents scurry across his path. Shadowy creatures appeared deep in the woods. Shimmering insects flew against the windshield and bats dove down out of the trees. He glimpsed a pair of frightful eyes glaring out of the darkness, or so he thought. The strangely hypnotic droning of the windshield wipers rhythmically pulsing across the glass played tricks with his mind; as did the darkness.

Suddenly, a Kinkajou darted across the road. He jammed on the brakes, jarring awake his cargo. The jaguars banged in their cages and growled. The animals sensed the rainforest beyond and the freedom that was within reach.

The road became heavily vegetated. Long snake-like vines twisted endlessly along the path scrapping the sides of the van. Inside the cab the sound echoed. The muddy rutted road tossed the vehicle from side to side. Gaston fought the wheel and kept the vehicle in a straight line until the heavy brush overwhelmed it.

Gaston braked to a halt. He'd gone as far as he could. He turned on the dome light and checked his map and the corresponding GPS reading. He was right on target. The Reserva Forestal. Los Santos was near.

After climbing out of the vehicle, he thrashed the wet vines from his face and sidled to the rear doors, opened them, and stared in at the jaguars. What magnificent creatures they were. What power they possessed. The strength in their jaws – their sharp teeth – their powerful shoulders and razor-like claws – their amazing agility and speed. He loved these animals. His mother had once accused him of loving his animals more than her. But she'd been lost to him a long time ago. First from his heart and later from his life as she chose strangers to her own blood. Maybe they were more alike than either knew.

If only his mother could understand the importance of his experiment. He had an opportunity to reshape nature. Brooding on their hurtful words and arguments did no good. Deep in the forest a howler monkey cried, a shrill voice echoing the pain Gaston felt. *You remember things you should forget.*

His mind clicked into place as he pondered which method would be best to release his dangerous cargo. He decided he would lie on top of the cages, because opening the doors from above would allow the doors to swing outward, with nothing between the animals and the vast rainforest.

Once Gaston confirmed the transmitters were operative, he opened the van's side door and climbed inside. The cages were sturdily built. Solid sides with air vents. Bars over the front. As Gaston slid onto the first cage, the jaguar below hissed and struck the sides with his powerful claws.

Flipping the first lock open he eased the door outward and waited. The first jaguar bolted from the cage and blazed a trail through the dark woods. Now, cage two.

The remaining jaguar thrashed about, slamming its head into the cage while Gaston reached toward the second lock. It happened so quickly. The razor-like claw swept upward, through the opening, slicing through his heavy gloves like a knife through butter, and lashing his palm. As Gaston felt the flesh tear away from the bone a searing pain burned through his body, he struggled to get out of harm's way.

The jaguar overpowered the door and lunged from its cage. Instead of escaping like the other – its haunting eyes glared at Gaston and moved toward him. But Gaston was not dying today. Crawling with one hand injured, he managed to grasp a textbook one of the students had left behind and threw it over his shoulder. The book struck the jaguar in the face and it was enough to dissuade the animal from a second attack. The jaguar lurched out of the van and disappeared into the dark.

Gaston, not daring to leave the vehicle now, not with the scent of blood in the air, managed to hook the back doors with his good hand and pulled them closed. He sighed with relief and allowed his racing heart to return to normal.

He removed his undershirt. It was damp, and rank under the arms, but something was desperately needed to soak up the blood immediately. So he wrapped the smelly cloth around the injured site as best he could and felt a sudden jolt of pain when the salty perspiration reached his open wound.

He climbed to the front of the vehicle and searched his medical bags for bandages and sutures. After he stitched the gaping cut closed and dressed the wound, he formulated a plan. Hoping to reach his next destination by daybreak, his mind calculated the exact mix of amphetamines and opiates to cope with sleep deprivation and pain.

At dawn, near Empalme, on the outskirts of Rio Navarro, the white panel van turned off the *Carretera Interamericana* and picked its way down another rutted dirt road.

The Cabécars were scattered about the region of the Central Highlands, and like other tribes, they sought out remote locations, seeking fertile lands and privacy over convenience. The federal government land allotments were often unproductive tracts of land that provided little means of support. So the tribes moved from one region to another in search of a permanent parcel of the fertile soil they needed before commercial development threatened to forever change their lifestyle.

Gaston had discovered the indigenous people during graduate school. His studies had required his frequent visits to several of the villages to complete biological research. It was during this period that the tribal leaders had come to know him and over the years a semblance of trust had formed between them. His mother an anthropologist also adopted this tribe as her own. At least that's what

Gaston needed to believe. Later as a scientist with some political influence, he had seen to it that several of the medicines the Indian tribe had used for centuries to cure minor skin rashes and stomach ulcers had been protected. When a U.S. pharmaceutical company attempted to pirate them, Gaston had negotiated monetary rights for the tribe. Unbeknownst to the tribe, the Instituto also received a portion of the money as payment for services, which Gaston was putting to good use. He had something they needed and they provided what Gaston craved – living proof that commerce and nature could live in balance.

The van rolled to a stop at the road's end. Before him plains of green grass were surrounded by what appeared to be unending hills and rainforest. It was fertile, remote and the perfect location for an indigenous village. Having the road end miles from them was how the Cabécars liked it.

Gaston climbed out of the van, retied his hiking boots, grabbed a canteen of water from the passenger seat and strapped it to his daypack. He started trekking along a narrow trail which disappeared into the rainforest. Holding his injured hand up over his heart quelled the physical pain and quieted his soul. It also shielded the wound from public view. Eventually, the forest gave way to a clearing where a number of huts constructed from the areas hardwoods and palms stood guard over its residents.

There were cattle and horses and chickens running loose in a fenced pasture, children running about naked, women in colorful dresses, weaving or washing clothing by hand. The chief elder had a hut in the center of the village, the most sacred and protected of all places. However, it was not there that Gaston was headed. He skirted the village and continued walking to a small hut by a meandering creek. Gentle sounds of palm leaves rustling in the warm breeze helped him transition from an obsessed drug addled scientist to a gentle compassionate son.

It was there, standing outside the door to the hut that the chief elder's daughter, Leela, greeted Gaston.

"I need to tell you a few things," she said sadly.

Gaston immediately noticed her mournful eyes, it troubled him deeply.

"She has not long, but she was asking about you this morning – if you were coming."

"I have brought her some medication from the city."

"She does not want your morphine."

Leela was everything that his former mistress Cecelia was not – strong, caring, and homely by modern standards. Her body, a *corteza amarilla* in bloom, had no breasts to speak of. Her hips and arms were slender and long. Her legs and hands were coarse and stocky. Her body was a contradiction but somehow in perfect balance. She was unlike any women he had ever known. And he found her very attractive. But it was too late for that. Aside from a few clumsy sexual encounters with her during graduate school, he had chosen modern life and left her deflowered and degraded. She later married a local boy and moved on with her life. She appeared to have no regrets about her choices, unlike him.

"Leela – she is dying of pancreatic cancer."

"She has insisted, no modern medicine."

The one thing Gaston could do for his mother was to ease her pain and that was being denied. He felt the rejection as keenly as any slap his mother had ever given him.

Head bowed, Gaston quietly followed Leela inside.

He crossed the animal skin rug and sat his things down on a small wooden table. The heavy scent of cedar floated like a perfume cloud above the small bed in the corner, lighted by four candles at each edge, where an old woman lay sleeping. Her face was aged and wrinkled. Quilts covered her body. Beads and dried flowers hung above her on the wall and dried petals were scattered about the floor. Save for an oil lamp resting on a small bureau, no other furniture occupied the space.

By even Costa Rican standards, the hut was small. Lately, Gaston had had trouble breathing there. These suffocating moments were often followed by severe panic attacks. Gaston believed it had to do with the ancient spirits visiting his mother in her final days.

"I will leave you two alone now, and tell father you have arrived."

Gaston turned to watch Leela go and fought the desire to leave with her. He knew his mother's time was near and as a son he should be by her side, but he had other business to attend to. Secretly, he willed her dead. He had even considered facilitating her passing peacefully today, but unless she would allow an injection, that plan was moot. Behind him he heard a gasp and then a weak voice call out, "Gaston? Is it you, son?"

"Yes, mama."

"Come closer, please."

Kneeling down at her side, he reluctantly took her hand, which rested on the wool blanket the Chief had given her. "Aren't you warm, mama?"

"No, Gaston. My body feels as cold as a river in winter."

"I have brought you pain relief. Please take it."

"No, Gaston."

"This is absurd."

"Gaston – don't argue. That is not why I sent for you."

Gaston held his mother's hand. It was like a damp piece of clay formed to resemble an appendage. It was tiny and held very little life or warmth. Perhaps this time Leela had been right.

"I'm sorry. I should have come sooner. I have been working very hard at the Instituto. There seems no end to the things I must do."

"Gaston, you are my son, but I hear things in the wind that concern me, even in my last days. What are you plotting?"

It was remarkable to him that she had any mind left at all. Many years ago after his pet monkey, Jake, failed reentry into nature, he had explained in detail his plans, expecting his mother's full support. Even then they had clashed on the role of man in nature.

"Mama, don't worry about such things. It is too complicated to discuss now."

"Just because my body has left me invalid, doesn't mean my mind has."

Gaston thought it over. His mother had made sacrifices all her life for anthropology, often at his expense, as had his father, now long dead. Still, it had been his mother who had provided him with the introductions to the tribal leaders. It had been his mother who insisted he be placed in private schools. She had pushed him to succeed beyond all others. His father had been a successful businessman who had left his life at a young age but had also provided for them financially.

Why was it a surprise that after a lifetime of anthropological studies of Central American indigenous tribes, his mother would ask to live among the Cabécars in her final days instead of with her only son? It was his mother, as well as a number of other dedicated individuals, who spoke out and whose relentless lobbying efforts eventually helped secure legal rights for indigenous people. He had always been proud of her and sought her maternal love, but she had never returned the favor.

"It's a variation on survival of the fittest," he said finally. "I want to strengthen a species within my lifetime. I have chosen a member of the primate family as my ultimate goal of change."

"Jake again," his mother closed her eyes. Then, she let out a gasping sound.

"I can tell it is upsetting you. You should rest."

"Gaston, I must understand this desire of yours. For we fear what we do not understand. I worry you are making a terrible mistake."

"Don't say that, mama. Please."

She coughed. "I have spent a lifetime pursuing things, Gaston, in an effort to understand. I forced this on you, too. From when you were a child, I wanted great things for you. I wanted you to have a rich mental life, so you could understand the things I never could. All this education and studies have come at a great cost to you. I see that now. You must stop this experiment Gaston. Live with nature. Do not attempt to alter it – or in the end, nature will destroy you."

Her words ended as abruptly as they seemed to emerge from her flattened chest. Her limbs quivered and her eyes closed, her chest palpated back and forth through the blanket like something was trying to escape. Then she fell silent.

"Mama?"

No sounds came from her pale lips. Just a few empty breaths and then that too ended. He felt her spirit lift up and hover over them.

How could you leave me without a single word of love?

After a long while, Gaston released her hand and covered her face with the blanket. He wanted to crawl next to her and wail like the lost child he had become. Instead he removed a stack of cash from his backpack and placed it on the table. Perhaps the money from Senor Héctor would balance the scale for what his mother felt was being taken from nature by his work. Feeling devoid of any real emotion, other than freedom, Gaston walked out of the hut for the last time.

Chapter 21

As the car pulled in and parked, Vu turned and looked out the passenger window. The streets in front of Carlos' apartment building overflowed with celebration. People danced and clapped their hands to music. Patriotic flags fluttered in the wind. Fireworks snapped off in little bursts on every street corner. General mayhem reigned. A group of children ran by the car screaming with delight as they tagged the car's window with a water balloon. Vu knew they were going to draw some attention when they got out of the car but decided the chaotic atmosphere provided the perfect cover for them. Crazy circumstances require crazier actions.

Carlos turned off the engine and sat back.

"Anybody got any ideas?"

Vu turned and looked in the back seat where Jiménez appeared anxious, staring out the window. Of course, of the three, he looked the most ridiculous in his plaid shirt/diaper. And then there were the shower caps on their heads and bags on their hands and feet.

Vu glanced down at his own yellow silk boxers and a plan began to form. Betty was always telling him to loosen up and go with the flow. Buddha would put it a different way – if one learns to live one day at a time then they can become happy and free. Nirvana. Vu smiled. Time to live a little.

"Where is your apartment from here?" Vu asked Carlos.

Carlos pointed to the second story unit in the building down the street.

"Can't we get a little closer?" Jiménez said.

"What are you bitching about?" Carlos said. "This is my neighborhood." Carlos was not so eager to move.

Without a word, Vu opened the door and climbed out into the bright sunlight, stretching his arms wide.

A small group of children gathered around pointing and laughing at the ridiculous little Asian man in his underwear. Vu bowed deeply to the crowd and began advancing toward Carlos' door, performing tai chi moves against an invisible opponent. The crowd howled approval.

Vu heard another car door slam. Carlos joined him on the sidewalk.

"A little lonely, isn't it?" he said, smiling over at him, and then began shadowboxing and ducking next to Vu. Together, they bounced and ducked down the street.

Jiménez wasn't budging from the car's back seat. He rolled down the window, shouting to Carlos, "Why don't you bring me back some clothes?"

Carlos shook his head. "Man up."

Jiménez opened the back door, and climbed out with his hand firmly planted over his family jewels and pretended to bull whip the boxer and martial artist toward their goal.

Together these pantomiming musketeers hurried along the sidewalk among the shouts and laughter from pedestrians who stopped in their tracks to catch a glimpse at these clearly drunk idiots.

Eventually, they reached the building. Carlos fumbled around for the key.

Jiménez whined, "Jesus, now what's the hold up?"

Carlos smiled. "Look up."

On the balcony two floors up, a young woman in a bikini was leaning over the railing, pointing her cell phone. She had ripped off video of the three gyrating men. Her breasts were practically hanging out of the skimpy garment.

"Hey Carlos!" she shouted down, cheerfully. "Nice show. Having another party? These two are cuter then that drunk senorita you had over the other night."

Carlos kept a straight face. Jiménez looked down at his bony legs and blushed. Vu puffed out his chest and placed his hands on his hips. He wondered if anybody he knew would even recognize him if his image was blasted across YouTube. Betty would never believe him if he told her how he got these three to the apartment, but actual footage, that was another story.

"I'm going to have to confiscate any incriminating videos," Carlos shouted as he herded the men through his front door. Once inside his smile evaporated as he walked over and pulled the curtains.

The apartment was a loft style environment where the main room was the entire living area. By the look of things, Carlos appeared to be single. The room certainly lacked a feminine touch. The Oriental rug patterned with Roman warriors covered most of the living room floor. A few macho oil paintings broke up the white-washed walls. On the far side of the room sat a dark leather sofa with two carved hardwood end tables. Each had a brass lamp and a little extra frill, small African Art sculptures. There was a small hallway off to one corner that lead to what Vu figured would be the bathroom. Jiménez took a quick look around.

The room had a tasteful but somber quality which Vu felt was reflected in the young detective's mannerism. He noticed a trash can in the corner where a large four-poster bed sat. He walked over to retrieve it to use during his evidence gathering.

By the bed Vu detected the decidedly un-masculine scent of perfume. He couldn't place it, but it was a scent with which he was familiar.

Curiosity got the better of him after he walked back to the kitchen and set it down by the table. At the bottom of the can were a few personal hygiene items, and what looked like a used condom wrapper. It then dawned on him where he had smelled the perfume before. He looked directly at a smiling Carlos who had watched Vu sniff and snoop and put two and two together.

"I think there are *cervezas* in the icebox," Carlos said. "Help yourself." Then he disappeared into the bathroom and closed the door before Vu could stop him.

Vu turned toward Jiménez, frowning. "We must not contaminate the evidence. Please allow me to collect the samples from you first."

"Relax," Jiménez said. "I'm having a Dos Equis. I suggest you do the same."

Much to Vu's dismay, Jiménez wasted no time and walked into the kitchen. He pulled open the refrigerator and fumbled around inside with his big plastic paws. After removing two bottles of beer from a lower shelf, nearly dropping one, he offered the other to Vu, who flatly declined.

He set the second bottle down on the counter and eventually managed to twist the cap off without tearing the bags on his hands. He left the cap lying on the counter and took a long pull on his beer.

What a man would go through for a drink, Vu thought.

"How long have you worked with Ms. Sanchez?"

"Not long. Why?"

"She seems most driven."

"That's an understatement," Jiménez said. "Since her father was executed by the Cartel, or so the rumor mill says, she's been so determined to find his killer she's taken such wild chances. Most of the department is afraid to work with her."

"But you are different?"

"I had no choice. My orders came from higher up."

Carlos entered the room, overhearing the tail end of Jiménez's comment. "What was that about higher up?"

"I was telling Vu," Jiménez blurted out, "about how Sanchez's old man was killed by the Cartel."

The news pained Carlos, who started to say something and then held off. Vu noticed that the young detective appeared to be thinking about something other than collecting bits and pieces of the corpse's skin from their person.

"So Sanchez intends to bring the killer to justice?" he finally said.

"With or without the department's help."

"Why is the department against this?" Vu asked.

"It's complicated," Jiménez said.

Carlos handed Vu some towels and a manicure kit containing nail clippers, scissors, tweezers and files. "There are some Ziplocs in the kitchen," he said to him. "What else do you think you'll need?"

"Perhaps a tape measure and a felt-tip marker."

"I'll see if I can find them in my tool box."

"Perhaps it would be better if I retrieved the items," Vu said, eyes filled with concerned the men would destroy what evidence remained on them.

"It'll be quicker if I do it."

Carlos walked off. When he returned he had the items Vu requested. Vu suggested they move to the kitchen bar, where the light was better.

The men chose opposite sides of the kitchen bar, still sizing up each other. Each seemed to be weighing the others motives or intentions, a futile attempt at determining who had the most accurate intel on Sanchez and her father. Vu remained neutral trying to keep balance in the room.

"Investigations involving organized crime are messy, no matter what country you work for."

Jiménez nodded. "Her father was deep undercover when it happened."

Vu understood what Jiménez was implying. "So the records have been sealed?"

"Something like that."

"Why? Unless your office has something to hide…" Carlos challenged.

"Or perhaps they have *someone* to hide," Vu added.

"Nah, they're politicians. They just don't want any more bad press."

Vu started to lay out the items on the marble bar and noticed what looked like a large smudged imprint on the shiny surface. He took a closer look, not wanting to put his tools down on a dirty counter. Upon examination, the smudge appeared to be a perfect imprint of a small buttock. Vu found a wash cloth by the sink, wetted it, and then wiped the counter top clean as if it was all part of the job and perfectly fine with the two men who were still intent on staring each other down, paying no attention to Vu's discovery.

Jiménez downed the remainder of his beer. "Mind if I grab another?" he said to Carlos.

"No!" Vu snapped. "Enough of this. Sit!"

Jiménez ignored him and walked into the kitchen. "Hey, so what's this about Sanchez stealing cash?"

Vu took a deep breath and let it out slowly – found his center again.

"It was missing from a photograph I saw earlier on her camera. Where the body was found, there was money lying on the ground. When we arrived today, it was gone. Only Sanchez knew about it."

"That is not true. There are the murderers and you had the knowledge too, as did your partner," Vu offered in a neutral voice. He was beginning to feel like a hairdresser stuck between two battling divas.

Jiménez returned with a fresh beer, chugging back a slug and stared over the top of his bottle at Carlos. "Yeah, maybe you took it?" he said, smiling. "She also told me you recovered her stolen camera. How convenient..."

Carlos stared the detective in the eye.

"I was working a case last night."

"That happens to be the truth. I saw the detective retrieve Detective Sanchez's case in a drug bust in Quepos," Vu added.

"What?" Carlos looked at Vu.

"I was drinking *Blue Moons* in the bar across the street."

Both men then turned to check out Vu.

"Okay, can we begin?" Vu said, after he returned the washcloth to the sink, and wiped the counter top dry with a paper towel. "Carlos, let's start with you."

He began by carefully removing the bags from Carlos' hands and feet. Within a matter of minutes, Vu used the tweezers to pick bits and pieces of corpse's skin off both, bagging the samples and labeling it accordingly.

Jiménez looked at Carlos. "If what you're implying about Sanchez turns out to be true, you would like that, wouldn't you? Your office has always been in a pissing match with the Feds. Any shit that goes down along your coastline or in your territory and you get all bent out of shape if someone else wants in."

"We know about the mule teams..."

"Sanchez mentioned as much. You fuck her to get some dirt against us?" Jiménez lowered the bottle, but Carlos wasn't taking the bait. Vu knew the perfume he smelled in Carlos apartment was the same worn by Sanchez. Earlier he had also observed the way Carlos and Sanchez had looked and acted toward each other. It was clear they had had a connection and from the contents of the trashcan, it wasn't hard to deduce it had been sexual. Perhaps Jiménez was jealous of his co-worker's affections. Or, that Jiménez had his own reasons to stir up trouble.

Carlos remained steely eyed and though he acted as if he had more to say about the matter, he calmly turned and looked at Vu.

Vu stepped in. "Let me finish here and then you two can go out in the alley and duke it out if you must."

Vu snipped hair from each man where some of the goo had dried, collected debris from under their nails. He swiped their hands and faces, the skin on their arms, even inside the small cervices of their ears with a wet paper towel and then bagged these. The whole thing took under an hour.

Jiménez wouldn't drop it. "You have any proof Sanchez or her old man were dirty?"

Carlos started to answer and then thought better of it and stopped. "Vu's right. We should drop it."

The issues between Carlos and Jiménez were far from over but Carlos gave Jiménez permission to use the shower after him. Carlos needed to get downtown to the station to check the computer for missing persons and they had to swing back for Jiménez's car so Vu and he could get the evidence back to the Instituto as soon as possible.

Carlos carried in clothing for Vu and apologized up front for his selection. He had very little clothing that would fit a man of Vu's stature. Yet, something one of his cousins had left behind during his last visit, might work. He handed Vu a pair of plaid golfing shorts and a green V-neck shirt with a pelican logo over the breast pocket. Vu fought back an urge to ask for something besides plaid, thinking immediately of how Betty would perceive his choice and accepted the detective's generous offer. Carlos then disappeared for a second time, returning moments later with a set of clothing for Jiménez. He handed the man a pair of striped slacks, a long-sleeve silk shirt, and a fedora, something a mobster would wear.

"Gangster attire?" Jiménez questioned.

"Vu cut more evidence off your head than you realize. Trust me Gangster beats Moth-Eaten every time."

Chapter 22

At the Instituto, a group of curious students pressed their faces against the glass windows of the laboratory attempting to catch a glimpse of the corpse.

"Why'd they bring it here?" One of the students asked, straining for a closer look.

"Maybe it died of some secret contaminant," another replied. "After all we are a government funded lab."

"I heard the police found it."

"I'll bet it was a jaguar attack." Another guessed.

"How could you tell? It looks like a rotten dead pig."

"Has anyone seen Dr. Trujillo today? I'll bet that is why they brought it here."

"I haven't seen him in a couple of days, and I heard his assistant hasn't been able to reach him."

"Merde! Maybe it's him!"

This stirred the crowd as the conjecture and stories multiplied as more students gathered. And, then, from the very back, an impatient woman's voice shouted. "Hey, people! We need to get through here!"

Sanchez barged her way through the crowd, clearing a path for Jiménez and Vu.

"This crowd is getting larger by the minute. We gotta cover the windows." Sanchez knocked on the locked door. Dr. Trujillo's assistant cracked the door open to let them in, pressing it closed against the craning faces looking for a quick peek.

The five squeezed in to the private laboratory and Vu locked the door behind him. Inside, Betty looked up at Vu and smiled, until her eyes dropped down his body to his baggy green plaid pants.

Vu shrugged, "Try to think of me as the Plaid Panther."

"Well it is an improvement on the Pink Panther from this morning."

Sanchez looked to Jiménez, "What's the deal with the hat?"

Vu stepped in. "I was very conscientious collecting trace evidence, and there was a large amount on Detective Jiménez's head, resulting in a rather unusual haircut."

"It can't look any stupider than that hat." Sanchez turned to Jiménez, "Let me see."

Jiménez lifted his hat and held it skyward while Sanchez slowly surveyed the damage. Suppressing a smile, she turned to Vu. "I was wrong."

Jiménez lowered the hat, dipping the brim rakishly over one eye.

"It looks a hell of a lot better than Jack's fashion statement," Betty said.

"I think it makes you look like a detective from the old Dragnet show," the assistant said. "I watch all the old television shows. My favorite is Rockford Files."

Sanchez cut off the gabfest. "Jiménez, find something to cover the windows."

"Who are you to be giving me orders?" Jiménez took a step toward Sanchez. Sanchez opened her mouth to make it clear to her babysitter exactly who was in charge, but before the moment could escalate further, the young assistant chimed in.

"I'll do it," and headed toward a cabinet across the brightly lit room to look for something inside one of the bottom cupboards.

"When do you expect the director back?" Sanchez asked her. The woman had bent over to remove a roll of butcher paper from a lower cupboard. Her navy colored skirt inched up slightly in back exposing more flesh and caught Jiménez's immediate interest.

The assistant stood. "I haven't been able to reach him on his cell phone," she said, and dumped the heavy load on the counter. "I've left him several messages."

Eager to assist, Jiménez approached her. "Let me carry that," he said, smiling.

Vu walked over to the examining table. "Where do you want me to put the evidence?"

"Over on that counter." Betty pointed with her chin.

Vu placed his evidence bags on the counter, put on a pair of latex gloves and joined Betty as she examined the decomposed body.

Students howled in protest outside the room as brown paper obscured their view.

Sanchez turned and frowned at her partner. "Can you hurry up there? The quicker you finish the sooner that crowd will disperse."

Jiménez's back stiffened at the comment. "You haven't mentioned anything about the money? What's up with that?"

"I told you before, I left it behind. It was evidence. Why would I mess with evidence? Hell, maybe the fuckin' monkey stole it."

Jiménez frowned. "You should have logged it on the spot."

"I was losing daylight. I didn't want to disturb a possible crime scene. I didn't figure it would go anywhere. It's not like tourists stroll through that area of the park. I was planning on coming back the next day. That is until you got assigned to the case."

Jiménez blew the comment off. "How much are we talking about?"

"A healthy stack of bills."

"What were the denominations?" Jiménez asked.

"Haven't you been listening?" Sanchez swallowed hard. "It was getting dark. They were covered in blood and mud. I didn't touch them. Besides, I was more interested in what Lyman was up to."

"Maybe he came back for the money," Betty said. "Besides you and him, who else knew about it?"

Sanchez started to reply and then stopped herself.

Vu appeared lost in thought then seemed to snap out of it when he heard them mention the soldier. "Lyman may be many things. But a thief he is not."

"How would you know?" Jiménez asked.

"It's not part of his karmic path."

"Karmic path? Are you kidding me? Or is that Air Force jargon for I got no idea how he did it?"

Vu ignored the two officers and approached the operating table and examined the corpse up close. Betty had already picked up a penlight and was examining areas around the face and ears. She pressed the tips of her fingers along the abdomen, probed just above the waistline, releasing sulfur laced off-gassing odors. Vu had a fleeting image of the Killing Fields as the noxious smell flooded his nose and opened a door in his mind that he was careful to keep under control. He closed his eyes a moment and concentrated. *I am Jim Rockford. This is not a real body. I am shooting a television scene and this is a dummy.* He opened his eyes and said goodbye to long dead memories.

Back in the now, Vu observed the appearance of what looked like fluid filled blisters on the skin of the arms where sections of the epidermis had sloughed off. Overall, the skin had a greenish discoloration.

Betty stopped and looked at him. "The body is in early stages of putrefaction. I suspected this in the jungle, but it's quite clear under better lighting. Look at the color of face and lips and I suspect after we get his pants off, you'll see distension of tissue around his groin."

Betty looked over at Sanchez. "Where's your camera?"

Sanchez had it stowed away in a bag across the room. She retrieved it, snapped off a half-dozen shots of the corpse and handed it to Betty who took several more close-up photographs of the head, hands and feet, and then set the camera down. Next, she picked up a pair of scissors from a tray of medical instruments placed by the table and carefully cut along the seam of the pant leg. She cut up one leg then the other, put the scissors down, and began to pull the material away from the skin.

"So how long has he been dead?" Sanchez looked as if the odor was getting the best of her and moved back from the table.

"Wetter environments increase the decay cycle. At this point electrolytes are rapidly leeching out of the body. I suspect both aerobic and anaerobic bacteria are present in large numbers. I'll need to collect some samples to be certain. Then I'll have a better idea about the time of death."

A slimy larva crawled out of the corpse's nasal cavity having no effect on Betty's concentration. She carefully unbuckled the boy's silver belt buckle. Vu found her dexterity remarkable, given the way she had to negotiate around the bony waist as she peeled the clothing away inch by inch, using one hand to lift under the buttock and then each leg. Once the pants were off, she didn't seem the least bit surprised that the young man had not been wearing underwear. She studied the gray-green skin color around the groin, lifted the limp dark brown penis and examined the scrotum. Following that she inspected the upper and lower thighs, the knees, ankles, and between the toes. She picked up a pair of tweezers and removed several thorns from the bottom of each foot and placed them on a sterile tray. Then, she removed the larva that had inched down the hollow jawline and placed it on a glass slide to be examined later.

While Betty used the scissors to cut off the boy's t-shirt, Vu examined the belt buckle under the florescent light. He made out some initials hand engraved on the back side of the buckle, but, for the moment, he kept the discovery to himself.

Across the room, Jiménez and the assistant were still blocking out the windows, taping butcher paper over the glass. Sanchez started to say something then stopped, pulled out her cell phone that was buzzing to read a text message received. Outside, protests from students in the hall echoed through the laboratory as the last window got blacked out.

For the next few minutes, both Betty and Vu studied the body for any evidence they may have missed. Betty began humming softly.

Vu kept out of her way as she moved adroitly around the body and then picked up the camera, snapping off another round of close-up photographs of the torso area before putting the camera down. The probing continued.

Betty looked through cupboards and drawers and rounded up the items she needed. She took blood and tissue samples. She wielded a razor-sharp scalpel making a deep incision along the left side of the neck where additional tissue samples were collected and set aside. Several incisions just above the waist were made allowing trapped air to escape from the abdominal cavity, releasing another gurgling round of putrid odor into the room.

Following that she began to examine the scalp. Clumps of dark hair stuck to her gloved hand.

"Oops…" Betty placed the hair on the metal tray. "We're well into the late stages of putrefaction. I'm still holding to my original estimate that this boy is of Indian descent. Approximate age – fifteen or sixteen. Although he has considerable disfiguration, his features seem indigenous to the tribes of the highlands. Sanchez, didn't you mention the Cabécars? I'm still learning about these various groups so I'll need to do further research before I can be exact. And, I am still placing the time of death at approximately 7 to 8 days ago. With all the decomposition, any more accuracy will require further lab tests and I don't suppose at the moment that will add much to your investigation."

"Eight days, you say…" Sanchez said. "That would place the time of death around the time the first mule team was due to pass through this area."

Jiménez turned. "Based on whose intel?"

"Mine."

That seemed to shut Jiménez up. Besides, he was only partially interested in this corpse. His main focus seemed to be on the young assistant.

"We've wasted enough time. Let's call it a day," Jiménez said. "Ms. Caan? The test results won't be back for a few days, correct?" Betty looked at the lab assistant.

"We've never run blood work on a human corpse," the assistant said. "I don't know if our equipment can even do an adequate job. It's pretty rudimentary. We're waiting on grants to upgrade some of the testing equipment. Besides, DNA testing will take a week at least."

"What about the crime lab in San Jose?" Vu asked.

"That's a possibility. But I'll have to check with our Director." Sanchez paced the room. "This is a police matter. Send it."

"Face it. We're dead in the water here," Jiménez said. "We know he's an Indian boy in his teens and he was bitten by a poisonous snake. Right, Ms. Caan? We'll follow up with missing persons."

Betty took one of the tissue samples collected from the neck and examined it under a microscope. After a quick look at the slide, she turned and nodded. Vu took note.

"I just heard back from Carlos." Sanchez said, referring to her text message. "There are no reports of a missing person fitting the corpse's description."

Jiménez smiled at the lab assistant. "That's no surprise."

"You might want to focus your inquiries on the tribal villages next," Vu said.

Sanchez didn't want to hear that. "Look, I don't know how much either of you know about Indians around these parts. If the kid could be linked to illegal activities, the tribes will deny it. They distrust outsiders and protect their own. And they hate cops."

Vu didn't need an explanation to understand the gist of her comment.

"Perhaps they would be more inclined to speak with an Asian?" Jiménez laughed. "That your karmic path?"

"Curiosity is a strong lure. They may have never met someone like me."

Sanchez sort of drifted in and out, Vu noticed, half-watching Betty examining the corpse, half keeping an eye on him. The student's protests in the hall quieted. He wondered if he'd missed something at the crime scene that could possibly help the officers. But, Lyman's presence still had him rattled. Of all places...

Betty noticed the assistant watching and waved her over for a closer look.

"How's it coming there?" Jiménez asked them. "We about ready to wrap this up?"

"This isn't at all like the Anatomy and Physiology course I took last semester. We dissected a cat."

"If you are interested in law enforcement, I'd be happy to give you a ride along sometime." Jiménez smiled at the young woman.

Sanchez went over to snatch her camera from the table and asked Betty if she was finished using it. Betty told her that she was, but she needed another hour or so to examine the tissue samples collected.

Vu looked over at the assistant. "Do you think I could get a tour of the facility while Betty continues her work?"

The assistant nodded and then looked at the others. "Would anyone else like to join us?"

Jiménez glanced at Sanchez: "Couldn't hurt."

Sanchez frowned. "I'll stay here. You boys go have your fun."

Chapter 23

In the brightly lit hallway outside the laboratory, a few curious stragglers shot questions at the three leaving.

"Was it a drug overdose? What will you do with the corpse? Was it murder?"

"We are making no comment at this time" Jiménez puffed out his chest and took the lead as the three headed down the hall.

After they were clear of the students, Dr. Trujillo's assistant apologized for the disturbance.

"You can't blame them for being curious." Jiménez said, giving her his best gangster smile, before adjusting the fedora sitting tilted on his head.

"What area would you like to see first?"

"Well, now," Jiménez blurted, zeroing in on the young eager face. "I'd like to see where the cafeteria is. I could use something to eat. It's been a very long day."

She turned. "What about you Mr. Vu?"

"I prefer to see the facility, if you don't mind."

Jiménez made a friendly shrug. "Did you introduce yourself earlier?" he asked her. "In all the rush, I don't remember."

"It's Angelia."

"Angelia, how long have you been a student here?" Vu asked.

"I'm a senior," she replied with pride.

"What's your major?"

"It was going to be anthropology."

"Sounds like that's changed?" Jiménez joined in.

"I've applied to Medical School but I won't hear the results for several weeks. Dr. Trujillo, I'm afraid, is rather unhappy about my decision."

"Why is that?" Vu asked.

"Well, he likes to see his assistants pursue careers in his areas of research, and he spends an exceptional amount of time with his chosen assistants."

"Sounds like you admire Dr. Trujillo?"

"He's driven and very intelligent. He's done great things for the Instituto. But I feel now like I want to explore working with humans instead of their second cousins, the primates."

"Has Dr. Trujillo voiced his disapproval?" Vu asked.

"No, I didn't mean to suggest that. It's just, well, you'll have to meet him yourself sometime. He can be very persuasive about his passions."

Jiménez pried. "Like how?"

"Fundraising, for one. He's solely responsible for much of what is around you."

And with that Angelia stopped at the door to another laboratory. She opened it slowly and held her finger up to her lips so the men would get the message that class was in session. The men looked inside. "This is our anatomy and physiology classroom," she whispered.

Vu poked his head inside the room. Several students were busy along the far wall. A series of microscopes sat on counters cluttered with textbooks. Students were examining slides. Others appeared to be studying for a test in front of a pull-down anatomy chart. A few more were dissecting what looked like different breeds of water fowl.

"Most of the programs require students to perform six complete dissections to graduate. We can specialize in one of three areas. Birds. Primates. Or, small mammals."

Jiménez looked as if he was going to comment and then kept his thoughts to himself.

They followed Angelia down the hall while she pointed out several more classrooms along the way. Two faculty offices at the end of the hall had their doors closed and Vu could also hear heated conversations beyond the doors.

Lining the hallways, there were trophy cases filled with pictures and awards touting the accomplishments of the school. Vu studied the numerous photographs. "Which of these is Dr. Trujillo?" He asked Angelia.

She pointed to various photos, some showing him shaking hands with politicians, with scientists, with prominent businessmen, and yet another showing him with his arms around a group of Indians.

"Does Dr. Trujillo work with indigenous Indians?"

"Yes, but I don't know the specifics. I believe it has to do with the corridor project."

"Corridor?" Vu asked.

"It's an area of clear cut land that connects areas otherwise blocked off by nature. Dr. Trujillo has been working very hard to secure the land for the Instituto. It's like a single-lane road slicing through privately owned undeveloped land. Most of the borderland is owned by the government, and is already off limits. But officials have been selling it off at an alarming rate. Multinational corporations are zeroing in on it. As we speak, there are precious areas that are under proposal for development. This could have a devastating effect on wildlife. Dr. Trujillo wants to ensure that primates can move from one environment to the next, so that the population will not become too inbred as it has already done."

"Is this corridor open to the public?"

"Well, not in so many words."

"What does that mean?" Vu asked.

Jiménez interrupted. "It's part of the regions political rhetoric. Corporations have been bribing politicians for rulings. Our bureau believes even the cartels are in on the action, using the corridor to move drugs from one country to the next. But the evidence is not conclusive."

Vu looked at him. "Didn't Sanchez mention something about this?"

Jiménez bit down hard on his lip. "Sanchez believes what she wants to believe."

"There is a dead body upstairs that might indicate otherwise."

"It's way too early to start tossing around theories," Jiménez said.

Vu took out his cell phone and took a photo of the picture.

Angelia looked around furtively, uncomfortable with his actions, so Vu reassured her saying: "I just want to remember what he looks like so when I meet him, I can address him by name."

This seemed to appease her.

Near the stairs, Vu noticed a sign indicating more classrooms were on the upper and lower floors. The uppermost floor was the Research Department.

"What happens upstairs?" Vu asked.

"That is our special research section where Dr. Trujillo has an office and laboratory."

"May we see the laboratory?"

She paused. "If you're still thinking of getting beverages the cafeteria is on the first floor and classes will be letting out soon. We should get going."

Jiménez seemed to think Angelia looked as if she could use a break. He smiled at her. "You read my mind. In fact, drinks are on me."

Vu was not interested in refreshments. He was curious about the research area upstairs and persisted. "First, could we possibly view the Doctor's laboratory?"

"I'm afraid that area is off-limits," Angelia said. "It is where Dr. Trujillo is working on a special project. He feels it has great monetary potential for the Instituto. What I can tell you is that it has to do with tracing the development of a species. Certain genes found in primates. But, Dr. Trujillo is the expert."

"Like Darwinism?" Vu asked.

"Who's Darwin?" Jiménez inquired.

Angelia smiled. "You're joking?"

Jiménez frowned. "In school I focused on other things."

"You probably specialized in partying," Angelia teased.

"I did my share. Isn't that part of getting an education?"

Angelia seemed to find Jiménez's ignorance cute. Sharing her superior knowledge seemed to please her. "Darwin actually studied Theology and law. He stumbled onto science quite by accident. His work in the Galapagos Islands changed how scientists now view the evolution of species."

"Why don't we let Vu wander off by himself," Jiménez threw out. "He can catch up with us at the cafeteria? That fine with you, Jack?"

Angelia thought it over.

"Well … I am supposed to escort you…."

"I will head back to the lab and see if the women would like me to bring some refreshments back to them."

Angelia shrugged. "Sure. You know the way. Go straight down the hall, take the stairs right. There's an elevator at the other end of the building, but trust me, it works only half the time. When you're finished join us in the cafeteria downstairs. If anyone stops you in the hall, just inform them you have my permission to be on the premises."

Vu wasted no time dawdling and scurried off like a freshman on the first day of class. As he was ascending the stairs to the forbidden laboratory, laughter from Angelia's soft voice seemed to echo through the stairwell like music from a violin. Vu had a strange feeling they were making fun of him. He unconsciously touched his large ears.

The area upstairs was mostly used for storage. Dark rooms filled with cardboard boxes, spare classroom furniture, and classroom supplies. Two of the rooms were classrooms. But their doors were closed and the lights were turned off. Vu took a peek inside each and then moved on.

Further down the hall there were three office doors, all closed. The plastic signs hanging on them indicated they were being used for building maintenance. Vu could hear someone talking on a telephone inside one of the offices. Dr. Trujillo's office was down at the far end by an emergency exit. The laboratory he used was across the hall and took up the space of three classrooms. Windows would face the noisy streets below. Vu pressed his head to the door and listened. He heard what sounded like a faint dog-like barking coming from inside and then tried the knob.

The door was locked.

He glanced down at the lock mechanism. Simple. Ten seconds tops, he could be inside. He stepped back and looked up and down the hall, then removed a notched credit card from his wallet, slipped it between the latch and the door with the notched area facing in. He felt it grab, twisted slightly and pulled the door open.

The light switch was to the right of the door. Vu flipped it on, put the card back inside his wallet, and closed the door behind him.

Across the room a series of metal cages lined the back walls. There was movement inside a number of the cages. The animal cries he had heard outside fell silent momentarily until he began to walk through the area. His tennis shoes squeaked on the linoleum. He stopped beside a trash can and looked inside before moving over to a small operating table where several used instruments sat out on a metal tray. He noticed some particles on the razor sharp blades suggesting they had been left there after use. A bottle of rubbing alcohol and a box of opened cotton swabs as well had been left out on the counter. Not like your typical researcher to leave contaminated instruments out on counters. Looked to Vu like somebody left in a hurry. A few of the cabinets contained glass beakers and precision measuring devices. A stainless steel sink sat in the corner with water droplets collecting in the basin. The laboratory was similar to those he'd been in downstairs with one difference. Those downstairs didn't contain eight primates locked in metal cages.

Vu walked up to the cages and peered inside. Each one contained only one primate. The primates seemed frightened of him. He counted three white-faced capuchins, two endangered spider monkeys and a lone squirrel monkey caged at a distance from the others, near the end. There were two separate cages along a different wall housing howler monkeys. The animals looked healthy and yet up near their neckline he noticed each one had a section of hair shaved bare. Tiny fresh scars were evident.

What type of research was Dr. Trujillo performing here?

A quick survey of Dr. Trujillo's desk revealed a log of numbers, dates and types of primates. Vu photographed the pages. A theory was forming that in order to track animals in the corridor to see if it was successful, they would need some type of built in GPS. It appeared that he had successfully implanted hundreds of devices. Across from some numbers were a red "X" and another date. Vu suspected these devices quit functioning and those animals were presumed dead. Then as he photographed another page, he realized that the names on this page were human. So Dr. Trujillo was tracking not just monkeys, but humans who frequented the corridor as well. Vu wondered how many boys like the one downstairs unwittingly were sending information to the lab of their exact locations at all times.

Vu walked over to a small table with a Bunsen burner and a large microscope. There were two tissue sample slides resting on the counter as if someone had been viewing them before they got called away. He took one of the slides, slid it under the microscope, and dialed in the focus. He sat back on his heels. He'd just seen the same effect in the tissue sample of the dead boy's neck. What was on the slide that could connect these monkeys with the dead boy and a cache of drug money? He pocketed the slides, asking blessings from Buddha to protect him from discovery. Suddenly, Vu heard the door knob move. He held his breath as the knob jiggled, and then heard the guard move on down the hall.

Trujillo, Cabécar Indians, politicians, mule teams and scientific experiments, possibly conducted on both humans and primates, it sounded to Vu like a perfect political thriller paperback to take on vacation. Only this wasn't fiction.

* * *

Jiménez had his hand resting on Angelia's leg when Vu walked up to the table and sat down opposite him. Jiménez sat back, placing his hands on the table as if he'd been caught doing something naughty.

"Did they find anything interesting?" Jiménez asked.

"Not really," Vu said, and smiled politely at Angelia who was sipping on a fruit drink. The two of them had seemed to hit it off rather quickly. Vu figured that Angelia was enjoying the edge she had over the older detective, the draw of her youth and over-eager appetite to experience everything, had the detective in her spell. Who could ignore it? Jiménez soaked it up like spring sunshine.

Angelia asked, "Mr. Vu did you want to grab a Coke or something for the ladies?"

He had almost forgotten. "Yes, thank you, Angelia, and then I will head back."

Jiménez leaned back and smirked. "Angelia and I will be along shortly."

* * *

Vu entered the lab to see Betty peering into a microscope and making notes with Sanchez pacing in the corner of the room. "I brought you ladies some refreshments," Vu said, handing Sanchez a sweating can of Coke.

"Where's Jiménez?"

"He's in the cafeteria entertaining Dr. Trujillo's assistant. They'll be joining us shortly."

"That's good. He'll probably need to call his wife." As if on cue, Sanchez' phone rang. She glanced down, grimaced and stepped out into the hallway to answer it.

Vu walked over to Betty and set her Coke on the counter beside her. "I brought you a little something extra." He pulled the slides from his pocket and set them next to the microscope."

"How sweet. Blood and tissue with my Coke."

"I took them from Dr. Trujillo's private laboratory. He has several primates in there with fresh surgeries on their necks. From what I could tell, they are implanting microchips or tracking devices in them."

"Next it will be us, Jack." Betty said grimly.

Vu smiled at his crackpot lover with the conspiracy theories and political intrigue ideas. "It appears it already is." He shared his information about the tracking chip in the belt buckle and the lists of names he had found."

"Chipping animals isn't that unusual. It is just the way scientists think," Betty said, "but chipping humans gives a different slant to the experiment."

"When I looked at one of these, it looked like the specimen you took from the boy's neck."

"How could that be possible?" Betty quickly shifted slides and looked at the new sample. "This is a sample with venom similar to the boy's bite mark."

"Lyman was burying a monkey under the tree. If his monkey died of a snake bite, then how did that sample get here to this lab?"

"There's more, Betty." Vu held up his cell phone and showed Betty the photo of Trujillo surrounded by Cabécar Indians. "Our doctor appears to be quite friendly with the local indigenous Indians."

"As you say Jack, there is a point of confluence, where everything links and merges. What do we have? Animal corridors which also service mule teams. Doctors, Drug Kingpins, and Money – lots of it, fueling both endeavors."

"But how does Lyman know Trujillo?"

"Maybe he just stumbled into this soup with us."

Vu mused. "There is a feeling of convergence...."

Betty smiled. "I'm all for this theory as long as everything links and merges in time for the Panama Canal."

Chapter 24

Sanchez cursed her day as she headed to her shoddy motel room, but at least she'd convinced her Captain to keep them on the case for another day. As she put the key into the lock she heard familiar laughter down the hall. She poked her head around the corner just in time to glimpse Jiménez steering the lab assistant into his room, his hands firmly planted on her ass. Normally she enjoyed out of town stopovers, just for the change in routine, but since Jiménez's room abutted hers, she hoped she wouldn't have to lie in bed listening to her co-worker get his rocks off. Given how the day had gone so far, it somehow seemed almost fitting that each of them in their own way were getting fucked.

Sanchez flopped down on her bed, and flipped on the television, only to find that her choices of entertainment were very limited. Unless she wanted to watch reruns of American TV, which conjured up Angelia's praise of Dragnet and Jiménez's stupid hat. Already Jiménez's laughter spilled through the thin walls, making it difficult to concentrate on anything. Before long, she heard some general banging about and figured by now they were tossing their clothes. It was only a matter of moments before the headboard started bumping against the wall. The girl was a squealer. And, who would have thought that Jiménez could talk so dirty?

Work will get your mind off Jiménez and his brainy putana.

Groaning, she rolled over and grabbed her camera from the nightstand and flipped back through the digital file for the "Bird Boy" so named for being found high in the branches of a tree. She stopped when she got to Lyman's picture, snapped on instinct an instant before he took control. He wasn't bad looking for an older guy. Definitely eccentric, and in a war all his own making, but his hardened power excited her. And, the more she studied his image, the more she heated up. *I'm young enough to be his daughter.* Was this some type of dysfunctional phase of mourning for her father? Hardly. Jiménez was with a woman half his age. She smiled as she remembered her dad once telling her he wasn't interested in dating anyone his own age. "The worst thing in the world for an old man is an old woman," he'd admonished her once when she caught him eyeing a college-aged Latina beauty at the market. Touching Lyman's image, she wondered what it would be like to experience his calloused, rough hands cupping her ass.

Next door, the lovemaking grew more intense. Sanchez propped Lyman's image against the pillow and rolled onto her side. Her dark eyes clicked into place on his photo as lovemaking cries pulsed through the paper thin walls. Sanchez joined the party and ran her fingers along her abdomen until she reached her panties, shoved them down and brusquely massaged her slit. Pinching her nipple with brute force, launched a series of small tremors down her thighs, which eventually exploded into a clenching climax. As she released herself, exhaling air slowly through her mouth in a silent whistle, she realized her partners next door had reached their conclusion simultaneously, leaving her feeling oddly voyeuristic and bashful. Sanchez sat up and retrieved the camera and her notes. Studying the images, she mentally mined the grisly scene and implausibility of the cast of characters already involved.

You can sleep when you're dead.

As the hours slipped by, she studied her notes and created a flow chart attempting to make connections that would allow her

Captain to keep her on the case until it was resolved.

Notes lay scattered on the bed when she woke the next morning. After a quick whore's bath and a weak attempt to comb her hair with her fingers, Sanchez banged on Jiménez's door, two cups of black coffee in hand. After no answer on the first knock, she kicked it with her boot. Eventually, the door opened on its chain. Jiménez peered out through the crack.

"Time to rise and shine, loverboy."

Jiménez rubbed his face, then removed the chain, and invited her in. Sanchez half-expected to find the girl in his cluttered room, but the bed was empty.

"Where's your girlfriend?"

"What girlfriend?"

"Oh, for Christ's sake, Jiménez, I heard you banging her last night."

Jiménez looked incredulous.

"Oh, baby! Oh, baby! Oh, baby! Right there, yeah ... yeah ... suck right there!" Sanchez mimicked humping motions.

"Jesus Sanchez, I'm a married man." Jiménez lowered his eyes. "Okay, you got me. I was watching porn on my computer. Sorry ... I'll turn it down in the future."

"Whatever." Sanchez shoved coffee at Jiménez.

Jiménez took a long pull. "Hey, did you hear anything from the Instituto?"

"Not yet. Drink up and get dressed."

"What's the rush?"

Sanchez flashed her watch. "It's after nine, Romeo. Time to hit the bricks."

Jiménez attempted a smile. "Give me a few minutes here."

"Well, hurry up," she barked. "I'll be waiting in the car."

Jiménez headed toward the bathroom. "I've been thinking about that Indian kid."

"And?"

"Maybe he crawled up in the tree because he was frightened."

Chapter 25

Senor Héctor walked past his library toward his desk to open the briefcase that the good doctor had given him. He'd grown weary of their arrangement, but it had been beneficial for both of them and it was going to come to an end soon enough.

Héctor pulled open the velvety curtains allowing the sunlight to spill across his large office onto one of his favorite 18th century oil paintings. Collecting art had been a nice way to balance the seedier side of his business. Also, it was an easy way to invest his questionable earnings and far more rewarding than purchasing real estate. His Cezanne's, Rothchild's, Dali's – even his more impulsive purchases of nude photographs by Art Kane, Serge A. Verriele McCabe, Cheri Hiser, and Robert Mapplethorpe. The more exotic nudes he kept in a private gallery near the cellar because they gave him immense pleasure and were rarely shared. Art calmed him. Women had occasionally provided the same affect, but not of late.

Today, the office's mahogany walls had a waxy glow and he noticed that his servant had put a fresh coat of lemon oil on the woodwork. His favorite leather armchair beckoned. The sculptures were dust free. The Indian rug vacuumed. All was right with his world.

As Héctor stored the legal documents into his wall safe, he heard someone quietly enter the room from behind. He turned in time to see Cecelia padding barefoot into the room wearing only a white long-sleeved shirt. Her thighs bore fresh reddened pock marks, like she'd been picking at them again. It came as no surprise really that Cecelia's eyes looked mournful and her appearance disheveled. Nor did the stress lines creasing her drawn face shock him. By the way she kept her hands pressed against her sides as she walked forward he saw the effects of withdrawal.

"Good morning, *Coca*."

"Baby doll I feel really, really awful this morning," Cecelia uttered, in a frail, fetal voice. "Can you give me a little bump?"

Personally, Héctor had never used the stuff. Heroin just wasn't his thing. But, he knew from others in the business at all costs withdrawals were to be avoided.

Héctor sat down behind his desk. "Come, *Coca*. Let me see you up close."

Cecelia padded over like an obedient child.

Looking into her hollow eyes, Héctor felt nothing. Within a few short months, Cecelia had gone from the perky sex kitten to a nagging, addicted whore. It was just as well that he had found out about her relationship with the good doctor when he did. It had put him in an awkward position. One that she would dearly pay for.

Cecelia moved in closer and Héctor could smell the unkempt odor on her person. Not even expensive perfume could camouflage it. Her lusterless lips reminded him of wilted orchids. The lovely dark skin that had so attracted him in the beginning now appeared flaxen and smelled of urine.

"Baby doll please don't make me beg."

"Is it very bad?" he asked.

"Yes."

With Cecelia watching intently, Héctor opened his desk drawer to remove a small bag of white powder. "*Coca*, my lovely. I'm afraid it is time we do something about this bad habit of yours."

Cecelia reached out to take the bag of dope but Héctor had a change of heart and dropped it back into his desk and closed the drawer.

"No, baby doll … I'll do anything … anything."

"Of course you will."

Héctor sat back in his chair and stared at her. She wasted no time in dropping to her knees before him and reaching for his pants. Héctor allowed her to unzip his trousers and fish around inside until she found his penis. Slipping the flaccid penis out of his pants, she stooped down over it and began kissing its head. Once erect, she took it all into her mouth and looked up at him.

Héctor said with a superior smile. "You are my precious, kitty cat."

And with that, Cecelia stroked the large penis with her lips and hands until Héctor shot off his semen into her mouth. With traces of the creamy juices oozing from her purplish lips, she took the edge of her shirt and wiped his member dry and gently slipped it back inside his trousers, then dabbed the corners of her mouth.

As if her legs were numb from kneeling, Cecelia didn't move from the floor, patiently waiting like an obedient pet for her reward.

Héctor couldn't stand her desperate staring. From his desk, he removed a special bag of dope and tossed it to her.

"Go enjoy yourself, *Coca*."

Cecelia rose unsteadily and clutched the bag of dope to her chest. "Thank you, baby doll."

After Cecelia left, Héctor checked his trousers to see if she had been careless with her wiping and saw two little wet spots. Héctor took a Kleenex, wetted it with his tongue, and dabbed the area. About then his bodyguard knocked on the office door, which Cecelia had left ajar.

"Come!"

The bodyguard entered and walked over to Héctor' desk. "The shipment has arrived," he said eagerly.

Héctor nodded. "Good. Then you know what to do next."

"Yes. Should I have Colonel Pierz prepare the full team?"

"This shipment is our largest. We will need everyone. I will go on this journey myself, to ensure we have no troubles."

"Shall I prepare a mule for Ms. Cecelia?"

"No, Edmund," Héctor said. "She is in no condition to travel. I want you to stay behind this time. Look after her. She is not feeling well."

Chapter 26

Aboard the *Sea Gypsy* a mutiny was afoot. Several of the passengers were demanding that something be done about the continued delay that was now in its second day. Captain Spartacus looked out over the crowded bar where moments earlier he'd told the guests to congregate. The latest news was the ship would be in port another day, possibly longer. Since the labor strike continued and the possibility of flying their clothing in from the Caribbean looked remote, they had made the decision to bring the luggage overland.

"There are transportation issues," he said in response to one of the passenger's questions. "A labor protest at the airport has caused many problems as well. All incoming and outgoing flights are behind schedule. Hopefully, everything will get ironed out soon. At any rate, your luggage is on its way here, unlike many other unlucky travelers stranded in our country."

"What do you propose we do now?" Another guest asked. "We have toured Manual Antonio and Quepos."

The crowd grumbled amongst themselves for what seemed like an eternity before one of the head guides stood up and offered a list of activities for the day.

Vu and Betty were returning to their room when Betty leaned over and whispered "If I didn't know better, I'd say you had a hand in this luggage snafu just so we can figure out our puzzle."

"I was looking at Dr. Trujillo's handwritten notes on the microchips this morning. I don't think they are exclusively for monkeys."

"You mean he's tracking other animals?"

"Yes, but the two legged variety. Dr. Trujillo may have somehow put microchips in the Indians."

"We didn't find one on the corpse."

"No, but there was something about the belt the boy was wearing that I connected with his notes last night. There were initials on the back of the buckle that match initials in his code."

"It would certainly be easy to give away free items that contained chips, but how could he be sure they would wear them? Or which person would get which belt?" Betty scrunched her face up in thought.

"Maybe Dr. Trujillo can shine some light on that." Vu smiled. "Use some of your Southern charm with him today and see what you can find out."

"Aren't you coming with me?"

Before Vu could answer, they bumped into Ginger on the aft deck, having just come in from a morning's swim.

"How's the water?" Vu asked.

"Porpoise free." Ginger wore a one-piece turquoise swimsuit with a beach towel wrapped around her waist. She brushed her hair and gleamed. "Where are you two off to?"

"We're on our way to grab a few things from our cabin before we head to shore. What about you?"

"I'm content to lounge in the sun. I've got a juicy novel to keep me company. But perhaps I'll join you later for a nip in the lounge."

"It's a date," Betty said.

Ginger stared at Vu. "How's the hunt going?"

"We turned the body over to the local authorities. So I guess the hunt is over."

"Bloody shame," Ginger piped in stroking the brush several more times through her wet hair. "I was hoping to get some really good stories to tell the little duffs back home. Well then, I'll see you tonight."

And with that Ginger sauntered off.

Back inside their cabin, Vu asked, "Shall we visit the Instituto first?"

Betty tugged on her stubborn damp hiking boot. "So you are coming with me? I'm rather interested in seeing the lab work."

"I have already done my lab research." Vu paused, thinking. "Would you object to my taking a cab to town after I drop you off at the Instituto?"

"Where are you going?"

"I'd like to snoop around a little."

"You're being vague, Jack?"

"I need to speak with Lyman."

Betty's brow wrinkled with worry. "I agreed to go along with this corpse thing, but now you're sounding like you want to dig up old dirt?"

"We have unfinished business."

Betty frowned. "Who doesn't? Let it go, Jack."

"Why don't we meet for lunch at that little outdoor café, say one?" Vu knew that any discussion of food brightened Betty's mood.

"Crumpys?"

"Yeah. I want to try their Crumpy Frumpy Fish Tacos."

"You're going to walk into a strange town, find a crazy SOB that doesn't have any contact with the locals, and meet me for lunch in a little over three hours – right?"

"You left out the part where I say I'm good at what I do."

She frowned, which caught him by surprise, but not as surprising as what came next.

"No you're not!" She said, but within moments, her face turned angelic and she clarified. "You're great at what you do. Just don't push Lyman. These monkeys have changed him. You don't point a gun at law enforcement personnel unless you're willing to go all the way."

"I agree."

"Why do you think he cares so much about the monkeys? They don't appear to be in danger?"

"Chips in primates?" Vu smiled. "Maybe he has the same kind of paranoid government conspiracy theories that you ponder."

By the time the Zodiac landed ashore, the sun crawled behind a cloud bank and the air grew swelteringly still. All the distant bird sounds in the rainforest suddenly ceased as the foreign invaders entered their private territory. The inflatable skittered over the sandy beach. The only sound immediately heard, besides the growling of Vu's stomach, was a distant plane flying overhead. All else seemed intent on silence.

They walked overland to the main road and passed very few tourists. The park seemed vacated. It was an eerie feeling to Vu, who had imagined seeing hundreds milling about. He turned to Betty and handed her a drink from his water bottle. "It's quiet out here, today."

Betty said, "Where is everyone?"

Vu shrugged. "Perhaps the labor protests have kept people away."

Up ahead, Vu could see the Instituto coming into clear view. Surrounded by immense trees and foliage the four large buildings made of white brick with red tile roofing stood out against the dark forest beyond. Almost military looking in its simplistic architecture and paint. "Do you remember the building from yesterday?" he asked Ricardo.

"Yes, yes," he said pointing toward the building to their right. "It is that one, I think?"

Betty corrected. "It is the building on the end. Over there," she pointed. "The one with the snake symbol over the door." Then turning to Vu she said, "Jack, are you sure you don't want to come inside with me? I won't be long. If the test results turn up something, we can pass the information along to Sanchez and the local authorities together."

"No, we will stick to our original plan."

"Okay, but it's your loss, because I know how excited you get when I put on my lab coat."

"I will visualize this, while I'm seeking Lyman."

Ricardo asked, "Will you be meeting with Dr. Trujillo today?"

"I hope to," Betty said. "I have several questions for him?"

And with that Ricardo led the way. Betty leaned back and kissed Vu's lips. "See you later, gator." Then she spun around and shouted. "Ricardo! Wait up!"

*   *   *

In the Instituto laboratory basement, Gaston paced back and forth in front of an incinerator, mumbling incoherently while clutching his bandaged hand. Voracious flames spilled from the open furnace doors, like a serpent's tongue, flickering in and out, the intense heat seared past him toward the tall ceiling. Nearby, on a rusted gurney lay the Indian corpse, covered from head to toe in a sheet. Nobody knew this boy or had any idea what he was doing in the tree. The big surprise was finding him in the laboratory this morning. Gaston stopped pacing and stood before the gurney. After restless thoughts, he pushed the gurney to the open door. Stepping to the left side of the gurney, he slid his hands underneath the corpse and hefted the body up and forward toward the flames. An ache rose in his hand and he lost his grip, leaving the sheet covered package slanting toward the floor. Then, all of sudden, a loud bang on the basement door startled him. He froze, recognizing the pleas of his newest assistant.

"Doctor Trujillo! I need you to come up right away!"

"I'm busy, right now," he shouted. "Can't this wait?"

"Dr. Trujillo! This is Detective Sanchez. I need you to open the door."

"All right. I'm coming."

Gaston slammed the incinerator doors closed. Hastily, he rolled the gurney into the service elevator and concealed it behind closed doors.

Climbing the basement steps to the first floor, he felt his heart thumping against his chest. Overweight and out of shape, he needed to smoke fewer cigars, and drink less. But it was his life. If he did what was best for his health all the time, he would have no enjoyment. What was the enjoyment in living a life of purity anyhow?

Stepping out into the bright light he expected to see the detective standing with his assistant. Instead just his assistant nervously paced the hall alone. Her clothing was rumpled, un-ironed and looked slept in. "I took the police to your office," she uttered. "And the lady doctor from the United States is back too. I put her in the lab room."

"What do they want?"

"They're asking if the test results taken yesterday have come back." His assistant frowned.

"An American pathologist ran tests on the Indian boy? I thought they just brought the body here for identification." Gaston knew the game had changed now. He was grateful he hadn't destroyed the body because it would cast unnecessary suspicion his way. They knew nothing of his tracking of Indians. To them this was just a runaway who died in the jungle. He'd checked the belt buckle and the chip was intact. His thoughts were interrupted by Angelia attempting to explain.

"I left you several messages regarding this – about the tests and the police."

"What tests were requested again?"

"Blood analysis, mostly … there was also a toxicity test that I'm not familiar with."

"And who is this pathologist? Has she been hired by the police?"

"No. As I understand it, she is a guest in our country."

"Which office are they with, did they say that much?"

"Yes. The *Policía de Fronteras*."

"What does the immigration want with us?"

It was a question requiring no answer. His assistant suddenly noticed his hand. "What happened?"

Chapter 27

When Gaston opened his office door, he saw a man and woman in uniform, waiting. The woman, who'd been pacing the small quarters, walked toward him and introduced herself as Officer Sanchez.

"You took your sweet time, Dr. Trujillo." Sanchez's remark seemed to have no effect on the doctor's professional temperament. He simply looked her in the eye and moved toward his desk. Jiménez walked up and offered a friendly handshake.

Gaston raised his bandaged hand, then thought better of it and lowered it back to his side. "You may call me Gaston, if you prefer. Most of the students do."

Sanchez glanced at his hand. "That looks like it hurt a little?"

Gaston flashed a disarming smile. "A little, yes. What can I do for you, officers? Does this have to do with the corpse of the boy that was brought here yesterday?"

Jiménez, who'd been reading the small inscription on one of Gaston's many trophies, placed the tiny bronze statue back on the shelf. The small plate on the bottom indicated that the award was from a civic group for accomplishments in biodiversity.

"You're quite a champion of the environment," Jiménez noted, referring back to the number of trophies and awards presented.

Gaston's voice tightened. "At present my studies are focused on primates and the new corridor that I assume you have read about since you are with Immigration."

"Look, Gaston," Sanchez said, "There were several tests run on the Indian boy's body yesterday…"

"I assume we are talking about the ones requested by the American pathologist, who I have not yet had the pleasure of meeting."

"Yes." Sanchez filled him in on the details. "Specifically, why I'm asking, is that our office believes the area around Manuel Antonia and even its perimeter is being used as a route for the cartels. The body was found in a location near here, on federal grounds, and our office has taken the lead to determine if there is a possible connection to this boy's death. What we are most wanting to know is, have you seen any activities that would indicate something illegal is occurring here?"

"You think the students are involved in these illegal activities?"

"No, please allow me to explain again," Sanchez said. "Not here at the Instituto per se, but on the grounds outside the doors?"

"That is where our students perform their studies…"

"They are not the area of our focus."

"You do know what we do here?" Gaston replied defensively.

"It has been explained to us," Sanchez replied. "I understand that you are primarily responsible for securing grants and funding to conduct experiments with primates traveling from one corridor to the next."

"That is a very simplistic version. The corridor is merely one area of our studies. We are studying the effect of different breeding habitats. Genetically, we are trying to alter a species. By introducing predators at a rate normally not occurring in the animal's lifetime, we can monitor how the animal defends itself, if it has the capability to adapt and survive. Many scientists believe Manuel Antonio is biologically undiversified. We are attempting to change that. The Instituto is hoping to reverse the weakness of a species; in essence to re-define nature."

Jiménez looked bored, with his hunched shoulders and his constant stares out the window. Sanchez cleared her throat as if she wanted him to get in the game.

"Doctor," Jiménez started. "Your assistant mentioned that you have indigenous family in the area. And we have seen photos of you with indigenous tribe members."

"My mother was an anthropologist and I myself spent several spans of time with the Cabécars."

"Is it possible you can identify the boy?"

Sure he knew about the Indian boy, and what he was doing in the tree, and how he died, but he knew they were clueless.

"What my colleague is trying to say," Sanchez interrupted. "Is that we have no idea why an Indian boy would be in these parts. And, more importantly, what was he doing in a tree? My theory is he was hired to scout. From previous cases, I've discovered that the Indian has an excellent knowledge of the rainforest terrain. They can maneuver through areas where others would be hopelessly lost. We all know the rainforest can be a dangerous place without a guide. If this boy was acting in that capacity, then we can assume the area is being used for illegal activities. Perhaps, with your help, we can surprise these transporters."

Gaston remained collected, however sweat beaded on his forehead. "This is the first I've heard of this sort of activity. I would be very surprised indeed if this is occurring. Getting back to the Indian boy. He is as big a mystery to me as he is to you two officers. These tests are to determine cause of death, I presume?"

Sanchez nodded.

"If the cause of death turns out to be from a snake, how will this information help your case?"

"We aren't sure how this all ties together. We were hoping you could help."

Gaston realized the two officers were on a fishing expedition. "Our Instituto is at your disposal. All I request is that you keep me informed of what you learn and try not to disturb the students. I'm afraid, I will also need billing information so that I can seek reimbursements for the costs of these tests, and any work my staff does on your behalf."

Sanchez bit her lip. "Yes, of course. Thank you for seeing us."

"If I learn anything I will be happy to contact you." Gaston walked the officers to the door. "It is a pleasure to assist Immigration with its efforts."

After he showed them out, he rang his assistant and told her to meet him at once in his office.

*   *   *

Betty looked around the lab, wondering where the body was being stored. All the evidence bags had been catalogued under the watchful eye of Detective Sanchez and placed in the walk-in refrigerator. The clothes were bagged and tagged and placed there as well. But the body had been moved. Betty looked at the belt buckle and photographed the markings on the back. She carried it out to the main room to examine it more closely under better lighting. On the counter were the lab results on the tissue samples she had taken. Cause of death was not straightforward. The thorns she'd removed from the boy's feet were from a barbed manchineel tree, whose poisonous sap is caustic, deadly and could have rendered a child unconscious in a matter of minutes and dead if left untreated. Betty posited that something scared the boy so badly that he ran through the poisonous plants, climbed the tree to hide, lost consciousness and was bitten by the eyelash viper.

That certainly put a different angle on the death. He could have been chased up that tree but would have never voluntarily subjected himself to the manchineel thorns unless under a life threatening situation. They could have also been administered as a torture device or even to make a homicide appear accidental. The poor boy – after finally finding a perch away from his tormentors, only to then die from an eyelash viper attack. It was so sad.

Lost in thought, with the now forgotten belt in her lap, she heard the door open behind her.

"I see our lab has produced results on the indigenous boy found on our property yesterday?" Betty swung around in her chair, putting her legs under the desk counter.

"Dr. Trujillo, it's a pleasure to meet you." Betty extended her hand.

Dr. Trujillo used his good hand to shake and sat across the table from her. "I see we have gotten lab results back. I assume they confirm an accidental death due to snakebite."

"Are eyelash vipers native to this area?"

"Not for many years. They were reintroduced as part of our program to add biodiversity."

"So ordinarily this child would not have had to worry about a snake in a tree had the Instituto not reintroduced it?"

"I don't like your tone, Dr. ... I'm sorry – I don't even know your name."

"Betty Caan. And it is I who should apologize. I have better manners than that." She tried her best disarming smile. "Besides, the snake didn't kill the boy. He died from manchineel poisoning."

Betty turned the results around to the shocked Gaston.

"The infamous *Hippomane Manicinella*, also called the "beach apple." These trees are native to the area and everybody is aware of their deadly nature. Not even a boy would subject himself to a dozen thorns in his feet unless he was forced to do so to escape a killer. The only consolation is that he was probably already unconscious when the viper struck."

Betty crossed her legs, effectively concealing the belt. She reached down and picked up her purse as Gaston stared at the lab results.

"Where is the body?" Betty wrote her cell phone number on the back of the sheet of paper. And pushed it across the table to Gaston.

"It is downstairs. An attempt will be made to find relatives, and then after 30 days it will be cremated." Gaston looked across at Betty with new eyes.

"Well now the body is evidence in a suspicious death or possible homicide."

"This is terrible news. What will happen to all our plans for the corridor?" Gaston put his head in his hands.

"You mean the crime scene?" Betty clarified.

"That will be up to Detectives Sanchez and Jiménez."

When she returned the items to her purse she slipped the belt inside. "I'll be contacting the detectives before I leave and bring them up-to-date on my conclusions."

Gaston had no idea that his day was going to get much worse.

Chapter 28

Vu was not having the best of mornings until he had the cab driver deliver him to the small animal hospital in Quepos. Though, it would still be another few minutes before he knew this.

He'd been unsuccessful at the Judicial Office, the Records Bureau, and the electric and cable companies. Tiresome lines of grumpy citizens. Then no files on Lyman. He even questioned several cab drivers. They informed him that there were hundreds of ex-pats, as they were called and yet no one in particular fit the bill. In all probability, Lyman was using an alias. Little hope now remained. Yet, Vu was determined. What if Lyman had given his address to the veterinarian? Hadn't he indicated yesterday he had tried to save the primate's life?

After telling the driver to keep the meter running, Vu climbed out of the cab. The clinic door was unlocked. Vu entered the narrow hall and knocked lightly on the door marked: *Aficina*, office. The door was ajar and eased open on Vu's tap. A man in his late thirties was standing in the middle of what looked to Vu to be a veterinarian clinic, holding a bloody Kleenex to his nose. There was noticeable swelling around the right eye.

Immediately, Vu surveyed the room, noticing a few items broken on the floor and some fresh liquid pooled near the operating table. A scuffle had taken place. Vu approached the man cautiously. Dr. Ramos looked pained by this intrusion.

"*Disculpe un momento, por favor*," he said, then repeated in English. "Excuse me one moment, please." The man rested his weight against a feeble table.

Vu had responded to innumerable bar fights in his early days, before transferring to The Office of Special Investigations. Recognizing assaults was second nature.

"Have they left the building?"

Dr. Phillip hesitated, then looked Vu in the eye, and replied. "Yes – ten minutes, now," he said. "He has broken my nose, I fear."

"Were you robbed?"

"No, nothing like that."

Vu moved in closer. "What happened?"

"I must ask – who are you?"

"I apologize for the sudden intrusion," Vu replied. "In the United States, I'm an investigator for the Air Force. I'm looking for a former soldier named Jim Lyman and I hope you can be of help. For the moment, though, I think it would be better if you took a seat. You look like you could use it."

Vu helped the man to a stool. He then searched for a box of Kleenex, spotted a box on a desk across the room, retrieved it and handed it to the veterinarian. Once the bleeding had stopped, Dr. Ramos tilted his head forward and looked Vu in the eye.

"I am fortunate my daughters are at school."

"How many daughters do you have?"

"Three. My wife wanted a boy but it wasn't in God's plan. Do you have children?"

"No."

Dr. Ramos sat up straighter. "Who is it you're looking for again?"

"He's an American. He may have recently brought an injured primate to you for medical attention."

Dr. Ramos slowly smiled. "Yes, I think I know of him. He has been here on several occasions, actually. The visits have been both pleasant and unpleasant."

"Explain, please."

"He is a very passionate person when it comes to his monkeys."

"*His* monkeys?"

"That is how he views them."

"Was one treated for a snake bite recently?"

"That is correct. There was nothing more I could do. The primate, unfortunately, died."

"He isn't responsible for your injuries, is he?"

"No, no. It was someone entirely different."

"Have you called the police?"

"Here, one does not call the police."

"I see," Vu said, and then handed the veterinarian a new Kleenex. Vu held up a metal container so the man could deposit the bloody tissue. "Were they drug seekers?"

"Yes."

"How many?"

"Just one."

"And does this happen often?"

The veterinarian shrugged in defeat.

"What did he steal?"

"Two syringes of Adrenaline."

"Heroin overdose?"

"That would be my first guess, yes. It is happening more and more."

The man showed no sign of wanting to pursue his attacker. He seemed resigned to the fact that he had been lucky this time. Yet his expression remained somber. "We have no army. We are situated between Nicaragua and Panama. They use our beautiful country as a drug corridor."

"What route are they using?"

"The corridor set up by the Instituto to connect the animals."

"And the police know?"

Again the veterinarian shrugged. "I've already said too much. Everybody knows."

"I need help, Doctor, locating Mr. Lyman…"

"He has nothing to do with this business."

"But he might be involved indirectly. He and his monkeys may have seen something they shouldn't."

"You are wasting your time."

"What about your daughters? Did they speak to him?"

Dr. Ramos paused and thought about the question. "Perhaps … But they are at school." He glanced at his wrist. His watch was gone. He seemed disturbed about this. He searched the floor. The inexpensive wristwatch lay by his feet with a broken band. He stooped over and picked it up. The dial seemed intact. He looked at Vu but then his nose began to bleed again and he pressed the Kleenex to it.

Across the room, the door burst open. Little Sabrina bounced in swinging her book bag, her playful expression quickly fading when she spotted her father in the corner, clutching a tissue to his bloody nose.

"Papa!"

* * *

The helicopter landed in a remote area of Provincia De Cartago, near the western border region at the entrance of the new corridor. After the whirling blades spun down, Senor Héctor climbed out and was immediately greeted by his contact on the ground, Colonel Juan Pierz, a stocky, tough-looking Columbian wearing soiled Army fatigues. The Colonel hustled over to briskly shake his hand.

"Welcome, Senor Héctor!" he shouted over the loud engine noise. "Follow me please!"

The two men joined a small group of dark-skinned men who Héctor knew to be made up of both Colombians and Nicaraguans. The men were part of a well-organized mule team that the Colonel had assembled weeks earlier. The thirteen members were assigned two pack animals, one to ride and one to pack the supplies, and enough rations for the long journey, along with rifles and machetes. The rifles were M-15s, outdated by today's standards but still very effective in getting the job done.

The mules drank from puddles of rainwater. Despite bulky cargo strapped to their backs, the animals still had plenty of energy to complete the long and arduous journey ahead. Weighted down cargo consisted of two wooden boxes strapped to their sides, that when taken together, contained enough cocaine to supply the western region of the U.S. with product. This impressed Senor Héctor.

Forming up his group of transporters, the Colonel discussed last minute details with his men. He pulled out a map and showed it to Héctor, and then asked the men if they had any questions.

"You all have a copy of the revised route with you. Should we run into any problems along the corridor, and you are forced to break from the team, you will make every effort to meet us at the next location. Does everyone understand? The boat we are meeting has been given clearance. It should be at our destination point within three days."

One of the men asked, "I see we are traveling near Manuel Antonio?"

"Yes."

"But there are risks of tourists, no?"

"We are skirting the perimeter only. The area has been secured by the Instituto for research purposes. There will be no problems. We have been assured of this."

When he was finished, he walked to the front of the line, retrieved a beautiful black stallion, and handed the reins to Héctor before giving him a boost up.

"Up you go, sir."

Once atop the horse, Colonel Pierz adjusted Héctor's stirrups for the long ride.

After Héctor was settled in, the Colonel climbed onto a second horse, a chestnut Stallion, with nice markings, and trotted out of the pack, circling the group, looking the team over carefully, one last time. Before leading the team onward, along a rugged trail leading into the heart of the rainforest, the Colonel's satellite-phone rang. He said a few brief words and then handed the phone over to Senor Héctor.

"Yes! What is it Edmund?"

* * *

Senor Héctor's mistress, Cecelia, was lying naked in a bathtub of cold water. Following his call to Colonel Pierz, Edmund returned to the room and re-checked her pulse for the last time. Nothing. Not even the two adrenaline syringes he'd muscled off the veterinarian in Quepos, now protruding from her chest, could revive the addict.

When Edmund finally spoke to Senor Héctor, it came as no surprise to learn that his mistress had overdosed. Edmund had been expecting the worst from his employer, since he had allowed Cecelia to die on his watch, but Senor Héctor had taken the news calmly, almost stoically. And it was then that Edmund realized that this had been the plan all along. He had been left behind to dispose of the body, a promotion in this line of business. He had thought he was being eased out by his employer but the opposite was true. This was his time to make a favorable impression.

From Cecelia's bedroom, Edmund removed her top sheet and returned with it to the bathroom. He spread it along the floor and then lifted the limp body out of the tub and laid it down on the edge of the sheet and wrapped the sheet around it. Later, when he returned, he would burn her bedding and belongings.

Senor Héctor's other staff had been conveniently given the afternoon off. So, there was no trouble concealing the body in the back of the suburban with its heavily tinted windows. Now, where to dispose of her? It would not be suitable to have the body turn up in a location that could be traced back to Senor Héctor. An idea formed. Disposing of Cecelia at Dr. Gaston Trujillo's residence seemed both dangerous and brilliant. Edmund knew the message would be evident, a reminder to the good doctor, never to betray Senor Héctor again.

Chapter 29

The cab rolled up the steep drive toward the house on the hill. Actually, it was more like a fortress than a house. Bars covered the front windows. Sturdy trees fenced in the plot of land on three sides. Even the main road had ended a kilometer before Lyman's driveway. It would be practically impossible to sneak up to the property unannounced because of its layout. Vu also noticed several remote cameras installed in the treetops, but did not point these out to the driver.

Along the roof a number of solar panels reflected sunlight. Large plastic collection tanks were located along the ground beneath four roof corners to collect rainwater. A towering storage tank off to one side of the property Vu presumed was used for more water storage. The electrical poles ended before they reached the property. By what Vu could tell with his precursory study of the house, Lyman was off the grid, which was why his name wasn't listed with the electric and cable companies.

Vu handed the driver a five-dollar bill, told him to relax for a few minutes while he visited the house.

Vu knew it was not the wisest move to come here. Lyman in all practically could shoot him then feed his body to any number of wild creatures living in the nearby rainforest. But something told him that even if he had a desire to kill it would not be him or the cabdriver. Lyman had been a soldier. Soldiers have a moral code, even when they aren't serving their country. Of course, this was only a theory.

There was an old pickup truck parked in the driveway, but Vu could see no lamps burning inside the house. The windows were not curtained, just barred over, and this caused Vu some uneasiness, like he was swimming in a fishbowl, unable to get out of the eye of the observer.

Vu stepped onto the front porch, knocked, and after no response, he tried again. After the third try, he gave up, and checked the rear of the house.

There was no backyard, just a large garden with row upon row of flowering plants and vegetables and a few wild chickens running about. The windows at the rear of the house were also barred and there was only one door leading to the outside and it was also barred. There were two more collection tanks and a garden hose strewn out to where someone had been watering the vegetables recently. In a caged area under what would normally be the patio, rested an oily generator. Along the side of the house was a small gun range with a number of different paper and steel targets. Whoever had been shooting at the paper targets had put nine shots directly into the forehead of all three targets. One bore Gaston's likeness. Vu's brain looped as he photographed the other two faces and headed back to the cab.

"Where now, senor?"

"Drop me off at a restaurant called Crumpys."

"You must try the fish tacos, senor. In this area, they are some of our finest."

Vu took a small table on the patio and waited for Betty to arrive. The waiter came over with a glass of ice water and asked if he wanted something from the bar. "I'll wait."

"As you wish..."

The waiter moved on to the next table and took a couple's order.

Vu picked up his water glass and started to take a sip when from behind a large man approached and without an invitation sat down at the table, facing him.

"What were you doing at my crib?" Lyman said in a cool tone.

Vu put his glass down, picked up a square napkin from beneath his glass, and dabbed the corners of his mouth, regaining his composure. "It would have been more convenient if you had just answered your door."

Lyman smiled, remaining stoic. "What do you want?"

Vu adjusted his glasses. "I'm not sure."

"You're going to have to do better, Jack." Lyman leaned back in his chair, sizing Vu up. "You're becoming an annoyance. I thought I made it clear I didn't want to be contacted."

"You did."

Lyman's expression softened as two strangers walked by their table. After they were out of earshot, he leaned forward and said, "If this is about old business, you're rattling the wrong cage."

Vu studied Lyman's chiseled face. The last few years had been tough on the ex-soldier. But no matter how much he listened to his inner Buddhist voice, nothing surfaced, other than a faint gut feeling that he had to contact Lyman again. And, this all seemed a bit out of character for even him. Finally, he said, "Why did you risk arrest? Was it really just to keep us from disturbing the primate's remains?"

Lyman reached out and took Vu's water glass and drank a good portion of the water before setting it down. "You, of all people, should understand the value of remains."

"I have this odd feeling about Manuel Antonio and the Instituto and about the officers who were with us. I do not think this is just about drug cartels moving product through the rainforest. I think all of us meeting has more significance than that."

"Buddhist bullshit." Lyman slid his chair back and made a move to stand. Vu reached across the table and grasped Lyman's wrist. Vu's inner strength, far superior to mere physicality, stopped Lyman in his tracks.

"Look," Lyman said, "I have become a little obsessed with a family of capuchins. Let's leave it at that."

Vu released his grip. "What is the nature of your obsession?"

"I'm not sure I can explain it to you. We've got each other's backs."

"You and the monkeys?" Vu smiled at the thought.

"Yes. I know how it sounds but there is innocence and yet sophistication to the way they do things that makes sense to me. I relate to them in a way I have never been able to do with humans."

"Speaking of humans – what happened to the woman you came here with? Emily, I believe was her name?"

Lyman paused. "I should have known you would know about her. Let's just say she and I had different ideas of what constitutes Paradise. Mine involved solitude and shutting out the real world, and hers involved a more urban view."

"Like running water and cable TV?" Vu asked.

"Exactly." Lyman sobered and his eyes bore into Vu's. "I'm not going back."

"Look, this is a vacation – the first one Betty and I have taken in a couple of years." Vu looked down at his watch. "I've told no one about you or how I even know you, nor do I intend to."

"What about your girlfriend?"

"She has threatened me with castration if I even think about work on this trip. I consider you to be a lot of work."

"That was a good answer. But I'm curious. Why wouldn't you turn me in?"

"What is there to be gained? It serves no purpose other than to embarrass the military."

"What about honor, duty and integrity, all those codes of conduct pounded into soldiers?"

"My core values are not strictly dictated by the military. They were developed in the Killing Fields."

"So why were you looking for me?" Lyman asked. "What do you want?"

"I need your help."

Lyman did a double take. "Help you with what?"

"This Indian boy – I sense there is more to his death than a mere drug connection. He had a GPS tracking chip in his belt buckle. I think your dead monkey may have had one too. What do you know about tribes living in the area?"

"That they prefer to keep to themselves. You should do the same." And then with that, Lyman stood up. "Don't get involved in this. You live in New Orleans, Jack. By now you should understand the mystery and power of their Cajun Voodoo. Believe me – Costa Rica has its own unique spirit world."

"Wait," Vu pleaded. "Let's discuss the corridor project. I have a few thoughts. They involve Dr. Trujillo and cocaine. I need to know who the other two targets are." Vu removed a compact camera from his pocket, turned it on, and clicked through the images until he located the one he wanted to show him. The photograph – two head shots taken at the gun range behind Lyman's house.

Lyman's color paled as he glimpsed around checking the perimeter. "The one on the right is Senor Héctor who is funding more than the corridor project. The other one is Colonel Pierz. Pierz provides the guns and transportation for the cocaine mule trains. All three need to be stopped if we are to restore order around here."

Lyman returned the camera and without another word marched off toward the exit.

Does he want me to follow?

As Lyman turned the corner, Betty's smiling face appeared. Lyman brushed passed her out the front door.

Betty sat down at the table beside Vu. "Was that who I think it was?"

Chapter 30

The door to the sweat lodge opened and Chief of the Cabécars walked out into the bright sunlight. Leela, his only daughter, waited until her father took a refreshing dip in the icy waters of Macaw Creek, had dried off thoroughly, before approaching him along the bank.

The last few years had aged her father. Once, his powerful chest magnificently empowered him with pride. But now, the muscles had atrophied, the chest hair had whitened; the skin had lost any semblance of strength and youth. No longer were his legs or arms capable of doing physical labor of a young man. His weakened body had become a handicap. On the other hand, his mind held wisdom and power beyond most elders, but it was old wisdom, which had its share of problems with the younger members of the tribe. He was the giant aging oak caught in a lightning storm whose core embodied questionable strength from the termite effects of life. In time, the wood would rot and the tree would be a memory.

Leela shouldered some blame for his condition. She had made a fateful choice as a young woman, which had put a knife into their relationship and weakened him prematurely. From the very beginning, her half breed child had been accepted by the tribe. Even her long dead husband had not doubted that his son was anything but his progeny, but her father had known from the first time he held his grandson that he was not pure Cabécar and to punish his daughter for diluting the purity of the tribe both spiritually and physically, he had treated the boy as a malevolent interloper. Leela became a ghost to her father. Leela raised the boy like other Indian boys, but at a great price. Without the Chief's mantle of acceptance the tribe's successor and future was a source of great turmoil. Her own mother had died many years ago and she had turned to Gaston's mother for support. All the lies. Another secret she had kept from the ones she loved. Gaston and his mother never knew the truth about their own blood. This great tragedy had played out over the course of fourteen years. Leela had never told the boy who his biological father was until his fifteenth birthday. He was becoming a man and deserved to know who he was. The disgrace over the years from her deceptions had overwhelmed him.

Leela stood before the great *cacique*, warrior chieftain. "Father, I have something to tell you."

The tall but frail man shivered in the cool breeze and pulled the towel tightly around his waist. "Yes, Leela?"

"I fear something has happened to Totem."

Her father stared at her. "And why would you think this?"

"He has been gone for a fortnight."

"He is a young man, Leela. You must not treat him like a boy. Young men must forge a way on their own. It is normal."

"He is fifteen, father."

"Fifteen is the age of manhood for a Cabécar, you know this. Young men seek adventures to prove their worth."

"I know this. But I fear he is on a different quest."

The chief turned and faced his daughter. "What have you done?"

"I told him who his father is."

The chief who had been slightly stooped in the shoulders stood straight and his haunting eyes glared at Leela. "So, finally the truth has surfaced. And with the child now diminished in his own mind, you have managed to destroy yet another life."

"I have told you this because I am leaving," Leela said forcefully. "With Gaston's mother gone, I have no reason to stay. I believe Totem may be in danger. I must go look for him."

"Where will you look first?"

"To the south."

"Toward the sea?"

"Yes, near Manuel Antonio and the Instituto."

"When will you leave?"

"My belongings are already packed. Goodbye, father."

The chief reached out and took her hand. "I am an old fool."

Leela felt her legs tremble.

"You have conducted yourself with dignity despite the slights I forced you to suffer all these years. My anger has done much damage to the entire tribe. If you return with your son and my grandson, things will be different. You have my word on this."

Chapter 31

The news reached the *Sea Gypsy* like all news does in small towns, scattered bits and pieces of truth, embedded in little white lies.

Out over the bow, Captain Spartacus watched a brown pelican dive below the surface of the water and popped back up with a fish in its beak. The birds had always fascinated Spartacus, because as they aged, they often went blind. The constant diving into the water damaged their eyes. Yet without diving they would die of starvation. It was damned if you do, damned if you don't. Sort of like the role of being a captain of the ship, Spartacus thought.

The young doctor aboard walked up from behind.

"Is everything alright, Leo?"

Spartacus turned around and stared at her. His eyes simmered molten lava. "That depends, doctor."

"I understand two of our passengers are disembarking."

"Word travels fast."

"I overheard Raymon mention it to Ricardo below deck. Will you be informing the passengers?"

"Yes. Loss of passengers for whatever reason is unsettling to those remaining aboard. And to lose them so that they can conduct an investigation into a local boy's death at the hand of the drug cartels casts a negative light on not just our beautiful Costa Rica, but on our staff as well." Spartacus paused, thinking. "Well, on the good side, their luggage is now in their possession."

"Raymon said that already some guests feel that someone has been rummaging through their luggage before delivering it to their rooms."

"Of course. We are now viewed not as guides and equals, but as opportunists to separate them from their money and possessions."

"Just like drug dealers." The doctor nodded.

"Exactly." Spartacus stared at the sea.

"Why don't you open up the bar?"

"That is an excellent idea. Would you have Ricardo join me on the bridge?"

Spartacus turned away and looked out over the water. The doctor left and in a few minutes, Ricardo sprang onto the foredeck, dressed in his crisp white uniform, and stood at attention.

"Sir, you wanted to see me?" he asked.

Spartacus looked him in the eye. "Have the crew open the bar to the passengers. Break out champagne and see that the steward has plenty of *Jugo de Naranja*, orange juice, on hand. Bring out a platter of *ceviche* and serve it with sesame crackers. I will be down in one hour to join the celebration.

Below deck, the crew moved through the crowded bar, re-filling champagne glasses. Many of the guests were well into their third glass of bubbly and the effects of alcohol were showing.

Vu and Betty slipped out a back door and stood on the aft-deck to watch the sunset. Ginger joined the couple moments later balancing two full glasses of champagne. She offered one of the glasses to Betty, who took it from her and set it down on the railing.

"That breeze feels nice, doesn't it?" Ginger said.

Vu felt the warm air dance over his face. "It is a nice change indeed."

"Yes, it is," Betty added.

"So what fun things did the two of you do today?" Ginger

asked. Betty filled her in on the day's activities, leaving out a few parts here and there, especially about running into Vu's old pal, Jim Lyman.

"Sorry to be losing you two. The thought of being here another few days, does not sound that appealing to me," Ginger said. "But I suppose the two of you are interested in wrapping up this case."

"I doubt we'll ever know the reason why the boy was in the tree," Betty said sadly. "At least we determined what killed him, but not how it all happened."

"What an awful way to die," Ginger said, grimacing. She took a big swig of bubbly, looked out over the water, shivering at the dark thought.

"The DNA will be in soon and we can at least determine where his parents are and bring them the news," Vu noted.

"Jack, please. Ginger doesn't want to hear it."

"You're bloody right, I don't. This is supposed to be a vacation."

"I'm sorry," he said. "This is not the vacation I had in mind."

"Nor me," Betty put in.

"Well at least you'll be rejoining us for the passage through the canal," Ginger added with a smile.

"Yes we will." Vu grabbed Betty around the waist. "Even if I have to commandeer a helicopter to get us there."

"Jack. After we get the DNA back, let's rent a car ourselves and see if we can locate the reservation where the boy lived. If nothing else, maybe we can find a relative of his. They have to know about the boy."

"That's ghastly," Ginger uttered. "I would avoid that at all costs."

Vu thought it over. The obligation to notify relatives was on Sanchez and Jiménez, even Carlos, not them. Was Betty insane? "It is a long shot. If we do happen to locate the reservation and we do happen to find the parents, what if the news comes as such a shock, they try to harm us."

"Jack, you're the one who says when things don't go as planned – that is when the adventure begins."

"What if they don't understand my Spanish, or they speak a dialect I don't understand?"

"It's still worth a try. Right?"

Vu thought it over.

"You could pretend you were looking to buy handmade items. Just some crazy tourists who wandered off the beaten path," Ginger pointed out.

"Ginger's got a point, Jack. We don't actually have to tell anyone we're there looking for the boy's parents. We could just sort of feel our way around and then if we turn up something, we could tell them."

Vu liked Ginger's plan. "Alright."

Betty spun around and hugged Vu. "Goody," she uttered, then faced Ginger. "You're brilliant, Ginger."

Ginger chugged the last of her champagne. "If only my two ex-husbands had been aware of that."

Chapter 32

On the beach, with the lights of the *Sea Gypsy* twinkling in the far distance, Sanchez lifted her own champagne flute and clinked glasses with Carlos.

"Cheers!"

"You don't find this too corny?" Carlos asked, smiling.

"A little, but it's also kind of romantic. Who would have thunk…"

"Was your partner miffed?"

"Jiménez couldn't wait to be dumped off at the hotel."

"What do you think of him?"

"He's unfaithful to his wife. The less I'm around him, the better."

It was work in the guise of a date. Sanchez privately acknowledged this. Carlos was on a stakeout. She wondered if Carlos had used the drug dealing story as a simple cover. That way, it wouldn't be like he asked her out on a real date. Yet, when he'd called Sanchez had been honest when she said she was excited to see him.

"So who are you watching again?"

Carlos nestled his glass in the sand and picked up a pair of special night-vision binoculars. "That boat over there. We got a tip they might be off-loading some product. But all it looks like to me is a bunch of drunks throwing a party aboard."

Sanchez struggled to make out the yacht Carlos was scoping in the marina. She glimpsed people partying topside and more she presumed partying in the cabin. "I got a call today," Sanchez said casually, "there is going to be a shipment of cocaine passing through the corridor in the next couple of days."

Carlos lowered the binoculars. "Really?"

"A boat left Golfo Dulce this morning. We believe the vessel will meet up with a mule team near Playa Matapalo to retrieve the product. It's an inventive plan – I've got to give them credit. Usually, they try and ship product out of Nicaragua on the Caribbean side. But we've been successful intercepting those shipments. This time, we believe the shipment crossed the border of western Nicaragua via a mule team somewhere in the vicinity of the Provincia De Heredia and followed the mountains down through Braulio Carillo and as we speak are somewhere in the vicinity of Provincia De Cartago. Whoever is leading the team is bringing it down through the connecting corridors and will meet up with the ship on the Pacific side, somewhere between Manuel Antonio and Marino Ballena. There are forty kilometers of isolated beaches and plenty of rainforest. It's the perfect cover."

Carlos looked her in the eye. "This is the first information I've heard. Are you bringing in any outside agencies?"

"No."

"Why not?"

"It's how our department works. All our information is coming from informants and they're unreliable. They want me to validate the intel and attempt to pinpoint the mule team's location, then call for reinforcements."

"That's suicide."

Sanchez threw off the comment and opened the picnic chest down by her feet. "You really made dinner?" she said, cheerfully, and peeked inside.

Carlos leaned forward and grabbed Sanchez's hand. "First let me re-fill our glasses and then we'll eat." As he poured, he laughed, "In case you didn't know, this is not real champagne."

"Oh that's right we are just a couple of lovers watching the sunset." Sanchez slammed back her drink, then tossed her glass aside. "Hell with champagne. I like kissing better."

She pushed Carlos back onto the blanket and playfully planted a long, passionate kiss on his lips.

Chapter 33

In the isolated region of Provincia De Cartago, near Salsipuedes, Leela spread out her blanket under the starlit sky. The new moon floated up out of the rainforest and like a smiling child brightened her surroundings. Earlier, she had collected an assortment of branches, which she laid around the perimeter of her sleeping area, so that if by chance any night intruders came around, she would hear them.

It was not particularly cold. Yet, her mind was troubled by the reoccurring images of her young son lost in the rainforest somewhere, or worse, lying injured somewhere, unable to seek help. She cast these pictures from her mind and listened to the sounds of the night, the leaf cutter ants marching, dipping bats, and the occasional four-legged animals skittering about. There was comfort in their familiar sounds, a lyrical heartbeat of the night world.

She closed her eyes and thought about Gaston. What must he be feeling now that his mother had passed on to the spirit world. He was no longer a son and had become a man with a son of his own. His son would find him and tell him what she had not been able to.

Leela stilled herself, breathed in the cooling air, and eventually found a moment of peace to drift to sleep.

* * *

Gaston was pulling into his driveway when his headlights illuminated something on his front porch. His mother had always been fond of swinging chaise lounges and so he kept one for her on the front stoop, but it unfortunately had collected many cobwebs because his mother had not visited him in a very long time.

After he parked his car, he followed the cobblestone path to the front of the house. When he got close enough to the front porch, he called out. "Who's there?"

There was no movement or response. "I have a gun!"

It was a lie of course. Still, he tucked his hand menacingly into his jacket pocket.

As he drew closer, he could see the dark image of what looked like a sleeping woman, leaning back on the lounge with her head rested to one side; her hair flowed down over bare shoulders. Bare feet poked out from beneath, exposing nails painted fire-engine red.

"Cecelia?"

No response. Gaston quickly moved in to touch her forehead. Ice cold skin. Then he checked for a pulse. Nothing.

He did not panic. He gently sat down beside her for a moment and collected his thoughts. He felt he was being watched. He forced himself to rise and calmly walk inside. Before he called the police, he had some thinking to do. The game had changed.

As he walked inside, Gaston knew what this meant. He looked forward to seeing Senor Héctor again.

* * *

At the side of the house, Lyman leaned back against the cold adobe wall, realizing that Dr. Trujillo had several skeletons in his closet. He decided to see how the good doctor handled this business before they met. The matter he wanted to discuss with him could wait.

Chapter 34

"I miss our teak berth on the boat" Betty yawned as she looked around at the modern hotel room at the marina, with its faux stucco walls and velour couch.

"I don't care where we are as long as I wake up next to you." Vu smiled.

"Good answer." Betty rolled into Vu's open arms. As the ceiling fan fluttered the sheets, they slowly lost all sense of a world outside their own. Just two runaways who'd found each other in this foreign, indifferent hotel room.

They'd watched the *Sea Gypsy* disappear into the darkness the evening before, feeding Vu's memory cache of yet another boat set adrift on the sea. He often mused on the role this liquid highway had played in his life. It had saved him by giving nourishment when he hovered near death and nearly killed him on several other occasions. His Betty had been born on the banks of the Mississippi and he on the Mekong Delta and through some astronomical continuation of circumstances they had crossed paths. Praise Buddha, Allah, God, and whatever other superior being allowed this random conjoining.

Vu whispered into Betty's ear. "This may not be the vacation we envisioned but it's certainly one that will be memorable."

"Hell, Jack, vacations can be overrated. If you and I sit on our butts for an hour in the sun we start thinking about the next case we're going to solve. It's our nature."

"Well, then it's time to get our butts out of bed."

As they exited their room there was still a chill in the air that revitalized. Betty had her hair stuffed up under a baseball cap and was shivering, even though she had put on an extra top. Vu slid up next to her to wrap his arm around her shoulder to provide warmth.

"What a beautiful day for a drive."

"I guess that's our car over there." Betty pointed to a plain gray sedan.

As they approached the car, Vu hurried to beat Betty to the driver's door. "I'll drive Sugar. You enjoy the scenery." Betty's driving was death defying on a good highway, but on these rutted back roads there was more than an even chance they'd be in a ditch within minutes.

"This car doesn't have a GPS. And there's no internet so no MapQuest." Betty's brow creased. "How will we get where we are going."

"We'll navigate, just like the whole world did five years ago."

* * *

Sanchez actually awoke before the alarm sounded, but laid in bed until the clock radio came on. The soft sunlight spilled in through the lacy curtains and reflected on the evening she'd had with Carlos.

The date had been cut short before any horsing around which kind of bummed Sanchez. But the life of a cop, especially one working narcotics, was full of surprises. Carlos had been ordered to move in on the yacht he'd been shadowing, along with a team of narcotic officers. Sanchez offered her assistance, but Carlos wouldn't allow it.

So, Sanchez had returned to her hotel room. Thankfully, Jiménez had already taken care of his libido by the time she returned and it had been relatively peaceful next door so she was able to enjoy a mental replay of the evening's events before hitting the pillow around midnight.

Sanchez crawled from bed and took a long hot shower and then made some instant coffee and choked it down with a PowerBar she had stashed in her purse. As she was getting dressed, she heard a knock on her hotel room door.

"Go away, Jiménez?" she called out.

"It's Carlos!"

How nice, Sanchez thought. She could have a little quickie before work. She hurried over to the door and released the deadbolt.

Carlos looked terrible with dark circles under his eyes. Like he'd been up all night. He still wore the clothing he had on from the previous night.

"Glad you're dressed," he told her, "we've got a morning date with the good doctor Trujillo across town."

Sanchez felt her heart sink to the floor. "What's up with Dr. Trujillo? He learned something new about the Indian boy?"

"No. Has nothing to do with that."

"Well, come on in," Sanchez said, "I just need to brush my teeth."

Carlos entered the room and immediately planted himself on the sofa in front of the bed. She left the door ajar so she could talk to Carlos.

"How'd it go last night?" she asked.

"It was a bust. I mean – a real bust."

"Meaning they walked?"

"Yeah."

"What happened to your intel?"

"The intel was accurate. I think someone dumped the product overboard."

"That sucks."

"Tell me about it. Is your partner still here?"

"I thought you were him just now. I haven't heard a peep from next door."

"Well, I'd like to leave Jiménez behind on this. That cool with you?"

The thought of dragging that lame partner of hers around again today wasn't appealing. "Sounds fine with me, but I'll have to give him a heads up. What's this about anyway?"

Sanchez looked in the mirror and watched Carlos's expression. Even having lost sleep and working most of the night, Carlos still looked damn handsome. His dark features, something she hadn't been so hooked on in the beginning, were starting to get under her skin in a good way. Something about the way he moved his eyes. That intensity seemed heightened this morning.

"Dr. Trujillo called me on the phone about twenty minutes ago. He said his old girlfriend dropped by last night as a dead body. Apparently, she overdosed. He thinks he knows who supplied her with the drugs."

"Why'd he wait until morning?"

"I guess he got in late and had trouble reaching me."

"And you're the one he thought of calling?"

"Since it involved narcotics, he called me first. Actually, he sounded rational. If he was involved, I doubt he'd be so forthright about things."

"This guy is a real mystery, isn't he? First the Indian boy at the Instituto. Now this?"

"This thing with Dr. Trujillo takes priority. It's just a matter of time before his enemies leak this to the press. I don't want the press to get hold of it until I've had time to hear his story."

"So why'd you stop for me?"

"Maybe I scratch your back, you scratch mine sometime."

Sanchez smiled hollowly as she stepped from the bathroom. *Okay. So maybe it is just business with this guy.*

A half-hour later, Carlos' sedan pulled in the drive of Dr. Trujillo's one-level house and parked. The two officers climbed out and approached the front door. Cecelia's body, still wrapped in a sheet, swung slowly back and forth on the front porch swing. The cloth made a swishing noise as it dragged across the floor.

Dr. Trujillo greeted them at the door in his suit holding a cup of steaming espresso. He addressed Carlos first. "I see you brought company. Good morning officer Sanchez. Would either of you like coffee?"

Both of the officers declined. Gaston stepped onto the porch and pointed to the swing. Carlos took out his notepad and pen. "This how you found her?"

Gaston nodded. "Someone must have carried her over from the drive. There were no tire marks in my lawn."

Sanchez surveyed the area. There were no neighbors to speak of. Gaston lived at the end of the street and the house was surrounded by trees. No one would have seen the body.

"You're sure she didn't OD here?"

"She was ice cold. Probably been dead for 24 hours."

"Why you?"

"I have known Cecelia for a number of years. We dated once a long time ago."

"Are you married, doctor?"

"No."

"What's the girl's name again?" Carlos asked, staring at the body.

Gaston supplied all pertinent details. "She was living with a Columbian. He goes by Senor Héctor. His first name is Marcus. He owns an estate near Jaco. Senor Héctor had been a very generous supporter of the Instituto in the past. His financial contributions to our research were invaluable. Cecelia didn't tell him about our relationship and when he found out we had a history, he was very jealous and severed his financial relationship with the Instituto."

Carlos made some quick notes. Sanchez thought over what was said. "This looks like someone wanted to send you a clear message," Sanchez pointed out. "Anything happen recently between you two?"

"Can this discussion continue inside?"

The interior of Gaston's house was modest and artful, a combination of handmade furniture and modern art. Sanchez followed Carlos into the center of the room, and while Carlos took a seat on the sofa across from her, Sanchez glanced down at the expensive Indian rug.

"You suspect Senor Héctor dropped this girl's body off at your doorstep."

"Yes, right," Gaston said, frowning. "As I said, Cecelia and I had a relationship years ago. This is something Senor Héctor didn't know about until very recently. I suspect he did not take kindly to the news."

"So you think he gave the girl a hot-load?"

"He's capable of that. And unfortunately Cecelia had developed a dependency on heroin."

"Then he stuffed her into his car and delivered her here to get his point across."

"Not him personally, he has bodyguards for that sort of thing."

"Still kind of stretching it," Carlos said.

"It matters not if you take my word for it," Gaston said, "because I can prove it."

Sanchez raised her eyebrows. "Yeah? How?"

"He will tell you himself."

"Really?" Carlos asked suspiciously.

"What are your plans today?" Gaston asked them.

Carlos looked at Sanchez. They both shrugged and looked back at the doctor.

"You will need to cancel all plans for today, perhaps even tomorrow. But I assure you it will be worth your time."

Chapter 35

The team drove the mules hard, across the Rio Cuerici, down through the Fila Quebrada Seca, upward through the steep hills known as Fila Pangolin. They had pushed day and night for over a week to reach this point. Colonel Pierz was a driven man and Senor Héctor highly approved of his tactics and the way he managed his men. Another day, perhaps two, and the journey would be over. Then, the Colonel and he could relax.

"Alfredo! Alfredo!" the Colonel shouted from his chestnut stallion. "You are lagging behind again! What is wrong with you?"

Alfredo was the newest member, barely old enough to vote, a high school dropout and one of older men's cousins. Alfredo had a wife and newborn waiting for him back in Nicaragua. He could not afford to lose this job. It was surely dangerous, but the money was very good. From the very beginning though, Alfredo had dragged the team behind schedule and it was now getting on the Colonel's nerves to the point that he wanted to dispose of this anchor.

Alfredo shouted back from the end of the pack. "Colonel my animals are tired. They need water."

"The only one who needs water, Alfredo, is you. You would have water had you not dropped your canteen, no?"

Alfredo's tiny head bobbed up and down. The Colonel circled back to the rear of the pack. "Alfredo, you are as dumb as your mules."

Alfredo yanked on the flimsy rope tied around his mule's neck. The animal jerked its head up slightly and skipped a step causing Alfredo to lose his balance but he didn't fall off the animal. As punishment for treating the mule so badly, the mule trailing behind snipped at Alfredo's leg.

"Ouch!" Alfredo cried. "Did you see what that stupid animal did just now?"

The Colonel laughed. "You are the only one the mules seem to bite. Now, pick it up and re-join the others before I decide to leave you behind for good."

The Colonel knew Alfredo was a city boy and was deathly afraid of being alone in the rainforest where other members of the team had told him about man-eating jaguars and snakes that could kill you with the spit of their venom.

"Yes, Colonel," Alfredo called out. "I hurry now. You have not to worry about me."

Up near the front, Senor Héctor's black stallion tripped on a broken stump, lost footing, and pitched him sidewise, ramming his shoulder into a large tree. The impact jarred the man. But he remained upright and got the horse back under control. The Colonel trotted over and checked on him.

"You are alright, sir?"

Senor Héctor swiped a twig from his collar. "Yes. What is wrong with your man back there?"

"He is not what I consider a man, sir, but he is trying. His mule dislikes him. In fact, both his mules dislike him. I dislike him presently, too. But we need him."

"Up until now you have done a good job keeping everyone in line. But, I think it is my turn next, if he does not improve."

"Yes sir."

Another hour into the journey the team had crossed Rio Savegre. They had altered their course. Heading more toward the east because the conditions of the forest had become increasingly difficult to maneuver, the team climbed a steep ridge. That put them on a smoother plain but the terrain was still treacherous, filled with potholes, fallen branches and rocks the size of truck tires. Nastic vines swung like the arms of a giant octopus waiting for the opportunity to knock one of the men from their mule.

The Colonel had moved to the front, to lead the way through the worst of it. Alfredo had fallen farther behind without the forceful encouragement of his leader. Presumably, the lack of water in his system was taking its toll. He swayed from side to side with each of the mule's labored steps and like a drunken man tumbled sidewise and fell to the ground, scraping his elbow on a jagged rock. His animal lost its footing and fell on top of him. He kicked and screamed and pushed the heavy beast off his leg and sat up, rubbing his leg as if it had been crushed.

The sudden jolt snapped him to his senses and he jumped up and grabbed the mule's rope and tugged but the animal would not get up. The mule moaned softly but would not respond to Alfredo's threats. "You tired old whore get up before I kick you senseless! Did you hear what I said! Up you fat whore!"

It was Senor Héctor who circled back this time, as the Colonel was busy up near the front helping the other men over a dangerous ridge.

Senor Héctor climbed down off his horse. "What is the problem with you?"

Alfredo glared and pointed at the mule. "It is the stupid animal that is the problem. He will not obey my commands."

Senor Héctor turned his attention to the mule. He stooped over and ran his hand down the mule's front leg. Falling, the animal had snapped a bone in his right leg, a compound fracture most likely. Not something that could be repaired.

"See. He does not respond!" Alfredo danced around shooting his mouth off like a fool.

Senor Héctor wasted no time. He pulled out a revolver, pressed it up to the animal's forehead and pulled the trigger. The thundering sound of the gunshot, echoed through the forest. Within moments, the Colonel trotted up, and hopped down off his horse.

"What has happened?" he demanded to know.

Alfredo was shivering with fright and couldn't speak. "I … ah, ah … I…"

Senor Héctor holstered his revolver. "The mule has a broken leg. It is useless to us. Have your boy load the cargo onto his other mule. He will walk the remainder of the journey."

The Colonel nodded and glared at Alfredo. "You heard Senor Héctor. What are you waiting for? Start unloading the supplies."

* * *

The gunshot had alerted Leela, who had stopped to wash in the Rio Savegre. Somebody was nearby. She must be cautious.

Leela wrung out the cloth she had used to wash her face and underarms and returned it to her leather backpack. She took out an apple and ate it while she hiked up to the top of a steep ridge where she could look out over the valley floor and perhaps see where the shot had come from.

From the ridge, she looked out over the landscape. Behind her was the endless expanse of rainforest. She remembered many trees and plant species from her studies on the reservation. What fascinated her more were the stories of spirits living among the rainforest. The fertility gods of Los Santos. The kindred spirits of the wind, sun, sky, moon, water, all of which she sensed were with her on her journey.

There were many gods, too many to remember them all. As chief her father passed down these stories of the gods to the elders who passed it down to their children. Doing her part, she too had passed the stories on to her young boy, but he was more interested in hunting. Killing his first wild pig at the age of ten had been a great achievement. The tribe honored him with a special celebration. It had been one of many moments where she felt so proud, her heart melted.

But this gunshot was not about hunting. Leela could identify different firearms sounds. She knew this shot came from a handgun, not a rifle. That could mean only one thing. Hunting was not the reason for the shot.

After squatting to relieve herself in the grass, Leela moved to higher ground. In the far distance to the west, she saw many men traveling with pack mules cutting a path through the rainforest. As she got a better look at the men, one thing was quite clear. They were not from Los Santos.

Chapter 36

As Vu and Betty reached their destination, the coolness of the morning had transformed like a butterfly into a beautiful warm afternoon. The preliminary DNA on the boy was back thanks to the intervention of the Air Force lab in Louisiana. And it was a shock. The boy was compared with DNA collected from various students and people involved in the government, virtually anybody in the data base the *Instituto* was using for their research.

The boy was a partial match for Dr. Trujillo. Apparently he had more in common with the Cabécars than anthropology studies.

Angelia had no idea where the Dr. Trujillo was. He had called in ill today. And she was not at liberty to release his home address, but was happy to give them his cell phone as well as maps to the Cabécars reservation. "His mother lives there," she told them. "She is a Tico and a famous anthropologist."

"Let's go to the reservation and see what we can discover about Dr. Trujillo's relationships there," Vu suggested.

"I looked him in the eye when we discussed the dead boy. I don't believe he has any idea this is his son." Betty shook her head. "This case keeps twisting on itself."

With Betty holding the map upside down half the time, she attempted to be a good co-pilot while Vu drove. Together, after a few false turns, they arrived at the jumping off point for the village.

They carried water and heavy backpacks, but no burden was heavier than delivering this surprising and sad news to unprepared family and friends.

Before they left the *Instituto*, Angelia had explained: "You are free to roam the reservation as you wish, but please be courteous. If you would like to purchase any of the merchandise they're selling, do so. But, it is not customary in Costa Rica to barter. The prices are low and are not negotiable; I think is what you would say. They have rules about going beyond fenced areas and that you respect their privacy. Do not enter any of the huts unless invited. Good luck with your hunt."

As they approached the first clearing Vu tried out his Spanish on a young boy, who pointed to an opening in the forest. Vu grabbed Betty's hand and as they followed a narrow path along the river until they reached an ancient sweat lodge with steam clouds, seeping out of its chimney.

Vu sat down on a bench and began to remove his shoes.

"What are you doing?" Betty asked.

"What does it look like?"

"You're going inside?"

"The boy said the chief is in the sweat lodge. If we want to gather information, this is where I think we should begin."

"You can't go barging in, Jack. As a show of respect, you must be invited. This is a sacred place."

Hanging on nails outside of the sweat lodge were several pairs of men's trousers and shirts and a few pairs of worn sandals. Betty stared at the old clothing. "I don't see any bras. I'm guessing just men are inside."

Vu continued to undress. "Betty you should go find the *mercado*, the artisan vendors, the boy mentioned, and do what you are an expert at."

"What's that?"

"Shopping."

"Everybody has special gifts." Betty smiled and pecked Vu's cheek before turning to go.

Vu knew Betty was right about being invited inside. He lifted the heavy door flap but didn't enter. A blast of heat slapped him back accompanied by what sounded like mythical voices of old warriors. Vu made the decision, there and then, to get permission to enter. He would not violate a sacred rite.

He sat down on the bench in his jockeys to wait. Before long an old Indian man appeared from the forest. He walked down the trail toward him. When he stopped at the bench where Vu was sitting he frowned down at him and then began to peel off his clothing, hanging his cotton shirt and baggy beige pants on an empty hook outside of the entrance. Naked, he turned toward the sweat lodge. He hesitated a moment, then turned and stared back at Vu.

"You come."

Vu jumped up and joined the man at the door. The Indian blocked his entry and pointed at Vu's underwear. "Off!"

Vu stripped quickly and hung the offending item on the hook with his other clothing. That seemed to please the Indian, who almost smiled as he held the flap open for Vu.

While his eyes adjusted to the dark, his lungs filled with hot, eucalyptus scented air. To his surprise they had not entered the actual sweat lodge, but a staging area. To get into the main enclosure they had to get down on their hands and knees and crawl through an opening about the size of a dog house. On the other side, he could see a fire burning, which he assumed was the source of intense heat.

The Indian nudged him forward. Vu got down on his knees, crawled through the dark opening toward the light. The temperature had doubled. The air was so hot, it felt like if he breathed in deeply, it would scorch his lungs.

Sweat droplets exploded down Vu's body, and his lips felt like they were starting to blister. He licked them and looked around for water to drink. There was a bucket sitting on the ground near the smoldering fire pit where a young man was in charge of using a la-dle to sprinkle water onto the hot volcanic rocks to generate steam. Once his eyes adjusted better to the dark interior, he saw a group of old Indians sitting across from the fire on a wooden, three-tier bench. The men seemed to be chanting in their native language. Rather quickly, he figured out that the bottom tier would be a few degrees cooler than the next level up. The top tier was for the very bravest. There was an old Indian sitting there by himself. The In-dian behind him squeezed by and took the last spot on the bottom tier. Vu felt his testicles starting to sag.

The old Indian sitting alone on the top tier scooted over and made room for Vu to join him. Vu reluctantly climbed and sat down on the hot cedar planking beside the old Indian. He tried to speak but his vocal cords felt singed by the intense heat.

"Take very shallow breaths," the Indian instructed.

Vu's heart pounded.

"Allow air to fill your lungs slowly. Talking – no good."

Vu panted like a Pekingese. What a great idea this had been.

An elder got up to add another chunk of wood to the fire, then returned to his seat. The men on the middle tier sang a spiritual song. Afterward, one of men reached into a leather pouch at his side, pinched out a small offering of powder and blew it toward the fire.

After ten minutes of hellish heat, Vu's lungs began to slowly acclimate. Still, he felt like his head was turning into a poached egg. Every pore on his body oozed sweat. Even his tongue sweated. *How was that even possible?*

An elder gripped his arm and pulled him from the sweat lodge. He crawled out through the opening, stood very slowly on shaky legs, then pushed out through the main flap into the harsh sunlight. Ten meters away was the icy Macaw Creek. Vu followed the Indian tip-toeing over the rocky dirt and waded down into the cold water. Within moments, he experienced the worst throbbing headache of his life. Was this really the true way to experience transformation?

The pain passed.

Vu climbed out, shivering while he pulled on his sun-warmed clothing. After a few minutes the remaining elders strolled out of the lodge. One by one they entered the creek and began to float about like contented seals.

Vu finished putting on his shoes. The elderly Indian that had the good sense to save him from the torturous heat stepped out of the creek and sat down beside Vu on the bench.

"My name is Chief Tinoco. I had not heard tourists were coming today. You must be from Quepos?"

Before Vu had time to answer, a young boy appeared and held a clean towel out to the chief. Chief Tinoco dried his face and chest and then returned the towel to the boy who ran off.

Vu, still shivering uncontrollably, struggled to speak. "I am Jack Vu," he said, offering a timid hand.

Chief Tinoco smiled. "You are very brave. How did you like the experience?"

"Transforming. Into what I am not sure."

Chief Tinoco nodded. "In the beginning that is not so unusual. From where do you come?"

"The United States."

"I would not have guessed that from your appearance."

"Both my parents were Vietnamese. I moved to the U.S. after a war."

"You were forced from your homeland?"

"Yes."

That seemed to strike a nerve in Chief Tinoco. "My Country does not have a military. But as a young man, I was involved in many border disputes. I don't know how much you know about us but in the old days we were a strong people. Not as thriving as the empires of the Mayan or Aztec but as proud. Culturally we were influenced by the Mesoamerican tribes from Central America and cultures from northern South America, what is today's Columbia. Before the Spanish arrived we had a population of 400,000. The Spanish wanted to tax us and turn us into slaves. To avoid this we moved back into the mountains. We split off into several small groups to better evade capture. Some of us fled deep into the jungle. Some moved from the central plains to the southern coastline. In this way, the Spanish could not as easily slaughter us with their guns and swords. We were too clever. But in the end they eventually killed most of us anyway with the diseases they brought here from Europe. The indigenous tribes living along the Northern Pacific and in the Central Valley – like the Talamanca, Chorotega, Quepo and Nicoya, developed a thriving trade route in the region of the Gulf of Nicoya on the Pacific coastline. We managed the best we could. Foreigners feared us because we were known to conduct human sacrifices. These are ceremonies we do not practice today." Chief Tinoco smiled good-naturedly. "Lucky for you."

"Today the *indios bravos* make up only one percent of the total Costa Rican population. You will find us still living to the south or along the western coastline. I will tell you that once I even killed to defend my family. Struggles never seem to leave us. Now, my only daughter is gone, searching for her lost son. And, I am to blame."

"What is your daughter's name?"

"Leela," he said. "She left yesterday. And I am too old to go search for them. Yet, I worry about their safety."

"Do you know where your daughter went exactly?"

Chief Tinoco pointed over his shoulder. "She is following the path to the sea."

"How long has your grandson been gone?"

"Leela believes a fortnight. A mother's intuition is usually right."

"Would you have photographs of your grandson or your daughter that I may look at?"

He shook his head. "Photographs are forbidden."

Vu knew historically many Indian tribes especially those in the United States were superstitious about losing their souls if somebody photographed them but he wasn't aware the practice was still being taken seriously in the 21st century. "I would not ask if I didn't think it was important. An Indian boy's body has been discovered in Manual Antonio Park. No one has reported anyone missing to the police and there was no identification found on the body. The only thing we could piece together is perhaps he belonged to a tribe in the area."

The chief frowned. "Totem is dead?"

"As I said, we have no idea who the boy is."

Chief Tinoco got up and immediately began to dress. "But a boy is dead?"

"Yes."

"How was he killed?"

"We believe he was poisoned by manchineel sap from stepping on thorns we found in his feet."

"My grandson would not be so careless."

"Chief Tinoco, it may not be your grandson. But, the boy is at least part Cabécar."

"What do you mean part Cabécar?"

"We believe his father is Gaston Trujillo."

Chief Tinoco's expression turned to stone. "Follow me."

The Chief rose to his feet and headed toward the huts on the edge of the village. Near the creek bank they entered a small shelter. In the corner on the floor was a bed with quilted blankets. There was a small table with an oil lamp on it and several animal skin rugs. There was some bead work on the walls and a few cooking utensils. A small wood stove sat in the corner.

"Who lives here?" Vu inquired.

"My daughter, Leela."

The Chief walked over to a shelf of books. He selected one and handed it to Vu. "Thumb through the pages."

Near the back, photographs spilled out onto the floor. Vu stooped over to pick them up.

"My daughter didn't know I knew of these. She kept many secrets."

The first photograph taken years ago by the obvious fading, he guessed, was certainly a striking resemblance to Dr. Gaston Trujillo. Vu turned it over and read the caption on the back, written in cursive writing: *Universidad de Paz, 1995, Gaston's graduation day.* There were more photographs, but this time some of them were

Leela holding a young son in her arms. Several were of Dr. Trujillo tending to some of the elderly Indians at the reservation. Vu found a last photograph stuck between some pages, a faded snapshot of Leela and Gaston sitting together around a campfire holding hands, looking innocent and happy.

Chief Tinoco took the pictures, glanced at them all, groaned at the snapshot of his daughter with Gaston, and pushed them all back at Vu who put them back inside the book as he found them and returned the book to the shelf.

"The man in the photograph is Dr. Gaston Trujillo," he said. "His mother was a treasured member of our tribe for a number of years. She passed on several days ago. It is her body that we are honoring today through fire. It is right that you purified yourself in the sweat lodge in preparation for this ceremony." Chief Tinoco lowered his head. "Dr. Trujillo was once a good friend of the reservation but he has disgraced himself and was not allowed to visit the village unless he came to visit his dying mother. And now he will not be allowed to ever return here again."

Vu remembered the image of the young son in Leela's arms and a strange sensation came over him, one that could ignite a whole series of problems if he was incorrect about what his gut was telling him.

"Chief Tinoco – is Dr. Trujillo the father of your daughter's son?"

Chief Tinoco stared at Vu for the longest moment with expressionless eyes. Then, he turned around and left the hut without another word spoken.

* * *

In another part of the reservation, Betty approached a young teenage Indian girl, stringing beads on her lap. The girl wore a beautiful turquoise dress and leather sandals. Her long black hair shimmered in the sunlight. Despite being picture perfect in all ways, her eyes were downcast and sad.

"Excuse me," Betty said, "Do you speak English?"

The girl looked up and mumbled shyly: *"Un poco oon."*

A little was better than none, Betty thought. She found her dark eyes enchanting, but painful to look at.

"What are you making?"

"Una pulsera para mi novio."

"A bracelet. How nice." Betty winked. "What's his name? *¿Cuál es su nombre?"*

"Totem."

"Totem is a lucky boy. *"Él es afortunado."*

The girl's eyes brightened.

Betty waited until the girl put her beads down. "Has any boy your age gone missing?"

The girl nodded. "Totem." The girl explained through gesture and broken English that Totem had left during the night and has not been seen since.

Betty took it all in. "Por qué?"

The girl hesitated, and then said. "To find *su padre."*

"Dónde?"

"No Dime…"

"He didn't tell you," Betty repeated. *"Tienes una fotografía de él?* Do you have a photograph of Totem?"

"No." She shook her head. *"Prohibida."* She disappeared inside her hut and returned carrying a leather necklace with three eagle claws hanging from it.

Betty held the necklace up to the light. *"Mucho bello."* And he was wearing one like this when he left?"

"Si."

"You're certain?"

She nodded. *"Por fortuna."*

"And you're sure you don't have a picture?"

The girl reached into her pocket and pulled out a worn drawing. She flattened it out and held it up for Betty to see. "Totem."

Chapter 37

The tribesmen finished stacking firewood beneath the small platform. The dried wood had been arranged haphazardly into a pile, along with bushels of dried grass. Next, hot perfumed wax was poured over the mixture and a number of elders by the old woman's body placed flowers on it. Nearby, Vu and Betty silently observed the ritual as old as time. Vu's mind drifted to the recent burial he had accidently uncovered a day earlier. It seemed impossible that when they landed in Costa Rica for some much needed rest and relaxation that they would experience the same death and suffering from which they had sought respite. Vu had quietly brought Betty up to speed on what was happening.

"The ceremony is for Gaston's mother. Chief Tinoco has allowed us to stay for the funeral ceremony since he believes our visit has spiritual importance."

Betty's expression remained somber. "It gets worse."

"You're going to tell me that our Indian boy is named Totem, right?"

"Yes. I met his girlfriend. A boy named Totem has been missing for over two weeks. She told me he went in search of his father ...

I've been looking for the mother, but no one seems to know where she is. I thought if I could talk to her..."

"She's gone after her son," Vu's words stopped Betty in her tracks. "She's Chief Tinoco's daughter."

Betty's mind seemed to be reeling through charts, reports and murder scene photographs.

Vu explained. "Gaston did not know Totem was his child when he walked away from his mother's deathbed." Betty stared in disbelief but allowed him to finish. "The tribe does not expect him today, although if he did come, it would be the last time he would be allowed in the village. He felt betrayed when his mother rejected his home and chose to live and die here instead, and they felt betrayed by his attempts to alter the course of nature."

"Does the Chief know that we believe Gaston to be Totem's father?"

"The Chief did not confirm this, and Leela was married to a tribe member when her son was born, but given the evidence you were able to provide, and the secret photographs his daughter kept, which he allowed me to see, it's as good as confirmed."

"Totem's girlfriend is so cute and in love. She showed me a drawing she had done of him. It's hardly more than a stick drawing so I couldn't tell what he looked like, but I know I didn't have the heart to tell her that he's probably dead..."

"We will only tell Chief Tinoco. He will know how the news is to be disseminated among the tribe," Vu whispered. "For obvious reasons Leela kept the identity of her son from Gaston, his mother and the Chief. Then the time came when she revealed the truth to Totem. That would certainly motivate the boy to run off in search of his father. It is only natural to want to learn who your parents are – no matter what the age. The mother probably grew very worried that he wasn't back after being gone so long. Chief Tinoco told me that to achieve manhood a young man must journey into the unknown, and that is what he believed Totem was doing."

Their discussion was cut short by the ceremony getting underway. In solemn silence, one by one, the tribe's men and women paid tribute to Gaston's mother, either whispering some prayer or chant or by tossing a flower onto the platform where the body lay, dressed in an elegant beaded robe. Vu and Betty stood to the back of the crowd and watched with interest. Death ceremonies, no matter what culture or country, mine a wave of personal memories and reflections to everyone involved, thought Vu. Betty had her eyes closed listening to the chants and hymns. Her lips moved in a silent prayer.

Within minutes, dancing broke out as Chief Tinoco and three other elders lit torches, walked over to where the wood and grass had been stacked and took turns lighting each of the four corners. The blazing fire hissed and roared. Flames licked the sky. Betty's nostrils flared and her eyes fluttered as the smoke reached her.

As the body was engulfed in fire, children danced about banging drums and women began removing articles of clothing and chanting in a foreign tongue. Men screamed toward the sky and passed around a clay demijohn filled with fermented spirits. Then everyone began to sing.

This went on for the better part of an hour before the fire burned out and what remained of the woman's body was now nothing but smoldering bone and ash. Vu saw images of death camps from his youth and charred bodies lying smoldering on the ground. He saw the killing fields and bodies floating on the open sea.

Betty was soaked in perspiration, her frame quivering. As she clung to Vu his vision changed to lotuses blooming and mothers giving birth and he wept openly.

Chapter 38

Officer Sanchez blew out a match used to light a cigarette and tossed it down by her feet. Gaston watched the flame peter out in the dirt. The fire seemed to fascinate him or perhaps he was just looking for any excuse to focus on something other than the grassy knoll where they sat waiting while the sun began its slow descent over the rainforest.

Gaston picked up a radio control box and flipped the switch to the "on" position. He watched the needle reset itself, then flicker back and forth on the dial as if it were picking up trace signals.

"And that thing is used to track monkeys?"

"And other wildlife," Gaston added.

Carlos lowered his binoculars. "What other wildlife?"

"Jaguars for example."

Sanchez scratched at her ankle where the rough .45 holster irritated her skin. "You're tracking jaguars now?"

"It's just one facet of the experiment that I explained to you earlier."

"Frankly, doctor," Carlos said, "I don't get your whole theory of evolution. Seems to me we should live and let live. Why fuck around with mother nature?"

"Is that why you are a policeman? To live and let live?"

"Okay, so maybe you have a point."

"Look, I do not expect you to appreciate my work. To some, it is very cruel indeed."

Sanchez pointed at the dial. "Your box has a hard-on, doc. How far away is this jaguar?"

Gaston's expression perked up as he did a minor calculation and searched out over the knoll. "According to the strength of signal, I suspect right over that valley there."

"Several kilometers, right?" Sanchez preferred to keep her distance.

"Yes, officer."

"So what makes you think the mule team is going to pass through the valley?"

"It would be the most practical way."

"What if they run into the jaguar and change course?"

"That would be interesting."

Sanchez glanced down at the doctor's bandaged hand.

Carlos passed the binoculars to Sanchez, got up and stretched his cramped legs. He walked back and forth, from one lookout position to the other, could see no signs of the mule team. He mentioned to Sanchez he thought he heard noises in the woods behind them, but after watching for several minutes, couldn't see anything and gave up searching for ghosts.

When he returned, Sanchez said she needed to pee and wandered off into the woods to find a tree where she could do her thing in private.

Gaston wandered back up to the panel van and replaced the batteries in his radio control box. When he closed the door and glanced down to where Carlos had been sitting, he noticed the spot was empty. Then he heard a twig crack behind him and felt the heavy blow of a rifle stock slam the back of his head. His world spun out of control as a dark chasm like the parting of the Red Sea opened and engulfed him.

Sanchez had forgotten the golden rule of surveillance, always bring plenty of tissue. She found threads wadded up in her pocket, but it would have to do. She wiped herself best she could, stood to refasten her belt, and then caught a glimpse of something silver out of the corner of her eye and before she had a chance to pull out her .45, the searing pain of the knife pressed against her throat.

"I would not advise it senorita," her capturer warned. "You will come with me now."

* * *

The men had set up camp for the evening in a clearing, south of where Gaston had expected. It had been by sheer luck that one of the men had spotted the panel van. And, Colonel Pierz, was taking no chances. He'd sent four of his most competent men into the forest to investigate. After nearly an hour of being gone, the men returned, and had not disappointed him.

Colonel Pierz walked up to the three prisoners and singled out Sanchez, grabbing a handful of her hair before yanking her head back, exposing her bare throat where a fine trickle of blood still remained. "Hello, Senorita," the Colonel said, in a menacing voice. "A lovely night is it not?"

Sanchez glared into the scarred face and hawked spittle at his eyes. The Colonel slammed her face into a tree trunk and then pushed her to the ground where he planted a boot on her ribcage. "You should be more cordial, senorita. You have very bad manners."

Blood oozed from Sanchez lips and nose as she tried to focus.

"Colonel," Gaston piped in, rubbing the back of his bleeding head, "We are all in danger unless we leave this area at once."

The Colonel laughed. "And who are you?"

Senor Héctor walked up. "That is the good doctor Gaston Trujillo. The doctor operates the *Instituto Nacional de Biodiversidad* in Quepos. And the man beside him I have seen before. I believe he is a policeman working for the narcotics division."

Carlos twisted his head around. "I don't know what you're talking about."

"Of course not," Senor Héctor said, smiling. Then turning his attention to Gaston, asked, "And what brings you out this evening, doctor. Perhaps you want to rescind on our little arrangement?"

"Cecelia left behind something for you."

Senor Héctor's confident expression faded. "And what would that be?"

"You were treating her drug habit, but I was treating her syphilis."

Rage boiled behind Senor Héctor's eyes. "Colonel, kill these people at once."

The colonel scowled. "Soon enough, but I would like to extract some information from them first."

The Colonel motioned to his men. "Tie them up to a tree and remove their shoes. I will be back."

Chapter 39

Leela lay in the thick brush watching the men beat on the woman in uniform. Her captors slapped her, cut her clothing off with machetes and taunted her with threats. The woman refused to talk. So they slapped her some more until blood spilled from her nose and mouth. One of the men took great pleasure in beating the bottoms of her feet with a heavy stick but still she told them nothing. Difficult as this was for Leela to witness, her own true strength merged with that of the woman's. Their spirits were one. And then she spotted the leather necklace with the eagle claws on one of the tormenters chest. Leela understood at that moment what had happened to her son, and that Totem's spirit was with them. They would not be beaten down by any man. Their bodies could be abused but their wills were incapable of breaking.

Despite her strong desire to scream out, Leela remained quiet, searching for ways to help. Seeing the men next beat the father of her lost son was unbearable. She wept and prayed to her Gods for mercy. Somewhere in the expanse of rainforest was her lost son's body. The journey to recover it could wait. For now she knew who was responsible for Totem's death and what she must do to avenge the loss of his life and love.

* * *

Chief Tinoco's spirit spoke to him in the night. He sat up, allowing the single wool blanket covering his frail body to fall to his lap. He stood up suddenly and walked across the hut to remove his traditional headgear and deerskin pants from a small bureau against the wall. After slipping on his warrior's clothing, he left his hut carrying his hunting bow and satchel of hand-carved arrows, to call upon the tribe's elders. Within a half-hour, a group of eleven of his strongest men gathered outside. The discussion was brief. The men understood the vision that Chief Tinoco shared with them. They would round up horses, cross the Tico's inhabited lands, enter the rainforest, and travel until they located his daughter. The spirit of the wind had spoken....

Chapter 40

The soft creaking outside the door awakened Vu from a restless sleep. But when he sat up the noise stopped. Beside him, Betty moaned softly and rolled on to her side her head buried in a pillow and wearing sound-deadening headphones. He stared at the door and windows, but saw only darkness, heard no other sounds. Then, he heard the door knob creak as if someone was trying to get inside, and sprang to his feet.

Vu treaded over to the door and touched the handle. He could feel pressure being returned and knew someone had their hand on the latch. Then, very softly, he heard a hushed voice.

"Jack! It's Lyman!"

Quietly, Vu opened the door and stepped outside. Menacing eyes beamed down at him. Lyman didn't seem the least bit concerned that his wetsuit jacket dripped water onto Vu's bare feet. At this hour of the morning, the ex-commando looked like something that had crawled out of the swamp. Every inch of exposed skin had been smeared with camouflage grease paint.

Lyman put his finger to his lips, but stayed close to the door. "Get dressed," he whispered.

"Why?"

"Your friends have been kidnapped."

"I don't have any friends here."

"You want to find out who killed the boy?"

"I've got to wake Betty."

Lyman shook his head. "Leave her a note."

As Vu left a note on his pillow Betty stirred and let out a purring sound, then rolled to her opposite side. Now, she had her face pressed into the pillow and it was blocking off her air supply and the room filled with a quaint snoring, a sound that Vu found endearing. He hated to leave her like this, but Lyman had a point, especially if it meant that she would be in harm's way.

Vu slipped on some jeans and a t-shirt, removed his pair of hiking shoes from beneath the bed, and closed the door quietly.

"Follow me," Lyman instructed.

The two men walked down to the harbor. Tied to the dock was a four-man Zodiac with a small outboard. Lyman climbed in to man the tiller. Vu pushed off and then jumped aboard. Once they had drifted far enough away that the engine noise would not alert anyone, Lyman fired up the outboard and pointed the boat.

Chapter 41

Despite the low tide, the Zodiac glided onto the beach. Vu jumped out and pulled the bow out of the water, steadying the boat while Lyman handed him two rifles, two backpacks containing first aid supplies, explosives and flashlights. Then, he climbed ashore. Vu slung one of the AR-15s over his shoulder and placed a backpack down at his feet. Lyman grabbed the other gear.

"We've got an hour to daylight," Lyman reminded him, then pulled out two full magazines of ammunition and passed them to Vu. "We've got to hurry. And, don't waste these. It's all we have."

Vu knew that dawn was the time to plan an attack. Changing light patterns made visibility difficult, almost surreal-like, and the aggressor had the advantage. He'd spent many a morning waiting for the sun to break over the horizon so that he could plan his next move. Sometimes, the reason had been for military training, other times it had been a matter of life and death. Today, Vu assumed it would be the latter.

"Which direction are they headed?" Vu asked.

"Northwest. Near Dos Bocas. I figure we're their only chance of survival. Most likely the mule team will head toward the coastline. If we head them off before they meet their contact, we have a chance. If I were them I'd use these guys as hostages to ensure safe passage to their contact point. Once they get there – they're excess baggage and at that point they'll kill 'em."

"Are you working undercover for the DEA?"

"Jack, I don't exist, remember?"

Vu looked confused. "Then, why?"

"Because I have finally found a place where I feel at peace. These drug bastards with the help of Gaston Trujillo are about to fuck it all up."

Lyman's face had an eerie glow as he moved to explain further, but before the words were out, abruptly, he changed the subject. "Don't fall behind. We've got a rough trail to cut."

Rough indeed. Strangler vines hung low like iron curtains blocking their path. Lyman swung the machete through the spider-like maze and Vu followed, holding the flashlight on the ground ahead of them. Images reappeared in Vu's mind. He was on a different island, younger, more frightened. Soldiers were chasing after him through the jungle.

Years earlier, his escape from the internment camp had been planned. For nearly a year he dreamed of escaping. Then when the day came, it all seemed so misguided. Just as the Viet Cong were rounding up the workers from a long day of digging in the fields, Vu saw his chance. He'd been digging a trench along the perimeter of the jungle and as the guard turned his back, he dropped his shovel, jumped from the ditch, and ran straight into the thick foliage. Dusk was approaching. A number of gunshots were fired, but he was not hit. He kept on running, slamming into vines and branches, slicing open wounds in his arms and legs, his face, his hands. But he knew if they re-captured him this time they would kill him. He pushed on through the night. The soldiers pursued him, but he had managed to evade capture by hiding in the jungle's canopy. Nightfall came and went, but he had outwitted his captors. His stomach ached from malnutrition, his body beaten from the difficult journey, but he kept on....

* * *

As the hazy glow of dawn began to break, Sanchez kept her good eye on something moving in the rainforest, a small shadowy object that darted back and forth through the trees. Despite the pounding headache, she kept searching the forest, but the object never reappeared.

Behind her, the men of the mule team were crawling from their sleeping bags, yawning, stretching, and farting. Colonel Pierz walked over and Sanchez pretended to be asleep. The Colonel stopped in front of her and threw a cup of cold water in her face.

"Rise and shine, senorita."

Sanchez's hatred ignited. Someday, this asshole would pay. If the bastard only knew…

"I need to pee."

"There will be time for that. Get up now. I need to see if you can walk."

The burning sensation at the bottom of her feet when she stood seared like flames through her heels to her spine where another throbbing pain announced itself. Sanchez braced herself on the tree trunk until the burning subsided and she could apply pressure to her feet. Every inch of her body ached.

"Take a few steps now."

Sanchez hobbled forward. The Colonel made his appraisement.

"Put on your boots."

"My feet are too swollen."

"You are lucky I like you. I could have driven manchineel thorns into your feet and left you to die."

"So you're the scum who tortured that young Cabécar near the Instituto."

The colonel untied her hands. "And like you, he said nothing helpful. Other than to say he was on a quest to find his father, a famous scientist." Behind her, Sanchez saw Gaston's face ashen visibly at what he had just overheard.

"Well he got away and managed to take with him your blood money."

The colonel smiled. "The man who allowed that to happen suffered a cut for every peso taken before he died." To his men he said, "Insure she does not escape as she relieves herself. Then, you will release the others. Tie them all to the mules."

Suddenly, deep in the rainforest, the piercing howl of a jaguar echoed through the trees. And at that moment, Sanchez realized that after escaping from the mule team the boy had used his last ounce of strength to climb the tree to avoid a predator.

"What was that?" one of the men asked, startled. They stopped escorting Sanchez.

"*Un gato grande!*" another man replied. "Quickly, move!"

The man escorting Sanchez jerked her pants down and pushed her down. "Do your business here." As she squatted in front of him to relieve herself, she watched him nervously stroke his eagle claw necklace as his eyes searched the forest. Though he still held her, she could feel him trembling with terror. Her own fear of the powerful creatures seemed secondary to what she had just been through.

Out of the corner of her eye, Sanchez saw something move. The Indian girl's dark face rose up out of the brush like a capuchin. Her eyes acknowledged Sanchez and then she slipped down out of sight.

Sanchez finished her business, stood and faced her captor. "Okay," Sanchez said in a raised voice, "Your turn."

The man had recovered his bearings and smirked as he roughly pulled Sanchez's pants to her waist. "Perhaps I fuck you before I kill you?"

Unless the Indian girl had a whole tribe with her, she could do nothing to stop this pig from his threat.

Chapter 42

Along the corridor fringe the trees thickened and the path grew steep and rugged. Chief Tinoco had traveled all night and would not have found evidence of the mule team had they not been so disrespectful to his native land. Slicing through vines and plants, tromping rare plant species, leaving behind a smoldering campfire, smothering the very life of the fertile, ancient soil, whoever these men were, they were not a friend of mother earth. Chief Tinoco raised his hand for the men behind to stop. One by one the Indians climbed off their horses and waited. Chief Tinoco told the men to feed and water their horses. They would take a short break before continuing on with the journey.

* * *

Not at all pleased with the distance they had covered, Colonel Pierz shouted over his shoulder. "What is wrong back there!"

Sanchez cursed every inch she had to walk, tethered to a dumb mule. She kept her eye on the forest, hoping to catch another glimpse of the Indian girl. Seeing her had been so odd, and yet,

Sanchez knew she had come for a purpose, and she suspected it had to do with the body they had discovered in Manual Antonio Park.

Sanchez felt a tug on the rope tied to her waist and glanced behind her. Carlos swayed from side to side, his forehead swollen. Blood oozed from an ugly gash above his right eye. His ribs were broken, his breathing irregular. They had taken turns kicking him with their boots and spitting in his face when they decided he would not reveal what they knew about the mule teams. He gasped and with no warning collapsed. Since he was tethered to a mule, his weakened, nearly unconscious body scraped rocks until the mule finally stopped.

Reaching his hand out, Gaston tried to pull Carlos to his feet but the mule driver behind him lashed out a wet vine like a rawhide whip, slicing his hand, and shouted. "Leave him!"

"You can't let the mule drag him," Sanchez shouted. "It'll kill him."

"He is already dead," the man smirked, "as are you all."

"What is going on back there?" The Colonel shouted.

"One of the prisoners has fallen," the man replied.

"Well, get him to his feet!"

The man walked over to the mule and commanded it to halt. Then, he stooped and yanked Carlos to his feet. Unsteady and bleeding from cuts on his hands and face, the man released him and returned to his own mule where he climbed on and swatted the animal's hindquarter.

Sanchez used the momentary break to tell Gaston they were not alone. An Indian girl was following them.

Gaston stared at her blankly. The team began moving again.

*   *   *

Time passed very slowly. Gaston's head throbbed. His thoughts raced. His heart pounded. His mind tormented. What had Sanchez said?

Was it Leela tracking them in the woods?

Gaston tried to block the memory of his last night with her when he deflowered her and then left without a backward glance.

* * *

They were coming, Vu observed, hidden in the thick brush. The heavy canopy of spidery vines and palms now a hazy glow from the dawning light, still provided an element of surprise, if they acted fast. But the plan Lyman had discussed earlier seemed sketchy at best. And Vu felt uncomfortable about an ambush. It would be like slaughtering cattle and he wanted no part of it. But what other options were there? Eventually, they came up with an alternative.

"Jack, get over here," Lyman said in a hushed voice. "Help me with this snare."

Lyman had rigged two trip snares using vines and willowy tree branches at the head of the trail. The idea, snag either a mule's hoof or a man's foot. Either way, it would provide a moment of chaos. And, a moment is all they needed. They had agreed Vu would take out the three men surrounding Sanchez and the doctor, if Lyman's plan didn't work. They would first attempt the rescue without resorting to gun fire, because there was always the possibility of an innocent person being hit. But they had only a short window to draw down on them. If the men had time to pull their rifles, it would be too late.

Vu tugged a vine Lyman was holding to get his attention. "One last thing…" he said. "What happened to the money?"

Lyman looked over at him, showing no emotion. "It's in the wind…"

After the snares were rigged, Vu took up his position behind a stand of trees. Lyman was ten meters away where the head of the mule team would be. Take out the front and the rear. That had been a battle strategy since the dawn of time. Like the jaws of a vise closing in on a metal pipe, eventually, with enough pressure applied, the ends collapse and compress the middle.

Chapter 43

Senor Héctor was the first to hear the sound. Suddenly, he raised a hand to stop the mule team, just mere meters from the trip snares. Colonel Pierz broke rank and trotted up to see what was the matter. Before he could reach Senor Héctor, a family of capuchins swung across his path and startled him. Acting on instinct, he pulled his revolver and fired into the trees. The gunshot seemed to echo forever. The team acted quickly, jumping from their mules, pulling rifles, ready for most anything.

"Stand down!" Senor Héctor laughed. "Why Colonel you almost shot yourself a monkey."

The Colonel holstered his revolver and then something ahead on the trail caught his eye. He motioned for his men to spread out.

With extreme caution, the Colonel moved forward on the path, keeping his revolver drawn, and his horse protecting him from one side. He stooped down at the snares and tripped them. The willowy branches snapped back and forth like a pair of windshield wipers stuck on high.

"What is it, Colonel?" Senor Héctor asked.

"Get down at once," the Colonel shouted, stepping back into the thick brush.

Gaston and Sanchez searched the forest as if they were expecting a team of law enforcement agents to spring out at any moment. The guards cut them from their mules, tugging them into the brush. Carlos, too beaten down to comprehend much, sagged to his knees. The man guarding him struck his ribs with the butt of his rifle. "Get up!"

A shot was fired. The man guarding Carlos fell over dead, blood spilling from a bullet wound to his forehead.

Within moments the men circled Sanchez and Gaston and pressed their rifles to their heads.

Colonel Pierz, still protecting himself from an ambush, shouted: "You want us to kill them? Show yourselves. Now!"

After a brief silence passed and no one appeared, Colonel Pierz motioned to one of his men. Without a moment's hesitation the man standing next to Sanchez pressed the rifle to her head and as his finger squeezed the trigger, Carlos, forgotten on the ground, used his final ounce of strength to kick the legs out from under the killer, sending the shot echoing into the canopy. The Colonel calmly shot his inattentive guard dead and turned his gun on Carlos, who was beyond comprehending, the heroic kick having driven his shattered ribs into his lungs. Sanchez saw his head loll to the side as blood began to pour from his lips and nose. The Colonel stared coldly down at the dying man. "Waste of a good bullet," he said as he turned his gun on Sanchez.

Seeing her friend expire before her eyes, Sanchez squirmed in her restraints, cursing and screaming at the top of her lungs.

But before Colonel could act, Leela stepped out of the woods holding a single-shot .22 rifle, which she turned over to one of the men as he hustled over and grabbed her.

Gaston looked at her with astonishment. "Leela?"

Colonel Pierz stepped out into the opening. "Who is this woman, doctor? Tell me at once or she dies, too. Why is she here?"

Gaston shrugged. "I have no idea."

Colonel Pierz walked up to Leela who remained rigid and yet fragile as an orchid, while the man squeezing her arm, held her under control.

The Colonel slapped her. "What is your reason for being here? And why did you shoot my man?"

Leela said nothing. She pretended to be mute or not speak in the Colonel's native tongue.

The Colonel slapped her again. "This is your last chance. Speak."

But Leela would not. Gaston was so overwhelmed at the sight of her that he could not find the words to prevent the men from striking her once again. Then, he said, in a controlled voice. "She is deaf. She does not understand your questions."

"Then why does she kill my soldier?"

"She is human. He was going to kill a helpless woman. It was instinctual, as was your shooting at the capuchins."

"We are kilometers from anything. What business does she have here?"

"She is indigenous to this area. She was probably out searching for plants. There are wild animals in the rainforest. She probably carries the rifle for protection."

"How do you know this woman?"

"I did research as a graduate student at her reservation. I remember her. She was Chief Tinoco's daughter. If harm comes to her, you will have a tribe of very angry warriors. They will hunt you down and kill you. She is next in line to lead her tribe."

The Colonel laughed. "You read too many books, doctor. The Indians are a backward, gentle people. They are not savages. They would never harm me. This one is different." Then, staring at the two bodies on the ground, he said to his men, "Tie her up. I will take her as a souvenir."

As the Colonel signaled to one of his men, Leela turned quickly to Gaston. "Totem is our son. Do you know where he is?"

Gaston dropped his head. "His spirit is with my mother, but his body is at the instituto." Leela screamed in grief as one of the men approached with a rope. Leela's eyes locked on her son's necklace swinging from his neck.

Just as Colonel Pierz turned his back to Leela, out of the forest soared an arrow that pierced the Colonel's back, the razor tip fracturing a rib as it seared through tissue and bone and protruded out of his chest. Gasping, the Colonel grasped the arrow, snapped the end off, and toppled over dead. Leela grabbed the necklace from the startled guard and jerked it off his neck as Gaston threw his bound hands around his neck from behind, pulling him to the ground and away from Leela.

Vu could not believe his eyes. He had waited for an opportunity to draw down without risking the other's lives. And that opportunity had not come. Then, an arrow, seemingly out of nowhere, killed the Colonel in a single shot. Buddhist's would say it was fate floating toward the earth. What followed was something out of a bizarre western flick. The Indians, riding in on horseback, arrows flying everywhere, old Winchester rifles blasting, bullets whistling through the rainforest. Out of the hazy light, Chief Tinoco appeared on the back of a black stallion, and proudly charged toward Leela swooping her to safety aboard his horse.

Fearless, aggressive, channeling the warrior's spirit, Vu raced into the action, reaching Sanchez before the others. He sliced the rope tethering her hands, and whisked her to safety, just as the horses trampled by. From a vantage point above the trail, Lyman fired on one of the men drawing down on one of the Indians on horseback. The bullet was on target. The dead man slumped to the ground.

Somehow, in the heat of the battle, Senor Héctor on horseback escaped down the path leading to the sea.

There was no one to go after him because Lyman sprang out of the woods to jump one of the Colonel's men, wrestling him to the ground, and Chief Tinoco was riding Leela to safety. The other Indians were surrounding the men on the ground. But, when all was done, no Indian had died; however, several of Colonel Pierz men weren't so fortunate. Vu's last sight of Lyman was as he was disarming and tying up the soldiers. Vu and Sanchez headed toward the sea.

Once he was free, Gaston wasted no time and jumped on Colonel Pierz's horse to chase after Senor Héctor.

Chapter 44

Gaston figured Senor Héctor was breathing easy, since he had escaped those crazy Indians. And, just ahead, he was sure of it, Senor Héctor believed his ticket to freedom awaited.

Every muscle in his body ached as he galloped along, ducking low hanging branches, swiping vines from his path, trusting his animal instincts to get him through. It was the reincarnation of his experiment, a survival of fittest. He was pursuing a man nearly twice his age, like the jaguars were pursuing the capuchins. If they were to survive, they had to learn new skills, defend themselves better, scavenge for food in more remote locations. Their species as a whole had to alter. It was a moment of clarity for Gaston. He was pushing nature to the limit but now it was pushing back.

Glimpsing the backside of Senor Héctor's horse as it rounded a twist in the trail, Gaston pushed his horse harder. His horse bolted out of the gate, which was the rainforest, and like lightening raining down from the sky, the thundering hooves ruptured the silence of the forest and ignited the spirit of Gaston. He was the hunter now. He was all powerful. He was the light.

Then he saw the flash of fur. The jaguar leapt from a tree top and attacked. Gaston felt the jagged hot teeth sink into his flesh as he tumbled off the horse and rolled over the ground. Locked in the cat's powerful jaws, Gaston could not move. His head was pinned to the ground. The jaguar's thirsty eyes glared down at him. He now understood what it meant to be the weaker of the two species.

The jaguar sunk his teeth into Gaston's neck and tore flesh and bone in one tremendously powerful bite. Gaston felt his life leaking out of him, the oozing blood running down his neck over his chest, saturating his clothing and the ground around him. It was over before he could cry out. As he stared through the towering trees toward the rising sun, he saw his mother and a boy he immediately recognized as his son smiling through the light streaming through the trees. Maybe this was how it was meant to end. He had found his family and home. His soul lifted up through the morning mist, finally free of his mortal struggle. As his blood repaid Mother Nature, he moved on.

* * *

Senor Héctor rode onto the beach where in the distance, the boat waited. He rode the horse straight into the waves and when the horse could no longer go any further he bailed off and began to swim, fearing the Indians would be firing down on him at any moment. Yet, the boat was in sight and hope reigned.

There was nothing that could stop him now. He had lost his cargo, lost the means to transport his cocaine through the corridor, lost his mistress. None of that mattered. Only reaching the boat mattered because he was sure he would be free.

Through the splashing waves he glimpsed a man on the boat waving his arms back and forth, signaling him. He kicked his tired legs and felt his heart thumping the sides of his chest. He was in good shape for a man of sixty. The best of shape. Just a little bit farther, and he would have his freedom.

As he hooked a hand on the collapsible ladder that hung into the water, he looked up at the man staring down at him from the deck of the boat. It was not the Columbian who had been signaling him earlier. Who was this man?

Then as the water cleared from his eyes and as the man reached down and pulled him from the water, he spotted the uniform, spotted the immigration badge, spotted the holster.

Jiménez yanked Senor Héctor upright and slapped handcuffs onto his wrists.

"What is the meaning of this?" Senor Héctor protested. And then Jiménez turned him around, and in the small cove to the south, surrounded by trees, he saw the small Coast Guard vessel that had delivered Jiménez to the Columbian's boat.

"You're under arrest, Senor Héctor. Where are the others?"

Senor Héctor could not utter a word. He felt the strength in his legs turn to wet clay. Three uniformed coast guard officers stepped out onto the deck, one escorting the Captain of the boat in handcuffs to the stern while they waited for the Coast Guard vessel to arrive.

Chapter 45

The Coast Guard helicopter landed on the beach near Quepos. From the forest Vu appeared with Sanchez at his side. Her battered body needed medical attention. She was dragging her heels, fighting every step of the way.

Jiménez ran over and slipped an arm around Sanchez's waist and the two men lifted Sanchez into the rear door of the CH-22 chopper where a medic began administering first aid.

Sanchez started to cry. "Why Jiménez, I didn't know you had it in you."

"When you said you were hunting the mule train with Carlos, I put it together."

"Carlos is dead..." Sanchez face crumbled. "He died saving my life."

Jiménez just stood there looking awkward. "And Gaston too," she gulped.

They had stumbled on Gaston's body just as they left the edge of the forest. Vu hoped she understood karma. His was to rescue her, Carlos' to die in order for Sanchez to live, so that she could then avenge her father's death.

Within an hour the place looked like a Hollywood movie set. The Bureau of Immigration arrived along with the local police and State Department. Even a second coast guard vessel had been called in.

Vu explained it all: His take on Lyman; how the Indians had rescued them; how Carlos had been killed; the mule team; even the details about the young Indian boy and how all this seemed to connect to Dr. Gaston Trujillo.

Since there was no evidence that any Indians had been in the area, because they had simply vanished after retrieving Leela, and the Colonel's men, who seemed filled with awe, like their tongues had been removed by the hand of God, were afraid to speak. They were claiming that it was just Vu and some other frogman who had captured them. But that didn't explain the arrow that had killed Colonel Pierz. So law enforcement was baffled by the story. Vu repeated his version to the State Department official. A brief meeting was held with those in charge.

While they rounded up the men, Vu saw the fear in their eyes. Later, he searched the area looking for any trace of Lyman, and found none. Even the AR-15s and backpacks were missing.

Vu led the investigators to Gaston's body with the help of the horse Gaston had been riding when the jaguar attacked.

At first, the local authorities were going to press charges against Vu, but the story was so bizarre that the head of the narcotics division and immigration, decided against it. Jiménez and Sanchez would take all the credit for bringing down a major cocaine drug lord and preventing a large shipment of cocaine from reaching the United States. They would escort Vu and Betty back to the *Sea Gypsy* and if he promised never to come back to their fine country again, everything would be forgotten.

Chapter 46

A brief squall swept along the rainforest fringing the beach, sending leaves, fronds and dirt swirling onto the hot white sand. The children turned their backs to the blast of greenery, laughing and running along the churning surf's edge. Another balmy gust of air jarred something else loose from the forest floor. It had not been lying there long. A family of nearby capuchins went scurrying off through the vines when the shrieking cry of a vulture spooked them.

The children stared skyward, captivated by the large-winged bird and didn't notice the bills float out of the jungle and tumble along the glittering water's edge. They were too busy giggling, running about and looking up – oblivious to the acrobatic dance of the paper currency beginning to blanket the beach.

Further down, their parents were busy too setting up the picnic area. The mothers laid out handmade blankets while the grandmothers unpacked baskets of food. The men were digging around in ice chests for cold bottles of beer. Everybody seemed unaware of the pesos swirling their direction.

Soon other guests began to arrive to share in the tranquil setting. Their backs to the forest, they turned their faces toward the water and the sun. Picnic baskets packed to the brim with freshly made sandwiches, snacks and soft drinks for the kids and wine for the adults were opened. Out came containers of mango, papaya and *carambeloa* – or starfruit, pasta salads, handmade tortillas, fried plantains, fresh tamales, spicy salsa and *gallo pinto*, black bean dip. The men opened bags of *chicharrones*, pork rinds and corn chips while the women laid out plates, silverware, and cloth napkins. A feast was about to begin.

The sky now clear of the looming vulture, out of the jungle scampered the curious family of capuchins. They raced through the money, shredding a few bills like confetti until the fresh scent of cold cuts caught their attention and drew them closer to the picnic. The parents jumped to their feet when they heard the chattering and saw the capuchins scamper to the food, snatching sandwiches from unattended plates like picking fruit from a tree. The scolding parents shooed the little thieves down the beach and the children chased them back into the jungle.

It was then that several people spotted the money hopscotching down the beach and began plucking it from the sand, never believing it to be real. Others joined in. The children chased after the scattering bills. It delighted them. This was far better than searching for turtle eggs.

Everyone got involved, and soon the forgotten monkeys had eaten all the picnic food while the families danced and gorged on the feast of pesos delivered from the heart of the rainforest.

Chapter 47

Betty was down in the bar having a champagne cocktail with Ginger who was draped in a wet towel, having just come in from her morning swim. When Vu poked his head in the door, Betty let out an excited cry, jumped up and ran over to hug him.

"I was just telling Ginger about how you are a hero. The captain heard it all on the radio, so everybody on board knows about you. Just promise me you'll never do that again?"

Betty turned to Ginger. "Do you know what note Jack wrote me when he left to go to war with the drug cartel?" Betty slid the note across the table. It said: *"Gone fishing. Back before you know it. Kisses, Jack."*

"That was some fishing trip." Ginger held her glass aloft in a salute.

Vu was still in a daze from the past few days events and he couldn't make sense of any of it. He told Betty he was going to take a shower and rest before dinner.

Returning to the cabin he flopped down on the bed and closed his eyes and didn't wake up until he heard the sound of the Ship's bell drone and felt the vessel begin to move.

He stepped out on the deck and wanted to get one last look at the country that held so much mystery.

In the distance he could make out a number of people waving to the ship as it made its slow departure toward Panama. He pulled out his binoculars. As he panned the beach something caught his eye. Down the coast, away from everyone else, on the edge of the forest was the silhouette of a man standing along the shoreline, with something darting about down at his feet. He focused in on the image along the shore.

Lyman's frogman face covered in camouflage face paint glistened as the sun shone on it like a stage light. A small playful capuchin danced about as other monkeys cavorted around him on the beach.

Waving toward shore, Vu put the binoculars down, skipped the shower and headed toward the bar.

– THE END –

AUTHOR'S NOTE AND ACKNOWLEDGEMENTS

The inspiration for the book came while I was vacationing in Costa Rica. My companion and I were traveling on a National Geographic Expedition aboard the *Sea Voyager*. During the trip down the Pacific Coast of Costa Rica and then transiting the Panama Canal we met a number of memorable fellow travelers and crew. One particular biologist named Gaston Trujillo intrigued me. He was 37 at the time, married and had a 6-year-old daughter. He learned to speak English in a German high school in Costa Rica. Formerly trained as a civil engineer, he'd returned to school to become a naturalist and later was hired by National Geographic as a guide aboard our vessel.

From the first moment I sat down with him, I was drawn in by his stories and theories on evolution. He believed that the only way to save a weakened species of primate living on one of the remote islands in the area was to introduce predators. You could do this by building a corridor that would allow all types of animals to move from one region to the next, but that in itself wasn't sufficient. It would also take more intervention, which we discussed in detail. After this conversation my imagination went wild. I knew I had found the topic of my next novel.

I had the good fortune to meet with Gaston on several more occasions privately. I told him over dinner one night that I was going to use him as a character in my next book. He laughed and said: "I'd make a good villain because I have a wicked imagination. But my parents ended that promising career because they were decent people. So, I missed my chance at becoming a criminal."

As we were leaving the ship on our final day at sea, Gaston stopped me on the dock and said farewell. "If you ever use me as a villain in your book, you can use my real name."

So, Gaston, thank you. I did my best to make you wicked.

At Floating Word, I'd like to thank my editor, Martha Cowen, for her masterful, yet at times brutal, editing. I walked away with many well-deserved bruises and the book is better for it.

I'd also like to give thanks to the following individuals for their insightful comments during the development of *Riff Raff*: Bill Ashworth; Lee Anna Bennett-Ashworth; Karl Gillespie; Steve Hanns; Jimmy and Suzanne Hendrickson; Dave Huitt; Bill Johnson; Kat Majors; Bennett McGough; Lenny Perrone; Harley L Sachs; and Laury #1 Swan.

And, without whom this book could not have been written, to my treasured companion, the very adorable and talented Birdie. Her endless readings, innumerable rewrite sessions and overall general advice were deeply appreciated. I also owe her much gratitude for keeping me afloat in life.

About The Author

Doc Macomber is a native Northwesterner. His previous books include: *The Killer Coin*, *Wolf's Remedy*, and *Snip*. He is a contributor to various national and international publications. Doc has a military affiliation that he does not discuss other than to say he formerly served in a Special Ops unit. He currently lives aboard a trawler in the Pacific Northwest.

(Author photograph by Serge A.McCabe)

Discover other titles by Doc Macomber at bookstores and on Amazon.com, Barnes & Noble.com, Smashwords.com, Kobo.com, Sony Books.com, Apple.com, Diesel.com, and Scrollmotion.com:

The Killer Coin

Wolf's Remedy

Snip

Connect with the Author online @ www.docmacomber.com or the Publisher: Floating Word Press, LLC @ www.floatingwordpress.com

COMING SOON!!!

The fifth novel in the Jack Vu Mysteries Series titled: *Little Tiger.*

The ebook version of Riff Raff is now available at the retailers mentioned above. The audiobook MP3 version of *Riff Raff,* and other Jack Vu mysteries are available on Audio.com.

Stay posted for upcoming releases by visiting: www.floatingwordpress.com

www.ingramcontent.com/pod-product-compliance
Lightning Source LLC
Chambersburg PA
CBHW020755250626
47155CB00003B/1089